THE FINAL RUN

The Final Run

TOMMY STEELE

COLLINS
8 Grafton Street, London W1
1983

William Collins Sons & Co Ltd
London · Glasgow · Sydney · Auckland
Toronto · Johannesburg

British Library Cataloguing in Publication Data
Steele, Tommy
The final run.
I. Title
823'.914[F] PR6069.T/

ISBN 0-00-222709-6

First published 1983

Photoset in Linotron Sabon by
Rowland Phototypesetting Ltd
Bury St Edmunds, Suffolk.
Made and printed in Great Britain by
William Collins Sons & Co Ltd, Glasgow

For my mother

'On May 24th, 1940, the German armour,
now within sight of Dunkirk and poised
along the canal between Gravelines and St Omer
for the final kill, received a strange –
and to the soldiers in the field, inexplicable –
order to halt their advance...
This delay allowed 338,580 soldiers of
the British Expeditionary Force to be rescued
from the beaches.'

Shirer: *The Rise and Fall of the Third Reich*

CONTENTS

Book I

The Beginning

The sound that greeted the inhabitants of the tiny Sussex village of Hamble that early morning of May 3rd, 1940 was not the usual melding of dawn chorus, church bell and milk churn. It came as a steady rhythmic beat, crunching from the gravel path, twisting between the thatched cottages.

Heads peered out from the tiny windows and a few braved the doorways and front gardens to look at the cause of the strange tune. The first to come into view was a regimental sergeant major of the Coldstream Guards, resplendent in his reds and golds, head fast front, hat balanced and feet crushing the stones of the country thoroughfare. No more than a second glance away came six more guardsmen; privates, but no less proud, no less quiet as they crunched after their NCO in tight ranks of two. The war was on and the villagers had read of such gatherings – but here in Hamble?

As the soldiers disappeared towards Lower Dell the more inquisitive came from their cottages and followed, and Marcus Ronay followed them.

They didn't notice this extra stranger, this tall sinewy man with the brown hair and bright blue eyes hidden beneath the snap brim of his trilby, his hands deep in his pockets. He walked slowly and purposefully, a soft bounce in his stride. He walked within the shade of the cottages – a habit – so no one in Hamble that morning was going to pay him more attention than the soldiers in Lower Dell.

He paused at the tip of the rise and looked down into the Dell – a small church crouched in the cover of a host of elms and over to the right of the covered gate he saw the guardsmen gathering in front of a single cottage. The front lawn of the dwelling was covered in neat rows of wreaths, and even from the rise, Ronay could see the colourful silks of a dozen regiments tied to the flowers with their messages of sympathy for the widow. One blazed the words "FAREWELL TO A WARRIOR". But the last thing Alex Villiers could be called was a warrior. A soldier – a general – but no warrior. In all the years Ronay had known him he had never heard of him leaving Whitehall. Alex was a planner of wars, a master of tactics and strategy. He had always been so and now, on his death and befitting his rank, he was due the honourable farewell of the guardsmen and the regimental wreaths. But why him? Why Ronay? Why did he get the telegram to come? Why, after all this time?

He felt in his coat pocket and took out the crushed pack of Woodbines. He lit one and drew on the nicotine deeply without taking his eyes off the movement below him. He would wait until the last moment before joining the ceremony. The villagers were closer now to the funeral and beginning to read the cards on the wreaths. Ronay smiled grimly. There was no dignity in death – flags, flowers, all camouflage. He'd seen more than his share of tight white skin and soulless eyes, and funerals. Only once, for a short moment with his beloved Cheney, for a few brief seconds, he had believed there might be something more to death. But the feeling passed. He'd followed the farewell ritual for her sake.

It was spring. Summer was close, yet he still felt the cold of winter. Cheney had said it was his age. He was forty-six. Along with his dreams his youth had gone. So had Cheney, his lovely lady. How long was it since her death? Four years?

Five? No, he'd left the factory three years ago and Cheney had died the following Christmas; it was two.

And now Alex Villiers was dead and below him on the lawn he saw Emily the widow. She looked smaller than he remembered, her tiny shoulders covered by a tartan shawl, taking the offered hands of her neighbours and gently fussing with the wreaths. Behind her at the open door of the cottage, Ronay saw the soldiers gathering. He moved down the path.

Suddenly Ronay stopped. A small square-faced man in a general's uniform preceded the coffin from the cottage. Ronay flicked the half-spent Woodbine behind him and walked closer. The General gave a humourless smile. That smile was a permanent fixture of Peter Pelluw.

'Marcus Aurelius, you old coot.' Pelluw's accent was high, affected, middle-class.

Ronay wished he had pressed his suit before leaving London that morning. He felt decidedly second-hand.

'You look remarkably retired, old chum,' the voice called again.

'And you, remarkably military,' he answered.

'Poor Alex,' the General murmured as the flag-draped coffin came into the sunshine.

Emily Villiers called to him. A faint tired call of welcome. Ronay went to her.

'Marcus, you look terrible,' she scolded.

Ronay shrugged, took her small head in his hands and kissed her gently.

'But you are both here and that is good, very good,' she said.

'Pelluw and I?' Ronay asked.

'Alex wanted it that way,' she said and followed the cortège without further explanation.

Ronay stood uneasily through the ceremony. Why was he here? He and Alex had known each other during Ronay's time at the Factory but Ronay was no longer there. An early retirement it had said on his exit paper, three years ago. He still felt the pangs of anger; three years since he was recalled from Spain; three years since his 'miscalculation'. That word creeping from the sterile lips of Charlie Peake still rang around Ronay's head – 'miscalculation'.

The volley of rifle shots brought him back to Alex and Emily and his questions. Apart from the soldiers around the grave there were just three mourners, Emily, Pelluw and himself.

Pelluw pressed the tightly folded Union Jack into Emily's hands and saluted.

Ronay felt her grip on his hand.

'Excuse us, Peter,' she said, leading him away.

'It's nearly over, Marcus,' she said with a sigh.

He knew it wasn't of course. He knew the nights to come, the lonely moments, the unbalance of living half a life. But it wasn't the time to talk of these things. Not yet. Before she thinks she is the only one to have such thoughts; he must tell her before then.

She took his arm and walked back towards the fresh grave. They stood there quietly, watching the grave diggers finish their task.

He was surprised that her voice was steady when she broke the silence.

'You know about the Ardennes, Marcus?'

'Only that it's a forest in Belgium,' he said.

'Do you remember Alex referring to a chap called Erwin Rommel?'

'Vaguely.'

'He's a general now, a tank man. He and Alex struck up a friendship during the late twenties and they corresponded on the strategies of modern tank warfare. Young Mr Rommel advocated the Ardennes theory. He believed that a tank division could penetrate the forest and achieve total surprise. Alex agreed with him.'

'Interesting. But I don't quite see the point.'

Emily looked at him. Her soft face became tight and anxious, her wide eyes watered and her hands trembled.

'We decided, Alex and I, that you should be here today to help us.'

'Us?' Ronay kept his face still, without expression.

'He always admired your style, Marcus – if anyone can help it's you.'

'What can I do?' he said. She seemed so vulnerable.

'Alex died without having his theory recognised. I have to do something. I don't know how. I just know that, somehow, I must do something. Please, Marcus, please.'

The tears spilled down her cheeks. But she went on.

'You saw Peter Pelluw today, his reaction. In the past he was embarrassed by Alex. They never agreed and now Alex is gone, no doubt he'll be relieved. But Marcus, I tell you I won't have it. I'll petition the Government, the King. . .'

He held her close to him and felt her sobs subside into a heavy sigh. It could have been Cheney there, huddled against his body, needing the strength of his arms and his counsel.

'I'll help you. If I can.'

She looked up at his face and silently pulled him into the cottage. Under the small staircase of the hall she opened a door that led to the basement.

'Follow close, Marcus, and mind the stairs. There's a rail loose in the middle,' she said, closing the door behind her. They stood in total darkness.

'Stay there and I'll get some light.'

Ronay murmured, 'I feel like I'm on the edge of the world.'

Suddenly the basement was filled with red light. Ronay blinked and steadied himself. He looked down and, at the foot of the stairs, and falling away to cover the entire basement of some five hundred square feet, was a complete model of Europe with the Channel and the British Isles.

Ronay gasped in astonishment.

'The red light gives it mystery, dear,' Emily said. 'Alex spent hours down here and he found the diffusion helped his eyes. Do come over to Holland and let me explain.'

For a moment Ronay had forgotten the reason for his being there. He was lost in amazement and sheer joy at the meticulous piece of work in front of him. She pushed him towards a chair, took an old army jacket from the back of it and laid it lovingly on a table.

'Marcus, do stop drooling and sit down,' she said, as she took up an army baton.

'Here to the left the British Expeditionary Force guards the Maginot Line with the French.'

Her soft voice changed and became almost gruff as she moved around the model, her whole being filled with passion and authority.

'They say here at the Maginot Line, the Hun will make his move.'

She looks like Alex, Ronay thought. It was quite uncanny. Old Alex the warhorse.

'Here to the south, is Belgium,' she continued. 'And here is the Forest of the Ardennes. According to the old brigade, an impassable labyrinth of trees. But if it could be penetrated, look what could happen. Enemy tanks could cross from Germany and into the forest in a matter of hours. At the same time a second front would engage. The French and British would be caught in a pincer-like trap. Alex estimated the campaign would take only about eight days and would lead to a full-scale Allied retreat to the Normandy coast in the direction of Le Havre or Calais. There, there'd be a decisive battle to cover a run for home.'

'By sea?' Ronay said.

'Given time,' she murmured.

'Time?'

'He said they'd need a week at least to get off the beach.'

Ronay was gentle but firm.

'With respect, m'dear, the War Cabinet would be aware of any penetration in the area.'

'Then why haven't they deployed men and armour to defend their flank?' Emily flared.

Ronay frowned. He wasn't sure of his ground.

'How do you know they haven't?' he parried.

'Marcus Ronay! You know as well as I do that Alex was privy to all military movements in the European theatre. Every signal concerning every regiment was passed on to him here.'

Ronay was silent. He glanced again at the model, searching for some words to explain the situation. But no revelation came. She was waiting for his next move, poised to crush any word that might suggest Alex was wrong. He didn't want to argue. He stepped carefully around the model towards the stairs. Emily's voice stopped him in his tracks.

'Rommel has just taken command of the Seventh Panzer Division at present stationed in a village sixty miles from the Ardennes.' The red lights of the basement snapped off.

'I'm not sorry for scolding you, Marcus,' she called in the darkness.

'I know you're not,' he laughed.

'I just hate to think that Peter Pelluw has had his way,' she said.

'Pelluw?' he repeated, trying to sound unconcerned.

'It's Pelluw who kept blocking the theory,' she shrugged. 'He could never believe that he and the others could be preparing for the wrong war.'

So that's why just Pelluw and he were invited; a ploy by Alex, the tactician. Very droll. Ronay had a hundred more questions now, but he knew many arose because of his feelings towards Pelluw. He had to get out of that habit. He asked no more and left for the station within the hour.

Pelluw was standing on the platform as Ronay arrived. The train had just crawled to a stop and the General approached him.

'Care to join me, Marcus?' he smiled, opening the First Class door of the front carriage.

'Afraid not, I'm on a Third Class day return,' Ronay muttered.

Pelluw called to his regimental sergeant major. The soldier marched towards him and crashed to attention.

'This gentleman will be joining me for the journey to Victoria – inform the guard,' Pelluw rasped.

Ronay did not attempt an argument, but accepted the offer without any pretence at gratitude.

They sat opposite each other. The doors of the carriages slammed home as the guard's whistle shrilled. The train gave a lurch forward and dragged itself out of the station, and steam clouded past the open window of the compartment. Ronay stared at the little General, the arrogant red face and tight combed hair. It took him back twenty-five years, back to his time at Westminster School, back to his childhood and 'Mad Pelluw'. He chuckled. Peter Pelluw, his nearly-friend and almost-enemy – how they had fought at Westminster and argued much later at Oxford. It seemed that every step Ronay had taken in his early years had brought him into the orbit of Peter Pelluw and it was really because of Pelluw that he had chosen the Factory instead of the Army. 'Mad Pelluw' had caused enough upsets. Sandhurst with him would have been too much.

Pelluw made the first move by sniffing the air.

'More Woodbine than St Bruno,' Ronay said.

'The compartment?'

'No, the suit, but then I've been on the scrap heap for three years.'

'Missing the cloak and daggers, heh?'

'I didn't, but since the balloon went up I've had a few pangs.'

'Heard much from Alex in the last year?' Pelluw asked. Ronay shrugged his shoulders.

'How about you?'

Pelluw moved in his seat uncomfortably.

'Quite a lot actually. He hardly left the War Room during November and frankly by January he became quite tiresome. You know Alex, he could be like that, damn tiresome.'

Ronay nodded without attempting to hold back a grin.

'Still, old soldiers never die, they only. . .'

The General interrupted.

'You always had that accursed habit of giving me the shits, Marcus,' he said.

'Oh you've got years yet, Peter. The War Room couldn't spare you!'

'Well, bugger all's happened since September and if someone doesn't shoot someone bloody quick we'll be arrested for loitering with intent.'

'Still better than nothing,' Ronay said grimly.

The General gave him a look of undiluted pity. Ronay felt cold and angry. Pelluw sat back with his usual smug self-satisfied look.

'You've got a sort of pension, Marcus,' he said. 'Not a fortune considering your early retirement but it should be ample, no gong I believe.'

Ronay lit a Woodbine and made a huge smoke screen between them.

'But then your line of work didn't rate one – with respect. Would you have accepted an OBE?'

Ronay shook his head.

'Another ten years' service would have been more welcome,' he said. He wished he could have resisted saying how he felt.

'Always the worker, heh Marcus. But then you couldn't be anything else could you? I often wondered how dear Cheney managed to take it – with respect.'

Ronay knew there wasn't an ounce of respect in Pelluw's body. Not for him. 'Mad Pelluw' gazed into the ice blue of Ronay's eyes.

'You give me the shits, Marcus,' he said.

'With respect,' Ronay smiled. He'd won some points.

An hour later the two men shook hands on the concourse of Victoria and Ronay stood watching his adversary strut away. He stayed motionless, taking in the sight and sounds of the huge expansive station. At times, it appeared calm and unhurried but at regular intervals, when the hollow sounds of the station announcer boomed from the loud speakers, small pockets of people would suddenly take life. They moved in whispers, as if every step were a secret and every person had something to hide. At one side was a tight pack of children with string-tied suitcases and huge labels hanging from their lapels. A mixture of red excited faces and white sad masks of tears and loneliness. They were destined for the countryside and safety from the German bombs that had to come soon.

Ronay walked towards a vacant bench at the side of the ticket office. He sat down facing the crowd. He remembered Charles Peake . . . old Charlie Peake, his chief inquisitor at the Factory. It was Charlie who had come into his dingy office years ago on that first day, taking him to Victoria and dumping him on the same bench at five o'clock one night in 1918.

'Watch 'em,' he growled.

'Watch who, Mr Peake?'

'All of them!' Charlie said, giving no other explanation.

Peake left Ronay watching the multitudes until the last train had departed early the next morning. And for twenty odd years, in various permutations of places and persons, that is exactly what Ronay had done. He watched – he waited – and, true to all Factory men, he'd performed his duties according to the articles of employment.

Before Ronay, the stage of a thousand plots unfolded. Fussing women, crying children, good-time girls, air raid wardens and servicemen. There were many servicemen. Boys and men were saying goodbye to prostitutes, parents, sweethearts. Uniforms of all denominations daubing the picture with flashes of colour. Ronay watched and played his mental game.

He thought of the Ardennes then. He thought of people, ordinary people, people shopping, looking, talking, hurrying, sitting; all content to live their lives. Life here and now was going along its normal way, but what of the forest – 'that impassable labyrinth of trees'? He left the station with a feeling of desperation.

He didn't reach his boarding house until late evening and his deliberations added to the tiredness of the day and the thought of his bed outweighed his hunger.

The untidy Fulham street was free of local kids at this hour and the light from the ground floor window of the boarding house showed Mrs Baylis was home for the night. He would get into the house and up the stairs as quickly and quietly as he could – he was not in a talking mood.

Once at the top of the staircase he breathed deeply – his lungs heaved and he coughed as though to waken the dead.

'You all right, Mr Ronay?' his landlady cackled.

'Yes thank you, Mrs Baylis' he groaned in reply.

He was inside the flat before another word was passed. The small room was becoming darker by the second as the day disappeared over the roof tops. He searched in his pockets for a sixpence and dropped it in the gas meter. The gas hissed from the ring as the coin dropped. He quickly lit a match and stabbed the jets with the flame, the gentle explosion sending a warm front into his face. He stood there for some time assessing his day. But just like the days before he could only remember how lonely it was and wasted. He was tired. He wished Cheney was there, but he'd been through those thoughts before and they didn't help. He pushed them away. He took off his suit and hung it on the back of the door then slipped on his pyjama jacket. The crumpled pack of Woodbines in the top pocket had one last cigarette to offer. He lit it thankfully from the gas ring. Within minutes the kettle was boiling and he opened the curtains to bring in the larder box from the window ledge. Inside was the cooked meat he kept wrapped in newspaper. He laid it on the side table, brushed away crumbs from an earlier meal and cut himself enough meat for a thick sandwich. Another cough sent ash down the front of his pyjamas. He shrugged and made the coffee.

His thoughts went back to Hamble and Emily and Alex and 'Mad Pelluw'. A relief from his usual thoughts of Cheney and the Factory and Spain, and Charlie Peake and his 'miscalculation'. He stretched on his bed and waited for the gas fire to burn itself out as the sixpence was finally spent. He lay in the darkness before at last he fell asleep.

It wasn't until three days later that the whole thing blew up again. He had gone to bed as usual – too early. He was watching the gas fire when the telephone rang. He pulled the instrument to him by the wire so as not to leave the warmth of his bed clothes.

'Is that you, Marcus?' It was Emily Villiers. 'A signal has just come for Alex, from France.'

Ronay lay back on the pillows. 'I'm listening,' he said grimly.

'Jerry's moved his Twenty-Third and Twenty-Ninth Armies to outside Namur. Looks like they're in reserve for Guderian on the Maginot front.'

'What do you mean "looks like"?'

'I mean Namur might be eighty miles from the Maginot but it's only sixty miles from the Ardennes Forest.'

There was a long pause as Ronay considered the information.

'Marcus, please go to Peter Pelluw,' he said. 'Go to the War Cabinet. Please, for Alex and me. If *you're* satisfied, then that's an end to it. It's so important don't you see?'

Ronay murmured down the line. Of course he could see, perhaps more than Emily could at that moment. He could see a caring little woman rushing from pillar to post in her endeavour to do the little things she couldn't do when Alex was there.

'Marcus, are you listening?'

'My dear Emily, what would he ever have done without you?' he said. He heard a muffled sob. The back of his throat closed and his hair tightened. What the hell, he thought. It wasn't that he had other things to do.

The next morning he was sitting in the waiting hall of

Pelluw's office. He watched countless officials, military and others, flock up and down the resplendent staircase, lined with glass-fronted cases full of military memorabilia. The giant crystal chandelier dominated the hall, hanging from a domed ceiling with softly painted murals of Mars, the god of War, courted by a collection of cherubs in various states of undress.

Pelluw appeared at the rail at the top of the staircase. He beamed down at Ronay like a latter-day god and signalled him to ascend to Olympus. Ronay followed him into a large room facing onto a vast expanse of parade ground. Pelluw nodded towards a high-backed leather chair and offered his cigarette box with the same self-satisfied smugness that he had had when he was made Captain of School and President of the Union at University.

Ronay gritted his teeth and determined that his opening sentence wouldn't sound apologetic. Pelluw cut him off while he was drawing breath.

'Did Emily call you before ten or after?' he said and then, not waiting for Ronay's answer: 'She found me at the War Room at seven. She's worse than Alex if you can believe that! And why the hell *you* got into the scenario escapes me.'

He moved to his desk and drew a large folder from a drawer, throwing it towards Ronay. It was obvious that Pelluw was not enjoying himself.

'That's everything known about the Ardennes Forest including a tree count. For your further information the Forest has been there for centuries y'know. So has the British Army and you must allow us to have the opinion that when the enemy comes they will not come through an impenetrable collection of lumber.'

'Then why do I feel they could?' Ronay said quietly.

'Because you're Marcus Ronay, ex-member of the faceless few. Your life was intrigue and seeing through what lesser beings accepted as fact. But do please, Marcus, for your own sake, enjoy your retirement and drop this crusade. It's a bloody affront anyway, a general explaining policy to a civilian. I ought to kick your arse for cheek. On the other hand, I ought to kick mine for gullibility. It's not enough that I had Alex Villiers driving me mad and then his wife, but now Marcus Ronay comes into the act. And what am I expected to do? Bare my soul and welcome the enquiry? Perhaps a glance at the overall strategy of the War Cabinet would suffice? Maybe we could pin it on the notice board of the Hamble church hall and invite the villagers to voice their opinions.'

The General huffed and puffed. In spite of the contempt that Ronay had for Pelluw he knew there was a lot of truth in his words. But verbal battles had to be fought and surrender was unforgivable. He decided on a token counter attack.

'Does this file mention any Fifth Column activity in the area?' he asked. Pelluw turned to the window and looked out onto the parade ground. Ronay wasn't certain whether he had made a breakthrough or not. 'If you can answer such a question?' he said, watching the back of his adversary for some sign.

'I don't see the relevance,' said Pelluw.

'The relevance is the normal practice of the German High Command: blitzkrieg, tanks, infantry. But always first, their Fifth Column agents stalking the area, preparing their intelligence dossiers. Look at Czechoslovakia and Poland, Peter. Heavens man, you know the drill!'

'I can't divulge such information at this time,' Pelluw said stiffly.

'Very well,' Ronay rose to go.

The General didn't turn, which was a good sign that Ronay must have hit home. As he walked into the hall, Pelluw came to the door and called after him. 'There'll be no surprises from Belgium this year, Marcus,' he said angrily. 'Look to Russia. It's Communist, unfriendly and available. You mark me, Marcus, it's Russia before the snows. Tell that to your Darby and Joan fan club in Hamble.'

Ronay walked away without replying. 'Mad Pelluw' was

in full cry and thoroughly ruffled. The Fifth Column question had hurt and Ronay was going to find out why. Emily and Alex no longer dominated his thoughts. From now on his investigations were for his own satisfaction. His step had a fresh spring in it, his head had cleared. He didn't feel cold any more.

The rest of the day was spent going through his old papers – notes referring to known Fifth Column exploits. It was all there: the shape of modern day German warfare – total blitzkrieg – the annihilation of the enemy with a blanket bombardment of heavy guns and air attacks; the combination of artillery and the Luftwaffe and information supplied by the Fifth Column. Men and women infiltrating the battle zone long before the attack – seeking out defences, supply depots, reserve forces and possible civilian and military collaborators for sabotage and yet more information. He didn't need a lot of reminding. The Fifth Column was a brilliant concept, something he wished the Factory could have emulated. He thought of Charles Peake who would have loved it, but his war was over long ago and Ronay's was just beginning.

He telephoned Emily and assured her he would have further meetings. With someone influential. He knew she would find comfort in that thought.

The next morning was warm. Ronay didn't wear an overcoat but stuffed his Woodbines into the top pocket of his waistcoat and took the bus to St James's Park. It was bathed in a sultry morning mist and was almost deserted. He would wait for Stone, the Factory gossip – his mine of information.

In the dull quietness Big Ben chimed seven forty-five. He sat by a heavy-leafed oak and never took his eyes off the houses that backed onto the park. The minutes passed and then Big Ben chimed again. It was eight o'clock. Seconds later, a small, red MG sports car skidded to a stop outside the gates and a man in his early fifties jumped out. He was tall and dapper, school tie, peaked cap and a carnation blooming from the lapel of his hacking jacket. Ronay jumped to his feet and waved. The tall man stared for a moment, then smiled and jogged across the grass. He shook Ronay's hand and gushed, 'Good morning, sir. Gosh what a shock I got, seeing you!'

Ronay looked at his watch. 'A little late as usual, Stone. What was it today? Traffic, 'flu, or bereavement?'

The man Stone reddened but smiled good-naturedly. 'Coming in to see the master and the chaps?'

Ronay shook his head. 'No, I'm still going through withdrawal symptoms. They never leave y'know. I thought just a look at the Factory and the occasional memory of past pleasures might help.'

'We miss you too, sir,' Stone said as he sat on the bench. Ronay offered him a cigarette.

'And what of you Stone, stalwart of the spies, agent provocateur, curse of the Fifth Column?

'I'm okay really. I've got the Belgium portfolio, don't y'know.'

'Good for you,' Ronay said, encouraging him. Stone would be as easy as he'd hoped. 'Belgium today, tomorrow the world, heh? Is there much movement there, on paper?'

'Not from us. I've got a contact with the Dutch crowd but it doesn't amount to any great master plan. I just send out the expenses and keep the general picture up to date but that's about all.'

'How about the Hun?' Ronay pressed. 'The same, I suppose?'

'No chance of that, sir. He's as busy as a beaver. He's all over Holland and at the moment he's having more than a casual sniff at Belgium. He's got his Fifth moving in and out of the place all the time.'

Ronay shifted closer to Stone and spoke in half a whisper: 'Has Head Office asked for a Company report? Hasn't the War Office asked for a breakdown of area movements?'

'Not so far, but you know the Factory, Mr Ronay. Keep

to your own shop floor, don't question anything and don't answer anyone.'

Ronay had heard enough. Another look at his watch and he reminded Stone of the time. Stone rose slowly and threw Ronay his boyish smile.

'Well if you'll excuse me, sir. It really was super seeing you again,' he said, offering his hand. Ronay eyed him closely and spoke confidentially.

'Keep this little meeting to yourself. It's a bit embarrassing my hanging around after all this time. I'd appreciate it.'

Stone put both his hands on Ronay's shoulders. 'They still talk about you, sir. You being the best, I mean. How did you do it?'

'By having nothing else,' Ronay said unguardedly. Stone looked bewildered and made no reply but turned and jogged away towards the house at the edge of the park.

Ronay walked towards Piccadilly. 'How now, Mad Pelluw,' he thought. There was much to be done. A return to the War Office was not on the itinerary. There would be no joy there. They had made their plans and he would have to make his.

That night he finished the last of the meat in the larder box and rounded off the meal with a packet of crisps and a bottle of Guinness. He felt more alone than he had ever been before. Cheney would have listened of course, but probably would have advised him to forget it. But how could he? He sensed the danger, and if he could see the signs why couldn't they? The boys, the dear old brigade. They had their game in progress and they were in no mood to listen, to believe they could be wrong. Then again there was something else, a thought floating in his subconscious tearing its way to the surface.

The Hyde in him, the someone Cheney would have run from, the dark him he would never allow in the open, squirmed inside, hoping that conflict was coming through that forest – begging fate to send him an enemy – someone, something to hunt, to bring to ground. He paced the room again and again. He had the chance to re-enter the arena – to feed again. The fact was that he believed Alex was right and that a rescue plan was needed for those men over there. Was it for them that he would devise such a plan – or for himself?

He started feeling cold again, his mind whirling with mists of anger and despair. He thought of Charles Peake. Wished Charlie was still alive. How many times did he walk the plank with Charlie?

'If you have a problem, dear boy, seek it out,' he would say, sucking his teeth in that ridiculous habit of his, 'and if all else fails, share it, but choose your confessor well, dear boy – he may not have the ear of God.'

Ronay made his decision. Once more the gas fire jumped into life as he selected a page of writing paper and in a few short sentences, wrote out his fears, his dilemma and his plan. He read it and re-read it and then went out into the night to post it. As the dull plop sounded within the postbox, he relaxed, his legs lost their tension and he walked back to the boarding house with a clear head. As he closed the front door, Mrs Baylis called from the ground floor flat, 'Goodnight Mr Ronay'. He muttered a reply and climbed up the stairs, tired, more tired than he'd been for years. But this time it was a good feeling. He had thrown down the gauntlet. He would await the reply.

On May 10th it came. Mrs Baylis had invited him into the kitchen for lunch. Her lamb was as exciting as her beef and whatever the menu offered there was the added luxury of taking the rest of the joint up to his box on the window ledge. They had absolutely nothing in common apart from being alone. She wasn't a bad old girl except her conversation was made up of 'them next door' and 'my Bill, God rest his soul', but her kindness was welcome. He was content to play his part.

A sharp rap at the front door interrupted the meal; Mrs Baylis padded into the hall to answer it and Ronay heard a muffled conversation. She came back into the room without a word, fussing at the stove before calling over her shoulder, 'I told the gent you was eating.'

She returned to pouring the hot custard over the mountain of syrup pudding, steaming in the middle of the table. Ronay fought down the urge to get up and go to the door. It was mid-meal and 'her Bill, rest his soul' wouldn't have left the table.

'Did he want me?' he asked.

Mrs Baylis pushed the steam pudding towards him. 'I don't want no strangers in my kitchen, so you can take your afters upstairs and eat it while it's hot,' she said without looking up.

Ronay took the dessert and covered the few yards to the front door in seconds. There, leaning on a tattered umbrella, was a small old man in a heavy overcoat. Ronay narrowed his eyes, concentrating. The man's face was familiar but half hidden by a black homburg hat. Just below the brim, a short forehead fell into a pair of large schoolboy spectacles that emphasised the little dark eyes that pierced Ronay's memory. The man lifted his right hand slowly and offered it, a slight smile on his paper-thin lips. Ronay gingerly transferred the steaming dessert to his left hand and greeted the man solemnly. He was astonished and showed it, but kept silent. He widened the door to allow the little man in, then led the way up the stairs towards his own room.

Ronay broke the silence. 'Your coat?' The man unbuttoned his overcoat and sat in the armchair. 'I'll keep it on,' he said, taking off his hat. Ronay saw that even the great Charlie Peake couldn't fight Father Time.

His head was quite bald, the skin covering his wily skull had crumbled into folds of lined parchment. His neck disappeared into the stiff collar which together with his old school tie dominated the upper part of his shoulders. It gave him the appearance of a turtle.

Christ, he's ancient, Ronay thought, but still as lethal. There was no mistaking the eyes and the cunning behind them. Charles Peake watched him search for a cigarette and waste a few matches lighting it.

Christ, I swore I'd never end up like him, Ronay thought. But he knew he was like Charlie. He was always like Charlie – in mind, in his every action. He couldn't credit it – yesterday he had despised himself, hating his past and dreading his memories. Now all of a sudden, his mind rang with its desire to remember the tricks and the training. He was Ronay and this was Charlie Peake – the Factory was open and he was approaching the gates again.

'For God's sake, eat your sweet,' Charlie growled.

Ronay pushed the plate away. He looked at the old man sucking his teeth, staring at him from the armchair. He didn't hold back the words boiling at the back of his throat.

'I thought you were dead.'

Charlie Peake shrugged and a hollow chuckle came from somewhere in the regions of his head.

Ronay felt the tiny eyes burning into him again. There had been other times when he had been in the same God-awful situation – Charlie Peake sucking his teeth and watching while Ronay stood or sat and waited.

'I read your letter.'

Charlie Peake's voice came like a Gatling gun. Ronay wanted to ask how the hell Charlie Peake knew about his letter. He had sent it to the Factory 'drop', Eyes Only for the Master. Charlie Peake had left the job just after Ronay's miscalculation – or so Ronay had believed. He had a silent chuckle. Crafty beggar, he thought, he's still at the bloody helm.

Charlie cut through his thoughts: 'It was most intriguing. You always could create more of a stir than anyone else at the Factory, Marcus. How did you compile your information?'

'I'd have thought the question should be: Is the theory viable?' Ronay said.

Charlie Peake sucked again.

'Let me be the judge of that, Marcus. I want to know where you got the information.'

'Are you cross-questioning me?' Ronay's temper was rising. Charlie Peake stared at him.

'Where did you get the information?' The question had a sharper edge.

'Alex Villiers.' Ronay capitulated to the will of the past master.

Charlie Peake gave a deep sigh and settled into an armchair. He pushed his spectacles back onto the bridge of his tiny nose.

'I have a brief. It's quite unofficial and has no recognition by any government department but then that has never bothered us before has it?'

Ronay shrugged. 'So let's look at you Ronay,' Charlie Peake said. His eyes searched Ronay's face. 'If I can give you your head, can you perform the task set out in your letter?'

Ronay didn't answer immediately. He had to be exact in his reply. 'Given the opportunity, I think I can,' he said.

Charlie Peake nodded and rose slowly from the armchair. 'I offer you the opportunity,' he said. 'Belgium was invaded two hours ago from the Ardennes Forest.'

Charlie Peake took off his overcoat. 'Now, take me through the plan in plain, simple words,' he said. If he were to give the go-ahead, he had to be sure Ronay was on top of the situation. The Spanish affair had brought an air of mistrust – Ronay had deviated from the official line, was known to have miscalculated. But Charlie Peake would be watching this time.

'By the way, a little extra news,' Charlie said suddenly. 'Chamberlain resigned a few hours ago. Winston took over this afternoon.'

Ronay couldn't believe his luck. Churchill would fit into his plan more easily. It was a safe feeling too, knowing Charlie was there. Just the two of them together. He, Ronay, and the old fox warming his hands and sucking his teeth.

'To the Factory,' Ronay said as he showed Charlie to the front door.

The look Charlie Peake gave was both fiery and mischievous. 'To you,' he said, 'to you, Marcus.'

Ronay accepted the compliment and closed the door with relief. He felt in his pocket for the packet of cigarettes and gave a dry laugh as he selected one. Suddenly he had no need of a crutch. There was no great habit to satisfy, just his desire to be back in the arena and to be as good as he always was. He crushed the cigarettes and put them in the dustbin in the hall.

Upstairs in the flat he searched out his best clothes and connected the electric iron – much later that night he had his first wet shave for years. He was back in favour. But the threat would still be there. He knew the Factory and Charlie Peake. Spain and Donna Maria would not be forgiven. But he was back and that was a start.

At three o'clock that afternoon, Charlie Peake took the next step. He went by taxi to Fleet Street. The interior of the Daily Express building was like the street outside, hectic. Screaming telephones, anxious faces. Copy boys in pairs grabbing at typed paper. To one side of the long newsroom, a group of people were studying a large blackboard on which an artist was preparing a cartoon, depicting the battles across the Channel: there were huge black trees bending in an ill wind, angry tanks crashing through the forest, spouting flame and fire. The artist worked quickly whilst the faces around murmured encouragement and suggestions.

From the group a small man emerged. He was in his sixties and wore an open shirt with thick red braces holding up a pair of pin-striped trousers. His head seemed too big for his small frame, on account of its full, lopsided, good natured smile. He signalled for Charlie Peake to follow him through the banks of animated desks. Lord Beaverbrook, news baron, was stalking his domain at a moment of history. His short fast steps led them to the quietness of a corridor.

'Well?' Beaverbrook said, unable to hide his anxiety.

'It's a good plan – I'm going for it,' Charlie said.

'Then I can tell Winston it's on. And this Ronay can get the Germans to delay once we're on those beaches?'

Charlie Peake sucked his teeth. 'This Ronay will *attempt to delay*,' he said.

'That's as much as we can hope for,' Beaverbrook muttered.

'It's what *he* wants that concerns me,' Charlie said.

At last light on the evening of May 12th, Ronay assembled a few necessities in a small case before slipping out of the house in Fulham. The car was waiting around the corner, for the less Mrs Baylis and his co-habitants knew of his trip, the better. Much later, he entered Northolt airport and boarded the waiting seaplane.

For hours, he sat huddled in one corner of the throbbing aircraft, his back against the freezing cold bulkhead. His body felt totally numbed. And yet he dreaded the moment that he would have to try and move.

The fuselage in which he sat was packed with boxes of supplies, a pile of army blankets had been pulled from one of the cases and placed around him like a tent. His overcoat and gloves were the only added protection he had against the cold. His face was aching from the oxygen mask he had been given after the aeroplane had climbed out of the dark air base.

The only other occupant of the fuselage was a crewman who sat next to the cockpit. Conversation between the two men had been limited to ape-like signals. Anything vocal was made impossible by the oxygen masks and the heavy drone and rattle of the engines of the aircraft. After vague attempts at semaphore, Ronay had opted out of any dialogue and concentrated on the rhythm of the engines. Eventually, in spite of the cold, he fell into an uneasy doze.

At some unearthly hour he was shaken half-awake – his eyes felt full of grit, but the quagmire that was his mouth was eased by a steaming mug of coffee. The crewman gave a thumbs up and shouted: 'Gibraltar – two hours sir.' Ronay nodded and sipped his coffee.

Back in the cockpit the co-pilot was preparing his chart for landing and the navigator's voice crackled in his ear-phones. 'Any ideas about him, John?'

The co-pilot smiled. 'I think he's the new Governor of Gibraltar making a surprise visit.'

The pilot switched into the conversation. 'Stick to the orders chaps,' he said in a matter-of-fact tone. 'No thinking, no speculating. If he's on the manifest, he's cargo, and if he's not on the manifest, he's. . . .'

'. . . he's not on the plane,' the other men joined in the chorus.

Ronay drained the mug and closed his eyes. Once more the drone of the engines teased his thoughts; Gibraltar, two hours – it didn't seem possible that he could be going back, back to Spain and Donna Maria.

Book II

The Miscalculation

The Domenquin family had been among the courtiers of Spanish kings since Isabella had married Ferdinand. They were knights of the Queen's family and had come to great power and wealth by the involvement of the King's wife and Columbus. It was said that it was mostly Domenquin money that had paid for the first trip to the Americas, but then most families of the aristocracy voiced that particular claim.

Donna Maria Domenquin remembered her father coming to a duel over such a story. She, an only child, had slept with her mother the night before the fight because her father had been unable to rest. She had still been able to hear him pacing the floor of the dressing room next door, muttering mixtures of prayer and revenge. The morning of the duel came. The family priest arrived at early light and held Mass for her proud father. Then came the two uncles. Then came the Contessa, her father's elder sister, a huge gaunt woman, the matriarch of the family. She wore the black of a widow with a high comb in her grey hair.

The priest led her father down into the open courtyard of their home. The uncles fell to their knees and crossed themselves as her father passed towards the confessional box in the tiny family chapel adjoining the west wing. Still in their night attire, she and her mother watched. The family had thrown down their challenge and this dear, lovely little man had to defend their honour.

A black carriage drawn by two black horses came to take him away. The uncles and the Contessa followed. She asked her mother why they were not going to the party too and her mother cried softly as they bathed together. She next saw her father as he lay in an open coffin in the family chapel. The funeral took place with the rain crashing down onto the neat, grey courtyard stones. During the service the Contessa must have said something terrible to her mother for the gentle, soft-spoken woman had become transformed into a raving fishwife, screaming violently and beating at the aunt. The uncles struggled to hold her. The servants too rushed to separate the women as they tore at each other's black weeds. It was a horrible day. She left with her mother for Malaga that winter and there she stayed until ten years later when her mother died.

And how strange it was for her then to return to Madrid. She was met at the station by servants and taken to her aunt's house, a huge gothic monstrosity outside the city. The servants were ill at ease and she herself vividly remembered her father and that final brawl between her mother and the ogre awaiting her.

As the carriage wound its way up the tree-lined drive she was mesmerised by the house. The gabled windows and arches glared down as though defying the girl to come nearer. She fancied a host of ghostly faces peering down from all angles. The closer the carriage the bigger the house, the bigger the house, the closer the windows. Then she saw a face, a real face; white, sullen features watching her alight and climb the steps guarded by the stone gargoyles of centuries of Domenquins.

The housekeeper curtsied at the staircase and took her to the topmost floor where they entered a light, airy room dominated by a four-poster bed and furnished sparingly. The room was windowed on both sides, giving a cross light, and a gentle constant breeze was blowing the soft curtains with a subtle scent that she would never forget. The housekeeper curtsied again as she left and informed her that dinner would be at seven and the Contessa would receive her then.

Donna Maria heard male voices below in the hall. She ventured to the head of the stairs and tried to hear the conversation. The voices were her uncles'. Seeing their faces brought back the memories of that dawn and her beloved father. Then the carved oak door leading from the hall to the drawing room opened slowly to reveal her first glimpse of the Contessa. Donna Maria could only see her ankles and the lower part of her heavy dress and the gnarled hands grasping her rosary. The wiry finger snapped the beads as if counting blessings on a Chinese wire.

The uncles assembled at the doorway and bowed. Donna Maria froze. She would have to make her entrance soon. She would be presented to the Contessa, she would curtsey and approach the chair, even though she could still see her mother, that morning long ago, shouting her anguish and beating into the blackness of the matriarch; her father's face after the confession; the storm, the rain, the black horses. Her parents, she believed, were together now and she was alone.

She was nineteen, and going to college was important for her future. She was also a Domenquin and prostrating herself before the enemy was unacceptable in the shape of things. She would wait until after seven before descending the stairs, just a little later than ordered. She would affect a demi-curtsey and she would kiss the cold hand of the Contessa with dry, unfeeling lips. From this mock homage would come her inheritance and from that would come her future. The evil old hag could not live forever and she would hate her later, when the danger from doing so had passed.

At three minutes past seven she knocked on the oak door. An uncle opened it and smiled gravely. No words. He merely stepped back to reveal the Contessa who had not moved since Donna Maria had first watched from the stairs. The old lady stiffened her pose haughtily. Donna Maria walked to the outstretched, unfriendly fingers. As her soft hand touched, the Contessa tilted her cheek for a kiss. Her stern eyes piercing Donna Maria's. There were to be no secrets here. But with her inheritance, her own mind and her determined will, she would be able to live her own life with no allegiance to any name and no love for anyone by right, only by desire.

Her first year at college was not particularly eventful. She sat for history and economics. Her personality was serious and introvert – the years alone with her mother had seen to that – but by the time she had weathered the storm of mixing with people of her own age, her confidence grew and she began to leave her books and seek companionship. Her first friends were the girls of the campus and then Miguel Maravall, a tough, intelligent boy from the Basque region. His ambition was to be an agricultural professor. She loved to hear him preach about the land and his beloved Basque country. His ridiculous black beret was forever perched on his mass of curls, his eyes like a pampas bull – alert, angry, always seeking argument. She would follow him to his lectures and leave him in the corridor with a long warm kiss. She would wait there at the door listening to the muffled voices and stretching to hear Miguel's rise above the others, asking a question or delivering an answer.

They went to dances and exhibitions, but never to their homes. He refused to let her see his family; their circumstances were no better than peons on a master's estate. She, on the other hand, had no wish to present him to *her* family. The Contessa would rule supreme without the luxury of dominating Miguel.

She became pregnant in her second year. The knowledge didn't come as a surprise, and they didn't feel threatened by it. They talked of marriage and of life in the Basque country together. She was deliriously happy. But there would be no mention of their plans to their respective families. For them, the fruit of their love was their affair and any interference from the outside was to be discouraged. They would tell the world when the child was born and marriage would come before or after; it was of no real importance.

That Easter she had gone home. As was the ritual of the family, a communal ride around the properties had been arranged when she and the other women of the family rode side-saddle. The Contessa followed in her carriage, the men rode as escort. They would join in prayer with their peons and accept Easter gifts as tribute. Whether it was the high-pitched chatter of the women or the pace of the ride, she could never be sure; only that the horse bolted and she fell heavily.

She came to her senses in the infirmary in Madrid. During that time her condition had been discovered and reported to the family. Her child, a boy, had been cut away. The Contessa was present to advise her that it was for the best; her social standing and the family's name would be preserved. Somehow she accepted it all without showing her tears. She would save her emotions and share them with Miguel.

Returning to the college after the summer she found that Miguel, too, had been cut away. Some un-named benefactor had provided better studies in America – what more could a young man ask for? She wandered aimlessly through her life after that. Love affairs came and went. Nothing seemed important any more.

Just before graduation, she was approached by the House of Silence. With her social standing she moved through the kind of corridors the House desired. At first she merely listened and noted. Reliance on her sexual prowess stayed untapped until the day it became necessary; when her tasks became difficult and more important. But still there was no warmth, no closeness, no love in her life.

In the autumn of 1935, came the beginnings of the Spanish Civil War. The House was under the control of the

Fascists. And, anxious about any communist infiltration of the country, Donna Maria was sent to the Punto Romano in Barcelona. One night in October – the House was expecting an important contact from Berlin – she was ordered to the Roman Bridge to meet him and prepare the House for his information. She waited in the dampness of the bridge till long past the agreed time. Then she saw a shadow and heard the dull thud of leather on leather as a click of heels echoed around the aged structure.

The man whispered his words. 'I am Baron von Zeiss. Good evening, meine Fräulein.'

'You are late, señor.'

'They did not take the train until last evening.'

She took his arm and led him from the coldness of the bridge to the bar on the edge of the river. White-coated barmen shook cocktails flamboyantly from side to side above their heads to the rhythm of a dance band jumping from a gramophone. The small leather booth at the back of the bar was vacant, a *reservado* card leaning against a bottle of champagne wedged in an ice-filled bucket.

Donna Maria slipped into the booth and the Baron sat down opposite her. She could see him clearly now: middle forties, a shock of brown hair emphasising brown eyes and moustache. A typical tall, dark, handsome aristocrat, she thought.

'Are they at the hotel?' she asked, taking a cigarette from her handbag. He jumped to his feet, and clicked his heels as he offered a match. She gazed up as she took the light.

'I do wish you would not click your heels, señor,' she said.

'In Germany, it is the mark of a gentleman,' he replied.

'In Spain, it means flamenco and I'm not in the mood to dance.' Her reply was accompanied by her warm smile. The Baron sat down again.

'The Russians have taken rooms above a photographic shop in the centre of Barcelona. A shop called Frans Lavasar, Photographer – 142a La Mancha Strasse.'

She nodded. 'Did they make any further contacts in Berlin?'

The Baron shook his head.

She pushed her empty glass towards him and he rose to open the bottle.

'No heel clicks, please,' she said. He smiled.

She assembled her information. She knew the photographic shop and Lavasar the owner. It was already known that he was part of the communist cell in Barcelona but up until now their exact function was unknown. Tonight, through the Baron following from Berlin, a direct contact with the Kremlin had been made. Surely this information would be enough to satisfy the House of Silence.

She joined the Baron in a half glass of champagne before going to the telephone booth at the other side of the room. She informed the House of the arrival of the Russians and the address and returned to the booth.

'We wait a little,' she said, answering the Baron's tense face. By the time they had started their third bottle he was relaxed. From the gramophone, a shrill clarinet solo rose above a combination of percussion and brass.

'*Bei mir bist du schön*, again and again.

Bei mir bist du schön, I love you.'

The Baron half sang, half talked the words. They were directed, not at Donna Maria, but to his empty glass. He was drunk and becoming loud. She would have to take him out of there. But she had to wait for the return telephone call. The Baron began to thump the table with the flat of his hands. There was no knowing how indiscreet this man might become. He might shout the communist meeting to the world, as he emulated Gene Krupa on the table top. She stood, trying to attract his attention.

'Hey, slow down,' she said, trying to sound relaxed. 'Don't spoil the evening.'

He stopped and looked up at her. Her eyes were sharp, chastising him.

'What evening? We can't stay here. We have to go. We

have to go to the camera shop.'

He shouted the words and then returned to his drumming. She should not have given him so much champagne. She had to get him out of that public place.

Donna Maria glanced over again to the telephone booth. One of the patrons was using it. The Baron thumped away and began singing again. He was drawing too much attention and she began to feel panic rising within her. She moved around to his side of the booth and sat close to him. He ignored her. She felt down along his thighs and then between his legs and gently stroked.

'Don't spoil the evening,' she whispered.

She felt him harden. His thighs quivered and his legs closed onto her hand. She leaned back into the high leather seat of the booth and saw him look down into the cleavage of her silk evening blouse. She glanced around the bar. They were in shadow save for the solitary candle twinkling in the centre of the table. She pinched it out with her free hand and then gently eased her left breast from her blouse. He was staring at her, his breathing heavy. She forced her eyes to gaze deeply into his. She whispered the command.

'Suck me,' she said, giving her voice a false vibrato.

He fell onto her nipple without hesitation. His tongue dug deeply into her firm roundness, as the full orchestra of '*Bei mir bist du schön*' enveloped the atmosphere. She closed her eyes and relaxed, confident that she was now in total control.

A firm touch on her neck jolted her up from the back of the booth. Swiftly she moved away from the Baron's mouth and turned.

'I'm sorry to interrupt, but I believe you know a very quiet house in the city?'

The question came from a tall man with a wide mischievous smile. He spoke with a soft English accent and repeated the question.

'I believe you know a quiet house in the city?' It was the identity code used by all Spanish operatives.

'I was waiting for a telephone call,' she said, still dazed by the interruption.

'I am the telephone call,' he replied, grinning again. 'Would you like to replace the puppy? It has a cold nose.' He stared hard at the bare breast which was still jutting from her blouse. She felt herself blush.

'Is this the chap from Berlin?' the Englishman gestured towards the Baron sitting sheepishly in the dark. She nodded.

'Is he sober enough to be of use?'

As the Baron continued to sit without speaking, she nodded again.

'Good.'

The Englishman sounded efficient and direct.

'The House has briefed me on Lavasar and the meeting tonight, señorita, so we know where we're going. But I'll need our friend here to point out the two chaps from Berlin if and when they leave the camera shop.'

'Am I to understand, señor, that you are only interested in the two men from the Berlin train,' she asked. She was anxious about Lavasar and the other occupants of the camera shop. What was she to do about *them*?

'The House would like the others to continue as if nothing had happened,' the Englishman said.

She moved wearily in her chair and caught the eye of the Baron. He too was puzzled.

'"As if nothing had happened", escapes my reason, señor.'

She was a little angry that the foreigner seemed to be taking command. His confidence was irritating. The Baron, too, spluttered questions. The Englishman paused for a moment's thought.

'We are interested in talking only to the two gentlemen,' he affirmed. 'Privately. Without the knowledge of the others who are waiting in the camera shop. You understand me?' They nodded.

'The House would like to keep the Spanish cell intact and

operating normally. Who knows how many more little lambs will call.'

The Baron emitted a puzzled sigh. Donna Maria displayed a cool acceptance but inside she felt a chill at the coldness of this Englishman. She did not like him. But he commanded more attention than any other man she had ever met.

'Well, señor, to work.' She spoke the words firmly, controlling her voice.

'And what do we call you?' she asked.

'Marcus will suffice,' the Englishman said, draining the warm glass of champagne before he led the way out of the bar.

There was the easy grace of the animal in her walk when Donna Maria followed him out to the waiting car, her slender legs brushing through her flimsy dress and singing the praises of Aphrodite. She was obviously a loose woman. They usually were in the field. Marcus decided that, once the operation was completed, a long night in her bed would not go amiss. Even Gomez, his driver, sitting outside in the darkened street waiting for him to come back from the bar, gave a low wolf whistle as she eased herself sensually into the rear of the car. It was still full of dust from their journey.

Gomez had met Marcus in La Linea secretly and they had made the long trip to Barcelona by road. Ronay had been in Gibraltar for a month, not knowing why he had been sent to the Mediterranean branch of the Factory. Cheney was left in London, expecting his return daily; that was usual in Factory business.

They closed the door of the car and sat silently in the dark as it pulled away from the kerbside. The Baron sat in the back seat, his hands restlessly trying to fumble Donna Maria. The girl started to talk to Gomez and skilfully ignored the advances.

The action commended her to Ronay. He looked forward even more to that long night with her.

Gomez stopped the car a few yards from the photographer's shop on the opposite side of La Mancha Street.

The street was dark, apart from a light above the shop. Shadows moved to and fro in the dim light. The Baron fidgeted, when the door to the shop opened and three men came out onto the street. The girl touched Ronay's shoulder.

'Lavasar and his brother,' she whispered.

'The other is the Russian,' the Baron murmured nervously.

Ronay noted the thick-set man with his hands in his pockets. He knew the face as well as his own but he kept this knowledge to himself. The man Lavasar walked to the kerbside and looked up at the room over the shop where a light shone. A figure gestured from the window. Suddenly the light went out, and the man came out of the door, closing it softly behind him.

'That's the other one.' The Baron choked the words from the back of the car.

Ronay recognised this man too. He was German. These were the two men the Factory had expected. Charlie Peake had been certain that they would break out and, as usual, he was right. And just so long as they were relaxed, just a little off-guard, they would not suspect they had been followed so soon.

The man Lavasar shook the hand of the Russian, kissed the other man on both cheeks and then walked away with his brother. Their business appeared to be completed.

The Russian and the German came towards the darkened car. Ronay eased back in his seat and motioned to the others to do likewise. Gomez the Gibraltarian smiled and flashed his ridiculous gold teeth and dribbled all over his lapel.

'They separate, Señor Marcus,' he whispered.

'We are in luck I think.'

'Keep the Baron with you,' Ronay rasped at the fat one. 'I'll walk on with the girl.'

He got out of the front seat and waited for Donna Maria to join him on the pavement.

'Take my arm and talk as we walk,' he said firmly. Her

arm crept inside his and her long slender fingers clasped on his. He couldn't understand a word of the Spanish she was cooing into his ear but it sounded natural and that was good. They followed the two men through four streets before hitting the main centre of Barcelona where the pavements were crowded. Ronay quickened his pace until what had been a gap of fifty yards was shortened to twenty. The crowd thickened, the distance became shorter. He knew the risk to himself if he stayed following much longer. The two men might be off-guard but they were professionals. Suddenly they stopped. No warning. They stopped so quickly that Ronay nearly walked into them. Their eyes narrowed with suspicion as they looked at him and the girl.

Suddenly she pulled him away into a small crowd of young people clapping hands to a flamenco guitarist.

'I'm sorry we couldn't find the others,' she shouted to a man clapping opposite her. He stared at the beauty calling him and tried to place the face.

'I don't know you,' he yelled over the noise.

'Forget it,' she yelled back. 'We're here now. Better late than never.'

The man shrugged and encouraged the guitarist with a high pitched '*Olé!*' Ronay clapped in time with the music, watching the two men out of the corner of his eye. They had relaxed again and were looking at the posters outside a cinema. They walked up to the box office and bought tickets.

'Got any money?' Ronay asked the girl.

She led him to the cinema and paid their entrance. They got to the rear of the dark auditorium in time to see the silhouettes of the two men excusing themselves along a line of patrons. Ronay stood motionless. If the men from Berlin were here to watch the film, luck had given him a chance to take them alone.

Ronay decided to make his move there and then, quickly, in the dark. He saw that the row of seats to which the men had gone was not full. The girl stood next to him and said nothing. He liked that quality. He waited another ten minutes, satisfying himself that the two men were engrossed in the plot of the film, then he whispered to the girl.

'We are going along their row of seats.'

She made no comment. She merely nodded. He liked her even more.

'Along the line past them and sit in the first vacant seats,' he said. 'You first. Do not stop for anything.'

A question rose to her lips, but she bit it back and moved down the aisle. Once opposite the row, she whispered her apologies to the first patron on her left who rose slowly from his seat without taking his eyes off the screen. One by one, the others did likewise slowly crouching forward from their seats, following the film and allowing her and Ronay to pass. Ronay felt the ice-pick in the left-hand pocket of his coat. He slowly drew it out and held it by his side.

As they approached, the Russian made an impatient comment as the girl bumped his leg. Ronay half fell against him as he passed, and apologised. The Russian didn't hear a word. The ice-pick had entered under his ribs and pierced his heart. The girl turned her head as she passed the German and saw the Russian crumple silently forward in his seat. Then she saw the sudden swift jab of the ice-pick as it went into his companion. Ronay gently pushed her onwards with his free hand. She longed to run but she controlled herself. Again Ronay admired her style.

They sat immediately next to the dead German, his glazed eyes bulging with shock. The eyes seemed to be watching the action on the screen in disbelief. She ached to move away from the smell of death. When would they leave, for God's sake? Please make it soon, she prayed.

A movement in the dark made her jump. Another couple were murmuring excuses as they passed along their row. The Englishman gripped her arm, holding her firmly in her seat. The man leading was stopped by the Russian's ill-mannered refusal to make room for the couple to pass. In spite of requests, the Russian sat, continuing to ignore them. Finally the man pushed the Russian angrily. The huddled body slowly tilted forward and crashed into the seat in front. This brought an angry retort from its burly occupant who stood and turned towards the Russian now lying crumpled on the row. The man, still trying to pass, nudged impatiently. Then his girl companion screamed. Two ushers rushed from the back of the auditorium, their torches flashing. By the time they had encouraged the couple out of the row the cinema was a mass of hissing and whistles.

One usher played his beam over the Russian. Finding no reaction, he bent down and touched the slumped figure. The white face and fish eyes told their grim tale. The usher backed out of the row and whispered to his colleague. Seconds later the film slowed to a stop and the cinema was bathed in a hard, white light. Manager and ushers paced the aisles, calming the audience. Groups began to file out of the auditorium. Ronay and the girl mingled with the crowd. As they reached the exit door, a startled shout came from the row they had left. The manager had discovered the German. Hysterical screams of the crowd echoed in unforgettable horror.

Ronay led Maria out onto the pavement. He took her arm. She had started to shake.

'I'm terribly cold,' she shivered. 'Please hold me.'

'It will pass, I promise.'

He held her close to him.

'Do we have to run?' she asked.

'I don't think so,' he grinned. 'We can just stay here and get to know each other.'

She felt so relaxed in his embrace.

'Would you like some dinner?' he asked.

'How can you think of food?' She shivered again.

He released her. 'Very well. I'll take you back to the car and leave you with your nightmares.' He turned.

She followed. 'I can do without your humour, Mr. . . .'

'Marcus. I told you, just call me Marcus.'

'Well, whoever you are, it isn't funny.'
'You're quite right. It isn't.'
She walked fast trying to keep alongside him.
'I would have appreciated a little warning. That's all.'
He stopped and held out his hand. 'You're right. Let us shake hands and start over again.'
She studied his face, her eyes taking in every line. Finally she took his hand.
'My name is Maria Domenquin.' She half smiled.
'I'm still Marcus,' he grinned. 'How about dinner?'
'Not tonight, thank you,' she said sweetly.
Ronay stalked off. She followed to the waiting car.
Gomez pulled down the window as they came level. The Englishman glanced up to the dark windows of the photo shop.
'Nobody's at home,' Gomez said.
The Baron in the rear seat gave a heavy snore.
'Nobody at home here either.' The fat one dribbled the joke and gave a hoarse chuckle.
'I'll take the dreamer here to a hotel and I'll take myself home,' Maria snapped curtly as she got into the rear seat.
Ronay seemed surprised. 'Is that all?' he asked.
'What else?' she flashed.
'What about reporting to the House?' He made the question sound like a reprimand.
She shook her head and leaned back into the darkness of the car.
'I can do that tomorrow.'
'They will want to know tonight,' he growled. He was becoming testy with this beauty.
She sat silent in the darkness.
Ronay spoke to Gomez. 'Take these passengers wherever they wish and meet me at the restaurant.' Gomez nodded and started the engine.
'Make your report and thank you for your help,' Ronay said into the darkness of the back seat as the car pulled away from the kerb.

He went to the restaurant and relaxed. By the time he had worked out the Spanish menu, the sweating face of Gomez was pressing into the window near his shoulder. The gold teeth flashed and Ronay knew he would have to invite the slob in. He waved tiredly and the filthy, once white, deeply-creased suit rolled across the dining floor. Gomez dragged the fedora off his greased hair and pressed it humbly to his heart.

'To join you, señor, is an honour,' he dribbled down his chin.

Ronay shifted in his chair and muttered, not looking at his companion. The sight of the Gibraltarian was distasteful when a meal was imminent. Gomez in his turn was also floundering. The atmosphere of the restaurant was clean and tasteful and to the eyes of the little man it appeared somewhat palatial. He constantly wiped his greasy hair with what had started out as a handkerchief. He perspired freely and tried to sit upright on the high-backed chair, causing his little fat legs to dangle embarrassingly one inch from the carpeted floor.

Ronay shut the little man out of his mind by composing a letter to Cheney on the back of the menu. He could be anywhere in the world and always in moments of calm or concern he thought of her. Whenever she came to mind he would write these *billets-doux*, short, long, always wishing he was with her. They never got posted. They went into his pocket and, when each particular trip was over, he would go home and the letter would come to light. At a chosen moment in the tranquillity of England, he would offer it, relax and listen to her gentle voice reading the words. Their hands would meet and cling lovingly.

It was a simple, very private ritual.

The sweating body opposite him stumbled into the table, shaking the condiments and rattling the tableware. The fat man had risen smiling at someone behind Ronay's shoulder. He turned to see Donna Maria. Her dark eyes were serious and anxious, her body on guard, yet vulnerable.

'I have just come from the House,' she said. 'I asked about the men in the cinema. My master refused at first to answer my question but he did eventually.'

Ronay returned to his letter, ignoring her. Gomez stumbled again as he offered her his chair. She looked down at Ronay, waiting for the invitation which didn't come. Gomez fidgeted, embarrassed by the rudeness of the Englishman.

'He told me about the two men, about the terrible things they did,' she continued. 'He told me why they were here. I would like to apologise.'

Ronay continued writing. 'Apologise for what?' he said without looking up. 'For not knowing that cowboys kill Indians.'

'Just because you wear a white hat doesn't make me feel any cleaner,' she said. 'I didn't realise how dangerous it all was. I've never been in such a situation before.'

He folded his letter and put it into his pocket.

'So now you have been in the situation,' he said harshly. 'After the event you feel a bit of an idiot having acted the way you did. Therefore, you prostrate yourself before your good knight and beg him to accept your favour.'

Gomez swallowed an ocean of saliva and waited for the lovely lady to respond. She flicked her dress and sat in the chair.

'I prostrate myself thus,' she said, picking up the menu. 'Not begging, merely accepting a once gallant offer of dinner, apologising only for my lateness. I am quite able to eat alone if at any time you should wish to leave.'

Gomez offered a prayer to his patron saint and shuffled out of the restaurant for safer climes. Ronay viewed this lady with respectful eyes.

He stayed for the meal. Afterwards, they walked to her apartment in the better part of town. By dawn she had slapped his face once and kissed him a thousand times and they loved for seven short weeks. He talked of Cheney and of England and of her, and she listened, understanding his words but mesmerised by him – she was completely taken by this Englishman.

With the eighth week of their affair, came the signal from the Factory and Ronay couldn't understand the sense of it. He asked for a confirmation but it said the same. He double-checked the code; again, no change.

Spanish Civil War imminent, it said. *Imperative communist faction free to confront fascists during hostilities. Promote communist friendship. Retire House operative Domenquin as gesture. Immediate. Peake.*

'A gesture!' Ronay muttered. The directive was a brutal shock. He had known them to change horses many times but this was Maria. It was like telling him to kill Cheney, but he had never deviated before and it was ridiculous to question policy because of an affair of the heart.

By the evening he had made up his mind. He dialled the number of Lavasar's photo shop. The voice at the other end confirmed Ronay's fears. Yes, the Factory had contacted them and yes, they had lost two operatives recently and yes, they would like to know who arranged the kill. Then Ronay told them of Maria and that he would present her to them that night.

He went to Maria's apartment. She heard him enter and moved her body under the sheets of the bed.

'Get dressed,' he said calmly from the semi-darkness.

She watched him walk around the other side of the bed to the dressing table and select one of the two hand guns from inside. She loved his seriousness at such times and leaned over the side of the bed to kiss the back of his neck.

Instead of scolding her he pushed her back onto the pillows and held her down. He kissed her gently, softly, slowly. She felt him relax on top of her and she eased herself deeply into the sheets, feeling his warm hand encircle her nipple and creep down her shining skin towards her thighs. Her muscles began to contract. She opened her legs, inviting him.

‘Can you hear me?’ he nibbled her ear.

‘Yes! yes!’ she cried, arching towards him.

‘Well get dressed then.’ He smacked her rump and jumped off the bed.

She chased him into the bathroom and jumped onto his back, squealing with laughter and frustration. Then the fun stopped.

‘Lavasar. The photographer,’ he said. ‘He’s broken out.’

Slowly she slid down. ‘When?’ she said, using his towel to wipe the soft film of sweat from her body.

‘Tonight. The House got wind of it too late. As usual. He has taken his brother and God knows what else,’ he said.

She went to the sink and began to flick cold water onto her face and breasts. ‘Were they warned?’ she asked.

He shook his head. ‘I’ve no idea, but if he has gone, the whole Barcelona operation goes with it.’

She dressed while he checked his gun. He saw her watching him, her eyes flashing with concern.

‘What has all this got to do with you?’ she asked.

He didn’t answer.

‘What do the Factory want?’ she asked. He snapped the barrel back into line with the chamber of the revolver and stood up.

‘We’re going for a drive,’ he said.

She followed him out of the flat and down to the waiting car. The man, Gomez, shuffled away from the front door when he saw them and dived into the vehicle. He pulled away from the kerb as they got into the back. They drove through the well-lit side of Barcelona, keeping to the main streets. Maria sat silently looking from left to right, hoping for that lucky chance sight of the photographer and his brother. Then her eyes caught a look between Ronay and the Gibraltarian crouched over the driving wheel. She saw the little fat man’s big wide eyes in the driving mirror and Ronay’s glint of a dark secret. She’d been around, she knew the game; she also knew the tall Englishman. That one glance told her enough.

Maria pulled herself into his ribs. The throb there at his heart affirmed what she had already guessed. She gave a quick look out of the rear window and saw the long, dark limousine following, just its lights showing life. Somewhere inside would be Lavasar or the brother or both, or someone from Moscow or Berlin or both. It stayed within twenty yards; its fearful presence menaced them. She fell back against Ronay.

'My God, Marcus, talk to me,' she breathed.

He lifted his arm and allowed her to tuck herself even closer to him.

'Lavasar knows about you, my little love,' he said, stroking her hair. 'I don't know how, but he does.'

She gripped him tightly. 'But why are we driving around Barcelona? Why can't we go to the House or away from the city?'

Ronay didn't answer and then she knew everything. 'You've set me up – you've used me to get them out, haven't you?'

Gomez gave a wet whistle. She waited for Ronay's answer. He spoke without showing her his eyes.

'I've had a note from Charlie Peake. There's been a change of policy – so Lavasar lives again.'

There was a short silence. 'That's not enough, Marcus,' she said. 'I want to hear it all.'

He glanced at Gomez in the rear mirror and the fat shoulders shrugged.

'Charlie Peake would like you retired – as a gesture.'

'They want you dead, señorita,' Gomez wailed as he skidded into another corner.

'As a gesture!' she gasped angrily.

'Lavasar wants your guts, so sit tight and be a good girl while I think.'

She watched him watch the limousine, she watched him calculate and then she pulled his lapel so that his face was touching hers. Her voice was bitter.

'It's all for you isn't it. You want Lavasar and I'm the bait.

You want it finished don't you and to hell with London and to hell with me!'

He pulled away.

'Marcus, bloody Ronay,' she said. She saw him laugh in the passing street lights, that boyish laugh that made her heart sing. He pushed Gomez in the back.

'You know the place?' he asked.

The fat one giggled. 'Si, señor.'

'Let's go then.'

Ronay took the revolver from his inside pocket and put it in his lap. He then took his jacket off and threw it onto the floor. The car skidded into a right turn and gathered speed.

Maria saw the limousine take up the chase. Twice, three times, four, Gomez swung the car into dark streets and the limousine after them.

'The cul-de-sac is the next bend, señor,' Gomez called as he pushed through the gears. Ronay took her roughly and pushed her onto the floor, onto his jacket.

'Stay there! Don't get up! And stop shaking!' he grinned.

The car gave another lurch. 'The cul-de-sac comes, señor,' Gomez yelled.

The car slowed as it turned into the narrow streets and, as it did so, Ronay hurled himself out of it and rolled onto the cobbles into the shadows. The Gibraltarian drove on for the last thirty yards of road before a high wall loomed out of the darkness. He stopped the car with its engine running. The limousine came into view, slowly entering the cul-de-sac and stopping within a few feet of the stationary car. For a few seconds the sounds of the two engines droned into the night. The headlights of the limousine suddenly switched on, bathing the area, but before anyone had moved from inside, Ronay pounced.

Coming from the rear, he had the advantage of surprise. He shot at the figure inside the limousine nearest to the window. There was a shrill scream of pain. Ronay ducked down and around the side of the car. The driver opened his door offering a perfect target but, before Ronay could aim, the driver fired. With a sharp flash of flame the bullet ricocheted off the wall behind Ronay's head.

The driver's door eased open a little more. It was enough. Ronay fired.

The bullet went straight through the driver's head. Ronay could hear the lead smash into the windscreen. He still didn't know how many more were inside the vehicle, so he rolled along the cobbled street and underneath it. He hoped that the silence would make them think he had been hit. He lay there holding his breath, listening, and then he saw a movement from his own car. He wanted to yell to Maria and Gomez to stay under cover. He heard her voice.

'Marcus! Marcus!'

He stayed silent. Above him he heard harsh voices. There were still two more in the limousine, he was sure now. One was in front next to the driver and the other was in the back, right above his head.

She called again. He could hear Gomez pleading with her to stay, but the rear door opened a little wider and he saw her slip into the street.

The person above Marcus moved towards the other side of the limousine and began to wind down the window. Maria was now a target.

'Marcus, are you all right?'

He stayed silent. He was in a perfect position to strike. And then he heard the click of a revolver cocking above him.

'Christ!' he murmured.

He heard the front door of the limousine ease open. He was faced with a two-sided attack. Which way should he go first, above or in front? He rolled sharply to his left, and pumped two bullets into the front door of the limousine. It swung open. The man's body fell out halfway onto the street and Ronay knew that that side of the car was safe. There was the sound of a shot from within the limousine. Ronay threw himself further into the street as the cry from Maria told him that she had been hit. In an instant he was on his feet. He must draw fire away from Maria. He felt a hot slash hit the shoulder of his shirt and a high-pitched whine pass his ear. He was the target now.

Ronay leapt up and landed flat on the roof of the limousine. He slid to the edge and emptied his bullets into the open window. He lay there waiting for some sign that the battle was over.

Gomez rushed out from his safety and went to the figure of Maria lying by the car in the soft light. Then he screamed and with an ungainly rush he ran to the limousine, shaking his fist. He glared into the back seat.

'I spit on you, I curse you!' he cried, venting his anger at whatever was there.

From around them lights sprang from darkened windows. Voices shouted down, doors opened, people gathered, questions echoed from one side of the street to the other. Ronay eased himself over the edge of the roof of the limousine, onto the road. He saw the bodies of Lavasar and his brother in the back seat. He climbed down and ran to Maria. Her head was a mask of blood but she was still alive. Gomez helped him lift her gently into their car and then Ronay drove the limousine onto the side pavement out of their way. He was totally oblivious to the barrage of questions being shouted at him from all sides. Gomez backed his car out onto the main street, waited for Ronay and then drove off, the car wheels screeching.

They drove through the night, searching the doorways of the passing houses for a sign. Then it was there: a brass plate shone in the street lights. Gomez pulled into the kerb. Ronay jumped out and rang the bell of the house; a minute passed before the door opened. Doctor Juan Beni peered into the night, his dressing gown hanging limply. Ronay pushed him roughly back into the corridor of the house.

'I have an emergency,' he snapped. At the same time the fat Gibraltarian puffed into the house with Maria in his arms. The doctor led the way into a back room.

'Put her over there, under the light,' he muttered as he

switched on a huge lamp over a long table. The Doctor turned. Ronay knew he was about to protest, the usual lines of 'I must report an injury. Who are you?'. But Ronay stopped him by thrusting him back towards Maria.

'Over the right temple. She's hurt,' he said, indicating the part of Maria's head that had congealed blood caked into the hair.

'It's a bullet wound,' the Doctor said, pulling back. Ronay took out his gun and pushed the muzzle into the Doctor's spine.

'Just relax, señor, and see to the patient,' he said.

Doctor Beni bent over her once more. He began to sweat as his fingers felt nervously around the girl's head.

'I don't think the bullet is still in there,' he said, prodding gently into the gash at the side of Maria's head.

The gun pressed firmly into his back again.

'Be sure. Be very sure,' Ronay whispered. He didn't know this doctor but where else could he go? The House was not to know of this night's work and any contact with the Factory would tell Charlie Peake that London's orders had been ignored. He had taken a decision. He had gambled. Even he did not know what price he might have to pay if he had made a miscalculation.

The Doctor prepared his potions and cleaned and stitched the wound. He stepped back an hour later, exhausted. The girl had begun to regain consciousness. Ronay bent low and talked to her in soft tones. Finally he turned from the girl and trained his steely gaze on Doctor Beni.

'Thank you, señor,' he said. 'Are there any dangers for her?'

The Doctor paused and thought for a moment. 'She will be clear of infection. The wound is clean but she has lost some blood. There is the slight possibility of her going into shock.' The girl slowly sat up on the table and looked at the Doctor. He tried to avoid her eyes but he could not turn away from her. Ronay lifted her in his arms and as he did so, he turned to the Doctor.

'I know where you live and I know who you are,' the Englishman's voice was quiet but coldly menacing. 'Forget us, and live your life.'

The car drove off as dawn was breaking. Out of Barcelona and into the far country, they drove on and on. Donna Maria slept uneasily, holding tightly to Ronay and becoming delirious at times. They came at last to the village of Istan. The car pulled its way to the top of the last hill and drove into the drive of the Domenquin Villa.

Ronay spent those last days at her bedside. Then, when he was satisfied that she was out of danger he took her into his arms and kissed her long and gravely. She watched him pack. 'Forever,' he said. He gave her one last look and then he was gone.

During the journey to Gibraltar, he never said a word to Gomez. Only when they had passed from Spain onto the Rock did he speak.

'Deliver these two letters,' he said. 'One is for the House, the other is for the Spanish police. They do not mention you, so you are safe.'

Gomez went about his task without question.

Ronay flew to London that day. His debriefing was clouded with suspicion. Charlie Peake sucked his teeth and listened how Ronay shot the girl only to be double-crossed by Lavasar and his brother. How he had killed them defending himself and then got the hell out of Spain with the House in full cry and the Spanish police demanding his head. Yes, he did understand that he had compromised the Factory, and yes he had badly miscalculated the situation.

That weekend he told Cheney of his early retirement. She accepted his quiet mood and he was glad she didn't ask any questions. Spain was yesterday and he would never see Maria again.

Book III

The Contact

The coasts of the south of Spain and North Africa were still bathed in moonlight as the cargo plane skimmed the cool Mediterranean sea and slipped between the two countries onto Gibraltar. Since 1704 the British flag had flown over this rock fortress. Not yet first light, the massive mounds of internal armaments sat silently at the ready, and deep inside the heart of the mountain the lights of the huge garrison were switching on and growing in number with every minute that passed.

The sea plane hit the hazardous water strip bordered crazily on one side by the mountain and on the other by the Spanish mainland. Its pontoons skimmed the waves and its airbrakes bit hard as the flaps sucked in the warming air beneath each wing. Some of the sacks and cases in the fuselage broke from their protective bindings and scattered from the force of the landing.

Suddenly the engine was silent and the bulkhead door was opened from the outside. An officer of the military police pushed the upper part of his torso into the fuselage. He wore a tropical white uniform and spoke with a high-pitched whine. ''Morning sergeant, welcome to Gibraltar.'

The crewman feinted a salute. 'On board medicaments, various, for the use of,' the officer said, referring to a manifest sheet in his hand. The crewman tapped each item as the officer read out loudly.

'Tropical socks, shirts and shoes, sizes various for the use of, etcetera, etcetera,' the officer called.

The crewman replied, 'Etcetera, etcetera, yes sir.'

During this whole action, the presence of Ronay was completely ignored by both men. He merely sat and admired the pantomime.

'I will unload in fifteen minutes,' the officer said to the crewman and, informing the silent Ronay, 'I'm taking the boat to the outer precincts of the airfield.'

The crewman looked at Ronay and gave a thumbs up sign. Ronay pulled himself to his feet and collected his small case. The crewman helped him out of the bulkhead door and lowered him into the boat. The air was warm and the soft breeze which rushed through Ronay's hair made him feel welcome.

The officer started the motor. Within five minutes the boat had reached the outer perimeter. Without a word, the officer got out, leaving the motor running, and started to undo a massive padlock on the door built into the high-wired fence which encircled the area.

Outside the fence was a small dark road that serviced the rear of the large dock buildings that backed onto the RAF landing area. A huge sign lit by a solitary low-power bulb announced that the place was off limits for unauthorised personnel.

The officer pushed the fence door open. Taking the hint, Ronay eased himself out of the boat and, with a stiff nod to the officer, carried his case onto the dock road. He heard the fence door close behind him, gears connecting in the boat and the motor pulling away, then silence. There were not even the tropical night sounds of the inevitable crickets. He stood, just out of the soft glow from the sign, the only source of light around.

He smiled. Who would have bet less than a week ago, that he would be standing there in the half-light on the dockside in Gibraltar? And how ridiculous time was.

He remembered Cheney. All those years she was there, happy, content, needing him and then within one moment of one afternoon she was gone. No warning. One afternoon and his life was stopped as dead as hers. He could still hear that clock, the clock which ticked and chimed as he sat in the room waiting for the man from Alby & Son. The doctor had called the funeral director for him and then left to attend to his living patients. With only the clock for company he waited, holding Cheney's ice-cold hand; waiting for the man from Alby & Son, waiting for a person neither of them had known existed an hour before.

A sharp explosion came from the direction of the far dock buildings. Then another louder bang pierced the night and somewhere distant a dog barked. Immediately others joined in, howling and barking.

Ronay caught sight of a dark object cranking around the bend of the road. It was a small, ancient saloon car. He stepped back into the darkness. The car's exhaust gave another sharp explosion and it finally lurched up to the airport gate, a few feet from where Ronay stood in the shadows.

A small shape poured itself out of the driver's seat and around the back of the car. Ronay's muscles throbbed as he steadied himself. Suddenly the shape pounced into his midriff. He fell against part of the perimeter fence and summoned every bone in his body to stay on his feet. He thrust his back into the fence and pushed hard with his buttocks into the wire which helped to keep him upright.

There was a thick, sweet smell of lemon mixed with grease and garlic wafting up from below his chin. He looked down onto the sweating, semi-bald head of his aggressor. It was covered by a thin layer of heavily brilliantined hair.

'Enough, Gomez,' he said with controlled anger.

The fat head spoke with its heavy Gibraltarian accent. 'Señor Marcus, to see you after so long make me forget. Forgive my embraces.'

Ronay studied this elderly fat man, looking up with heavy brown eyes and thick hooded lids, giving the impression that he was either intoxicated or about to fall asleep. Sweat was still pouring down his face. He caught Ronay's look and flashed a massive smile, showing an abundance of gold teeth that, in the shadows, gave the impression of wide gaps.

It was imperative that Ronay's arrival on the rock should be unannounced and yet he needed contact with someone local, someone he could trust. It hadn't taken long to remember Tomas Gomez. The little fat puppy forced a bigger smile. Saliva flowed from the gold teeth. Ronay grinned and relaxed, offering his hand. Gomez pounced on it and kissed it damply.

'Just shake the damn thing and get me out of here,' Ronay said. And Gomez dragged him towards the heap of automobile.

A gradual morning was breaking over the fortress as the Gomez car made its way through the tiny streets. It had no respect as it bumped one pavement in three, scratched at least two walls and left a dump of oil in most places like a dog marking new territory. Ronay watched Gomez huddled at the helm, his big brown eyes squinting nervously, his podgy hands overworking the wheel. The journey so far had consisted of continual braking, exasperated curses and gears screaming. It was a pure hate relationship between man and machine but was it ever different, Ronay mused, as he allowed the argument to continue uninterrupted. Gomez and the car, Gomez and the bike, in fact Gomez paired with anything mechanical was always going to be a disaster.

The little Gibraltarian was a loner. That's how Ronay had used him in the old days. If something urgent was to be done then Gomez did it, and Ronay couldn't trust another man more. Even Charlie Peake gave a murmur of approval when Ronay asked for Gomez. In him was a loyalty and a need to be needed, and if Ronay was going to slip into Spain, who better to guide him.

Ronay's eyes fixed on the passing scene as the light brightened. 'Three years and the Rock hasn't changed,' he said.

Gomez smiled. 'Outside perhaps, but inside there is the change, señor. Bigger guns and a machine they say sees a hundred miles in the dark. How about that, señor? They say you can see a camel shit in Morocco. That I would like to see.'

'How about the Factory?' Ronay said.

Gomez shrugged his shoulders, his nervous eyes never leaving the road. 'Not like when you had it, señor. Three years ago the Factory was a Factory. Now it is a schoolroom. They have two men. One works in Government House and the other has a business in the High Street. All no good, señor. What you call "second eleven".' Ronay smiled. Gomez continued. 'Not like us, señor, not quick to see. You remember, señor?'

'Vaguely,' Ronay said.

Do we do something quick, Señor Marcos. Like before?'

'I have to get into Spain,' Ronay replied.

Gomez smiled, his gold teeth flashed and his saliva flowed.

'Will it be difficult for you?' Ronay asked as the car buzzed through a small archway and skidded to a halt. Gomez turned from the wheel and fixed him with his enormous eyes.

'Over there they have peace at last. They do not like we bring our war over the border, so it is difficult. For the "second eleven". But for me, señor, it is easy.' He gave a broad grin, as he slammed the car back into gear and jerked it forward.

The warmness that Ronay knew as Gibraltar was easing itself through the open windows of the car as it clattered through the small thoroughfare. The squat houses of the locals were the same as he remembered. For him, his spell on the Rock had been a bore until that glorious last year. It was strange remembering those past incidents again after fighting to forget them forever. But Cheney wasn't there to hurt now, and so he allowed the memories to run free, bringing a warm smile to his face to match the breeze pushing through the window.

The car gave a final bang and moaned to a stop outside a shack on the outskirts of the town. From inside the dwelling came the noisy sound of human voices, dogs barking and flamenco music. Gomez took Ronay's case and led him through a broken fence into the open door of the shack. The entrance led immediately into a small room made even smaller by walls hung with a thousand gay, gaudy paintings of bullfights and biblical stories. The room was full of smoke from a large stove and an open spit over a log fire. At the stove, a large woman of around sixty stood in a black dress, her grey hair tied in a tight bun at the back of her head. She cooked in bad temper. In the middle of the room was an oak table. Seated around it, under it, and on top of it were thronged children and adults who were reading, smoking, eating, shouting, screaming, kicking, fighting and dancing to a radio that blared from a sideboard that also had on it a cradle with a sleeping baby.

Ronay remained at the small doorway, his tall frame filling the space. He was transfixed by the woman cooking. She was continually talking to herself in a foul temper and at regular intervals she smacked one of the four children hanging on to the bottom of her dress. She did this for no apparent reason except that they happened to be within range of her hand. But the children stayed and the noise went on. Gomez gave another wet smile.

'Welcome to my house, Señor Marcos,' he beamed.

He moved to the table and gave a young man in his twenties a deft kick which sent him from his chair onto the floor, yelling protest.

'This is my son-in-law, Paco,' Gomez laughed good-naturedly. 'He is married to Juanita over there, the pregnant one. Please have a chair. Your meal is prepared and my house is yours.' He then yelled at the top of his voice over the noise: '*Conchita*!'

The old lady at the stove turned and saw Ronay. She gave the children at her dress a mass smack and a torrent of abuse, then turned off the radio on the sideboard. The baby in the cradle awoke with a yell. She picked it up and waited for the room to quieten, which it did within a miraculous second. She crossed to Ronay and waited for an introduction.

'Señor Marcos, this is my wife Conchita and these are my children and my children's children,' Gomez said proudly.

The old lady rubbed her hand on the baby and shook Ronay's with a bow. Her dark eyes flashed with pride and pleasure.

'You eat with us, señor. You are family,' she said.

'That gives me great pleasure, señora,' Ronay bowed.

What had appeared to be a permanent frown on her tired face sprang into a beautiful smile at these words. She gave a girlish giggle and pushed the baby into Ronay's arms. The child started to yell again. Ronay sat down in a state of shock, holding the stricken infant, but for Gomez and his wife the whole event gave tremendous pleasure. They looked at each other with knowing pride. The old lady returned to the stove, turning on the radio as she went; the signal for the family to continue the uproar. Gomez leapt onto the table and threw himself into an ungainly flamenco with a young girl.

Ronay felt the smile returning to his face as he looked up at the dancing Gomez. The little fat body wobbled with the effort. The golden grin stayed firm, the heavy brilliantine shone with sweat. Gomez was a slob, Ronay always knew that, but there in the man's house, surrounded by his brood, watching him amusing his children from the table stage, there in that moment he began to doubt. If Gomez was a slob then what did that make him? It didn't bear thinking about.

Gomez gave a blood-curdling '*Olé*' and attempted to do the splits. '*Caramba*,' he screamed as his podgy legs parted. The little girl partner fell to her knees and grabbing Gomez by the neck she cried, 'Granpapa, I love you. Please don't die.'

Gomez smiled through the pain. 'For you, I don't die little one. I live for ever.' He crossed himself and looked at the heavens, holding her tight. The family gathered around and lifted the stricken patriarch from the table, singing something Spanish. Gomez conducted the ensemble as they paraded him to Conchita at the stove. She turned from the smoke and the heat, scolding, and then without breaking from the frown on her warm face, she took her husband's ample cheeks in her rough hands and kissed him passionately to a cheer from the crowd. Gomez the slob. Ronay thought how Cheney would have adored the rogue.

Breakfast with the family was hard going. Ronay felt himself slipping into a doze and only the continuous hubbub of the arguments and impromptu songs kept him reasonably on edge. He had been relieved of the baby and had tackled an enormous Spanish omelette crammed with potato and reeking of onions. It smelled ghastly but, in spite of the moat of grease around it, the taste was exquisite. He surprised himself by finishing everything put before him, first the omelette, then the hot bread soaked in *mantequilla*, oranges, a bruised apple and a savoury of fresh sardine on a bed of lettuce. The thick coffee chased down with cold bottled *agua* ran hot and stickily and cold and virginal across the membranes of his palate. He sat back finally, oblivious to the communal chatter, and allowed himself to sink into his first deep sleep since leaving London.

Gomez shook him awake at mid-day. It was ill-advised. Ronay snarled to his senses and glared around him; his eyes were aching and his tongue lay like a lizard at the back of his mouth. Gomez pushed a cup of coffee into his hands. It helped to ease Ronay's temper. Gomez sat opposite and waited to catch his eye.

'We go at fifty minutes after midday, Señor Marcos, ten minutes before thirteen hours, sharp.'

Ronay nodded. Then Gomez snapped something Spanish at the little boy who scampered out of the room. The two men sat there alone.

'Where did they go?' Ronay said, drinking the coffee slowly.

Gomez shrugged a golden smile. 'They leave us to talk, señor. A full meal, a full house and to talk of a full life.'

'Grasping at yesterdays is for pedestrians,' Ronay said testily.

'Cervantes,' Gomez mumbled.

'What?'

Cervantes, señor. Don Quixote. You speak of Quixote.'

'Yes I suppose I do.' Ronay was surprised at the fat man's answer.

'To be Quixote, Señor Marcos, takes a little imagination and, with respect, a little madness too. With regret I do not have these miracles.'

Ronay shrugged and Gomez stood and walked to the fire, tinkering with the dying embers.

'Then why are you here with me?' Ronay said.

'Because with you, señor, is a promise of danger.'

'The danger is to live, eh.'

'Si, señor. The rest is just waiting.'

Gomez was looking into the coals and Ronay watched him thoughtfully. Suddenly Gomez turned, his face shining once more.

'Now we go into Spain to Donna Maria, señor. Donna Maria Domenquin?'

Ronay nodded. 'We do,' he said.

'It is almost three years now, señor, but her beauty. Remember always her beauty,' Gomez wiped his saliva with his sleeve.

'Remember that time in Barcelona when we thought she was dead. How wonderful she looked, so white her face. A madonna, señor. The bullet had just touched her head. She was a lucky madonna that night. Do you have work for her this time, señor?'

Ronay ignored the question. Gomez chuckled. 'Now señor, we cross into Spain then to Istan and Donna Maria. Oh, Señor Marcos, we live again, eh?'

The little man rubbed his hands together and did a jig. Ronay smiled and drained the dregs of the coffee, the bitter last taste serving as a final sharp demand to his waking brain. He stood up, prepared.

Less than a mile away from the shack stood the colonial splendour of Government House. Its thin, elegant columns seemed brand new, its brave, wide sash windows glistened. Outside the Royal Marine on sentry duty also stood polished and alert.

On the third floor was Simon Forbes-Thompson. In his late forties, sporting a trim military moustache and spotless white civilian suit, he spoke grandly into a hand-held telephone set. 'Well, John, that's Factory business from this side. Are you bridging Sunday or do I have to invite Lady Jilkes again?'

At the other end of the line was John Paddersley, a man of similar age to Forbes-Thompson. He was taking the call in bed, his eyes full of cold and his voice hoarse from coughing, his accent rough to match. He was a Whitechapel man and cultivated the Cockney tone.

'No chance, I'm stuck here for a week of purgatory,' he rasped, half choking. 'This bloody Rock's bad enough in the middle of summer when I'm fighting fit, but when I'm laid up like this, it's a pain in the arsehole.'

'How about a little scandal to while away the hours?' Forbes-Thompson smirked.

'Scandal! Go on, surprise me.' Paddersley shifted his pillows.

'You wouldn't remember a Factory chap called Marcus Ronay would you? He was transferred to the knacker's yard three years ago.'

Paddersley thought for a moment. 'I've never met him, but I'd be pretty dumb if I hadn't heard of the crafty bastard. What's he up to?'

'He's on Gibraltar, dear boy.' Forbes-Thompson waited for Paddersley to urge him on.

Three floors below at the rear of the Governor's wine cellar, a man sat in the half-shadow. He looked like a ferret, with sharp features and high cheekbones that caused his spot-like eyes to pierce menacingly in their sockets. He was listening intently through a pair of earphones clipped to a terminal of the telephone line that ran down the wall of the cellar. As the voices of Forbes-Thompson and Paddersley crackled through to him, the man doodled nonchalantly on a piece of paper on his lap.

'He came in last evening on a cargo drop,' Forbes-Thompson continued.

'The bloody plot thickens.'

'Doesn't it just. He's come unannounced and I only got wind about it when the Governor arranged clearance for him this morning.'

'Marcus Ronay! But what's he doing here? It's not Factory business, is it? I mean surely we'd have heard. Christ, they wouldn't do anything without telling us, would they?' Paddersley half choked. 'The big prize is why is he here, dear boy.'

Forbes-Thompson considered. 'For my money, he's going into Spain if he's not already there.'

'But why, for Christ's sake,' Paddersley croaked.

'I know of only one man who can tell us and that's greasy Gomez. Ronay especially asked for him to be on hand.'

'Gomez! God, it's getting worse.'

'Isn't it? If I hear anything more, I'll keep you posted.'

'You'd better you sod, for Christ's sake keep a low profile. We don't want to screw up something important.'

'Mum's the word, John. I'll send you some grapes.'

The phone went dead. The Ferret sat in the darkness for

some time. He removed the earphones and sat with his eyes narrowed as he digested the conversation.

The outside of the Gomez shack was crowded with the family and a multitude of animals, mostly dogs barking madly at anything and everything. The children danced on the outside steps and chased each other around the family car. The older members of the group were preparing boxes and parcels which they piled onto the rusty roof-rack of the vehicle. As each second passed, the car became less visible. Onto the running board went various boxes of live animals. Gomez appeared from the rear of the shack carrying a long box of chickens poking their beaks through the wire tacked onto the front of it. He was followed by an elder boy who carried a roll of chicken wire and a hammer, and another with a large box. Behind them followed Ronay.

The three men approached the rear of the car, pushing their way through the children and animals. Gomez lifted the boot. 'If you will kindly step inside, Señor Marcos,' he said. Ronay looked bewildered.

The children stopped their games and surrounded him, edging him forward and into the contraption. Gomez flashed his teeth and spat saliva gleefully, 'It is very simple. You must have faith, señor. To pass into Spain is not like before, so we wait until siesta. At thirteen hours the Spanish border guards are not as they should be. We go, señor. Please get into the boot, *por favor*.'

Ronay eased his tall frame painfully into the small boot. The floor was covered with filth and straw and what looked like animal droppings. Once he was wedged inside, the older boys moved like lightning. One of them placed bottles of whisky and cigarettes between his legs and covered them and Ronay with a stinking blanket. Then they half closed the boot, leaving about a two foot opening into which Gomez quickly emptied the box of live chickens. They scattered over Ronay who protested loudly from inside the blanket. Quickly Gomez wrapped the chicken wire over the opening of the boot and hammered nails into the side bodywork of the car. Ronay was imprisoned with the chickens and the contraband.

Gomez shouted to some of the children to jump into the car, and the vehicle rocked. The chickens in the boot screamed over Ronay's cramped body. The whisky bottles rattled under the blanket. Gomez peered into the makeshift chicken run. 'Forgive me, señor, we do it all the time. It works. No trouble. You see,' he smiled, padding around to the driving seat.

The sun was high with not even a whisper of breeze. The Spanish inhabitants of Gibraltar were preparing for their siesta, a three-hour hibernation from the hottest part of the day, a time for a heavy meal and a deep sleep before continuing work into the late evening. Siesta, a tradition of the Spanish people, a heritage, an integral part of their culture. Without it an imbalance is brought about.

At thirteen hours there was a steady stream of men and women walking across the few hundred yards of causeway separating the British fortress from the Spanish border town of La Linea. These were the Spanish workers who for centuries have played a major role on the Rock, staffing and serving a host of offices and factories during the day and then joining the exodus home at night or, as now, for siesta.

The immediate area between the two countries is *campo neutral* – no man's land. The British side is guarded by military police immaculate in white uniforms and red caps, stiff and unsmiling; the Spanish side is in the hands of national soldiers and Guardia police; a more friendly and more relaxed atmosphere.

The Gomez car spluttered into the area and was brought to a bumpy halt by one of the British guards stepping out into its path. The guard peered into the open driver's window and winked at Gomez, calling over the din of the children and the animals.

'Morning Gomez. How's the family?'

'Anxious to see my dear mother who is to die soon,' Gomez said innocently.

The guard took a slow walk around the car with the children banging on the windows and making faces at him. He squatted and looked into the boxes strapped to the running board and then pulled himself up for a closer look at the boxes on the roof-rack. Gomez watched through the rear mirror as the guard approached the half-open boot. As he stooped to look into the boot, Gomez pushed the hooter. The loud, sudden burst sent the chickens inside screaming into the wire. The guard jumped back and laughed, waving the car through the barrier. The people at the gate waved and whistled as the car banged its way into Spain.

Among the cheering crowd the unsmiling face of the Ferret watched the amusing scene and then broke away towards a parked car. He drove towards the gate. The guard looked at his identification and searched the car. The Ferret didn't take his eyes off the Gomez car as it pulled its way towards the Spanish guards, who were waving as it approached the barrier to Spain. It was obvious that the fat little man had made the journey many times before. The guard rapped on the Ferret's roof, giving him permission to drive off.

Once in Spain the Gomez car turned off the main thoroughfare of La Linea and struggled into the back streets of the border town. Another turn and then the car stopped. The Ferret stopped too at a safe distance, watching. Gomez ushered the family out of the car, instructed them to take off the collection of boxes from the roof and running-board and then he opened the boot. The chickens ran amok. Ronay pulled himself out of the confined space and staggered onto the pavement and then into the rear of the car. Gomez kissed each child and left the box of whisky and cigarettes for the eldest to carry. He then drove away with a cheerful wave. The Ferret waited briefly before following.

Within a matter of minutes La Linea was behind them. It surprised Ronay that he was able to remember so many of the landmarks as the car picked up speed. He had done the journey so many times before. The first big town would be Estepona. On cue, the charming fishing harbour appeared just as it had before. Then, almost at once, San Pedro de Alcantara sparkled in the sun. It was a generous part of the world, inhabited by weather-beaten fishermen who loved their *cerveza, tapos* and dominoes and worshipped their small boats and the fruits of the sea.

Then came the sharp bend that left the road and led to the mountain village of Istan. As Ronay saw the rough sign jutting from the road, his heart leapt, his face felt on fire. The memories came flooding back. He saw her face as clearly as when he saw it last, three years before. He had been down this road then for the last time he'd thought. Now he was back, but would she be there?

Once the car had turned and their backs were to the sea, the scene changed entirely. There before them stood the mountain ranges of the Sierra de Ronda, their outline jutting into the clear sky like cut-outs in a child's pop-up book. The aged car was making very slow and very hard work of getting up the mountainside towards the hidden village. Hunched over the wheel, cursing and blasting long, loud horn signals at every bend, Gomez puffed with concentration. The track came straight and, without the bends, Gomez relaxed. He looked over his shoulder at Ronay and their eyes met, mirroring a gleam of excitement.

Ronay read the mind of his fat friend, 'I saw him first in La Linea.' He referred to the dust of the Ferret's car following in the distance.

Gomez cursed good-naturedly. 'I thought so, but you had the advantage of the boot. He couldn't see you for chicken shit.'

'Do you know him?'

'No, señor, and you?'

'I'd like to.'

'You think British? Or something else?'

'I think you'd better watch the road.'

Half a mile behind, the Ferret drove steadily and carefully, watching the dust of the distant Gomez car. He watched it turn yet another big bend and disappear from view.

Suddenly he heard a screech of brakes followed by a loud crunch and then the sound of a motor horn, stuck fast, came ringing through the mountains. The Ferret braked and listened carefully, his wits calculating calmly. He decided to drive closer. As he turned the bend, he breathed again. There before him, the Gomez car was bundled half-vertical against the hillside, the hooter still piercing the air. He saw Gomez hanging half out of the driver's door and Ronay sprawled in the road unconscious.

The Ferret stayed in his car and watched, his eyes taking in the scene before him. At last he got out of his car and slowly approached Ronay. As he did so, Gomez peered through his half-closed eyes, watching the Ferret's every move. Ronay, too, was concentrating on the shadow of the Ferret as it approached him. The trick was working. In that instant he thought of Charles Peake. 'When in doubt flush them out.' The advice of a pro.

The shadow loomed closer. A brutal kick crushed into Ronay's ribs as the Ferret turned him over and started to go through his pockets. Ronay kept still, his eyes closed, waiting to hear Gomez strike home. Suddenly fat arms grabbed the Ferret from behind. He fell back heavily onto Gomez who wrapped his tree-trunk legs around him as they hit the road. The two men rolled on the ground away from the car, but the Ferret dragged himself free and pulled an ugly looking knife from his pocket. With a flick the blade glistened in the sunshine.

Gomez stopped in his tracks with a nervous chuckle. He rubbed his hands on his trousers and then kept them out straight in front of him, circling the Ferret with a series of stop–start shuffles, but the Ferret was a little more nimble and with a sudden feint to the left he lunged to the right, catching Gomez off balance. Then with three quick slashes of the blade, Gomez staggered – his face a mess of blood. Unable to see clearly, he stumbled blindly. The Ferret went in again mercilessly and slashed into his chest. Gomez fell backwards with a scream.

The Ferret moved in to continue his ferocious attack. But Ronay had dragged himself to his feet, fighting the pain in his chest. He breathed deeply and felt all his confidence return. His balance was no longer suspect, his dexterity was sharp. He shouted and the Ferret turned to face him.

As his hands and feet followed combinations learned years before, he allowed the Ferret's knife to come inside his guard. Then with a left-hand parry to the blade his right hand, flat and hard, chopped into his assailant's rib-cage. He felt the bones cave in. The Ferret gave a grunt and fell to one knee. Again Ronay chopped. This time between the end of the man's nose and his upper lip. The action forced the nose bone up into the skull. Again a grunt, and now the Ferret was unarmed and cowering against his car's bonnet.

Ronay called to Gomez lying on the ground bleeding a few yards away. 'I'll get to you. Hold on,' he shouted without taking his eyes off the Ferret. He smiled grimly at the rat-faced man, his hands still holding the knife sticky with blood.

'You did a very professional job on my friend. You should be congratulated,' he said.

The Ferret did not return the grim smile. Like a trapped rodent, kneeling with his back to the front wing of his car, his eyes darted nervously looking for escape.

'Don't try it,' Ronay snarled. 'I can kill you with one finger and you know it.'

The Ferret stayed motionless. Looking up at the crouching Ronay, he searched the tall man's eyes for some sign of weakness and saw nothing but cold, controlled anger.

'Put your hands behind your head,' Ronay said.

The Ferret obeyed and flinched as Ronay jerked the tie

from his neck and knotted his thin wrists to the spokes of the wheel behind his head.

'Now for the usual procedure,' he said. 'I'm going to ask you who you are, you will not answer satisfactorily and I will be forced to make you talk. We will save time.' Ronay gave a sudden slash with the knife. The blow connected with the tip of the Ferret's elbow. He opened his mouth to scream but no sound came. His eyes rolled back to show just the whites, tears fell down onto his hollow cheeks. Ronay spoke finally and without emotion.

'Do you speak English?' he said. The Ferret, semi-conscious, nodded. Ronay had seen the reactions several times before. The utter shock of having the humerus bone dislocated from the ulna always brought that distant look in the eyes of the victim.

The Ferret's legs started to twitch; from somewhere inside the frail body a holocaust was raging. Charlie Peake explained it all in a brief afternoon at Guy's Hospital during the Twenties. He and a couple of Factory men had been working in Ireland when a group of Black and Tan soldiers attached to the Dublin police had interrogated a member of the IRA. According to Charlie, the Tans had an ingenious way of dealing with their enemy. They took a great deal of satisfaction in 'sending the bastards to St Vitas for a fox-trot'.

Ronay could still recall that time at Guy's when the orthopaedic registrar showed him the vital bones but didn't attempt to explain the excruciating pain that came about by cutting into the muscle of nerves. The only people with true knowledge of the pain were dead from it; except for the Ferret.

'It's called the funny bone,' he said loudly so the Ferret could hear above the scream inside him. 'But it isn't funny is it? You have another one on the other arm. Tell me who you are and tell me now.'

The Ferret was hardly able to form the words but finally spoke with a soft German accent.

'I work for German Intelligence.' Each word came separately, each syllable an effort of concentration.

'You are Gestapo. Working from where? For how long?'

'From Gibraltar for two years.'

'What is your cover?'

'I work at Government House in the kitchens.'

'What do you know of me?'

'Nothing. I know nothing.'

Without a second thought, Ronay struck the other arm. The Ferret managed a scream this time and thumped his head hard into the wing of the car. Ronay continued his interrogation.

'What do you know of me?'

'You are Ronay.'

'What do I do?'

'You come from England.'

'Why?'

'I don't know why.'

'You know my name, where I'm from. How do you know?'

'I listen.'

With that he began to faint. Ronay put his hands between the Ferret's legs, squeezing his genitals very hard. The Ferret groaned into a sort of sense and then screamed.

'Go on,' Ronay rasped.

'I listen. I listen to telephone at Government House. Forbes-Thompson, he talks to Paddersley. He talks, I listen.'

'Have you passed your knowledge of me to Germany?'

The Ferret was now delirious, his arms a mass of blood and the nerve ends of his body beginning to cause him to convulse.

'He talks, I listen,' he said again.

'Señor please, please Señor Marcos. Please.' Gomez called, painfully.

Ronay pulled open the closed eyes of the Ferret and saw that he had lapsed into unconsciousness. There was no more to be learned there so he delivered a swift final chop to the

German's throat. He felt the ridge of his hand connect with the vagus nerve. It was enough. The action sent the Ferret's head back. The vagus nerve did the rest. He lay there, his eyes wide and glassy.

Ronay moved over to Gomez and looked closely at his injuries. The fat man was a mass of wide cuts about the face and body.

'Can I move you?' Ronay spoke gently.

'*Si*. Please take me home, señor.'

'Come on. Help me. I've got to get you to the car,' Ronay said, getting Gomez up onto his feet.

Slowly and as gently as he could, Ronay managed to get the huge frame to the car and into the front seat.

'Sit tight for two minutes,' he said.

He returned to the Ferret, untied the blood red arms and dragged the body into its own car, then he started the engine and drove it to the edge of the mountain road. With a succession of short hard shoves, Ronay finally got the car to tip over the edge and with relief he watched it crash into the valley below. He watched the dust settle for a moment and then returned to Gomez. He pulled the wounded man as close to himself as he could, trying to make him comfortable. Then he reversed back onto the road and drove on up the mountain towards Istan and Donna Maria Domenquin.

The village of Istan stood atop the mountain dominating that area of the Costa del Sol. Standing majestic, the rolling mounds appeared to suffer without complaint the tiny road that crept between their thighs, and when at last a human felt he could go no further, the village came into view with startling suddenness. There on the last bend of the last kilometre she showed herself, her people mostly dressed in black, moving along white walls. It was busy, vital in its Spanish peon way. Donkeys dragged and carried the people, who had tough weather-beaten faces and had felt safe here for over a thousand years.

High up stood the church, and then to the left of the tiled roofs, a splendid collection of mimosa trees threw down their evergreen and yellow flowers. Behind them, almost hidden from the view of the people below, an exquisite terrace ran the full length of the ridge. Fifty yards of high polished marble melded with the hand-made terracotta tiles of the nearby Ronda. Back behind that, through an array of french windows, was a large, airy room running the full length of the terrace.

The room of obvious affluence was dominated by a splendid fireplace of carved marble. The walls were soft pastel with high-polished wood, the furniture was antique Spanish and the soft furnishings were the finest silks and brocades. The floors of Ronda tiles had shine and care and attention.

Seated on a deep sofa by the fireplace was Donna Maria Domenquin. She was dressed immaculately, her jet black hair swept back, revealing the high cheekbones of the classic Spanish woman. Her skin, soft and white, eyes black as her hair, she looked younger than her mid-thirty years. Standing near the open french window and halfway onto the terrace was Doctor Felipe, a tall man with a mass of long, black hair greying at the temples. He was looking down towards the road and the deep valley that fell away below the villa. He was older than Donna Maria but his manner was boyish.

'It's stopped now,' he said, calling over his shoulder to her. 'It must have been an argument. I've seen it happen on that road so many times before. Two vehicles unable to pass so they sit glaring like two bulls, hooting at each other in the belief that one of them will retreat. Of course they never do.'

He turned from the window and moved to Donna Maria. 'Now let's see you try again,' he said firmly.

Donna Maria held up an orange and slowly, deliberately pierced the skin with a long, hypodermic needle. The Doctor smothered a grin and fought to regain a more serious expression.

'Not bad,' he said as he took the items from her and held them out to demonstrate.

'You forgot to clear the syringe of air bubbles. Remember, vertical. Then push. Horizontal, prick and gently pressure the potion into the vein. There, try again.'

Donna Maria once more followed the directions, mouthing the Doctor's instructions as she went. He sat opposite her and watched, keeping his eyes on her face more than her actions. He watched her determination and her beauty. The cancer in her did not yet show in her face, but below the surface of that lovely person it was already preparing its rage. His eyes misted, so he hastily got up from the sofa and walked back to the french windows.

'There, how was that?' Donna Maria called, sitting back in satisfaction.

The Doctor kept his eyes turned away but spoke clearly enough for her to hear.

'You're sure this is the way you want to do it?' he said.

She nodded with a twinkle in her eye. He didn't see it but he knew it would be there.

'You definitely will not have a nurse?'

She shook her head mischievously.

'And I can only telephone for appointments,' he said.

She threw back her hair and laughed. 'That I know you won't do,' she said in a voice that vibrated with infinite texture. 'Keeping you at bay by telephone will not be successful.'

He smiled and shrugged. 'I have to give you the prescription for the drugs and I have to examine you regularly, but we can try the telephone if you insist.'

They paused in their private thoughts. His emotion was safely under control now and he returned to the sofa. She was pushing her finger into her arm, searching for a vein. He admired her tenacity. He admired everything about her.

'You had absolutely no pain last night?' he asked.

'I said I didn't, so I didn't.'

'I must be told the exact feelings you have. The body sends out its own signals.'

'I had no pain last night,' she said more sharply, a little irked by the interrogation.

'It will get a bit worse. Just a bit, but it *will* get worse. That's why you must tell me every symptom,' he said. His eyes were troubling him again.

'You will mix a stronger cocktail, keeping to our agreement,' she said flicking at a perfect vein standing protruding from her arm. She stopped and fixed her eyes into his. For a moment there, he saw her fear.

'You promise me that I will keep my mind,' she said. 'You know that is important to me.'

The Doctor took her arm and kissed the vein gently. 'It is just as important to me that you do not take more pain than you need to,' he said.

She nodded and returned to the orange. Once again she went through the ritual of inserting the hypodermic into the skin. The sound of a car approaching came from the drive below the terrace. It gave an impatient hoot. The Doctor went to the terrace and saw Ronay pulling the blood-soaked Gomez out of the car.

'Good heavens, it's like the Civil War again,' he called over into the room.

'What is it?' Donna Maria asked.

'Looks like someone's in trouble down in the drive.'

Donna Maria eased herself from the sofa slowly and joined him on the terrace. With one glance below, her eyes fixed on the tall frame of Ronay who was kneeling beside Gomez lying on the gravel drive. Unable to control the shock of seeing him she gave a soft cry. The Doctor moved to her side, taking her by the arms, but she brushed off his concern and leant on the terrace rail watching Ronay's every move.

When Gomez groaned with pain, the Doctor made his way down to the drive. A group of staff had gathered around the car by the time he reached it. Not one of them was willing to go near the blood-stained figure without some sort of lead.

Ronay looked around him, and summoned up enough Spanish to encourage at least water and a blanket. He saw the man come down the front steps of the villa and the pain of a single thought put everything out of focus. He saw Donna Maria's marriage veil and this man lifting it to take that first consummate kiss. He fought to cancel out the image.

The Doctor pushed past him and knelt at the side of Gomez. The fat man was ashen, the once white suit was saturated with red. The Doctor tore the soaking material off his body and roughly pulled open the gaping cuts. The blood flowed even faster from the seeping wounds. Gomez lay still, his sighs regular, not feeling anything any more. Ronay stood above the Doctor unable to help but anxious to hear someone who seemed knowledgeable give an opinion.

'How bad is he?' he asked.

The Doctor pulled himself to his feet and signalled the gathered staff to lift Gomez up off the drive.

'He's lost a lot of blood and he's in shock. If he's to survive, which I doubt, I'll have to take him to my Clinic.'

'You are a doctor, then. We are fortunate. And you live here?'

'I live in Istan, yes. But not in this villa.'

Ronay's heart leapt, as the Doctor followed the servants carrying Gomez out of the gates down towards the village.

Ronay sat on the front steps. He was suddenly very tired. It was then that he saw her – high on the terrace with the sun behind her – half silhouette but enough to tempt his very soul. She stood there, no wave, no movement, just her. Perhaps if he waited a moment longer, she might show some sign of recognition. If only she would acknowledge him, that would be welcome enough. If only she would – anything!

He rushed up the steps into the villa. He pushed past the

butler and housekeeper watching from the tall window on the mezzanine landing of the marble staircase. He twisted his aching bones sharply to the right and half slammed the polished oak door behind him. Then in five massive strides he entered the archway that led into her lounge. He stood breathless, searching the expanse of room for her. Then she was there, by the fireplace. She flashed her eyes at him, defying him to move. He felt vulnerable, his chest heaving for breath.

'Why do you always run about this house?' she chastised.

'Because it's too big. It was always too big. I've told you a hundred times.'

She smiled ruefully. She understood his predicament very well. 'It used to take you three seconds to get up here. This time it's taken three years. How do you account for that?' she teased.

Ronay didn't wait for her to say more. 'I lost my way,' he said, and covered the floor swiftly, taking her into his arms.

'Welcome home,' she whispered as he buried his head in her long white neck, pulling her close to him. He felt the tension inside her ease into a calm and then into a warmth that he never thought he would ever feel again. They stood there locked together and neither one of them dared to make the first move. He wanted to kiss her, to explore every inch of her, to search her. Then he felt her mouth on his earlobes and her tongue burn into his brain. He thought briefly of Cheney and then of the Doctor, but the insistence of Donna Maria's fingers pushed everything to infinity.

The french windows of the living room were open, with the sounds of crickets giving music to the sharp stars against the black sky. The butler of the Domenquin family had poured brandy and bid goodnight to Donna Maria and Ronay. The logs in the great fireplace crackled and two guitars were playing softly from the gramophone. Ronay sipped his brandy thoughtfully.

She sat on the floor, leaning against him staring into the

flames. They both knew that there was more to this moment than they had ever shared in the privacy of her bedroom. The flames licked around the logs sensuously, everything about the room was sensual, everything associated with Donna Maria was suggestive.

Donna Maria broke the soft silence. 'Why are you here, Marcus?' The question joined with the tranquil sound of the guitars. She asked it without probing, without insistence.

'Three brandies ago I could have answered you with consummate ease,' he said. 'But now I can't bring myself to break the spell.'

Her lovely back pressed between his thighs. She laid her head back into him, her long neck firing his loins. He closed his long legs around her and leant forward crossing his arms under her arms beneath the silk gown and feeling her warm breasts rise and fall against his skin.

'When I left you it was forever. You know that,' he said. 'That last morning we both knew what we were doing.'

She smiled, her fingers touching his fingers touching her. 'We were very brave in those days, darling. Action far outweighed sense,' she whispered.

He nipped gently on her ear. 'God I missed you. In England I composed a hundred letters to you. But I dared not send them. You were safe and I owed you my silence.'

'How is Cheney?' she said, not realising the effect her question would have. Ronay replied as softly and as unhurriedly as he could.

'She died.'

She kissed his hand. 'Is that why you're here?' she whispered with a sigh which pierced Ronay like a knife. He held her closer still. 'No. That's not why I'm here.' She kissed his hand again, trying to hide her hurt. He hated that moment.

'I knew you hadn't come back. Not really. Silly isn't it,' she said tossing her hair back. 'Maturity teaches us nothing. We still fall into the same traps, still follow the same stars.'

'I'm back my love. Believe that,' he said. 'And I love you more than you could know.'

She moved and knelt beneath him, looking up into his dangerous eyes.

'I'm on business,' he went on. 'I need you to *mark* a man, though I wish to God I didn't.'

He felt into the pocket of his jacket lying on the back of the sofa and took out his wallet. He pulled a worn, faded photograph from it and dropped it into her lap. 'Remember that day?' Donna Maria scanned the picture, nodded and smiled.

'The *feria* in Seville. It poured with rain just after this and ruined all the food.' She pointed to the picnic laid out around a group of figures.

'The chap standing behind me with a moustache and boater . . .' Ronay said, but he didn't get any further. She stood up and walked onto the terrace. After a few minutes he went to join her.

'I wouldn't ask if I saw any other way. I'm desperate,' he said.

'Desperate!' She spat the word. 'You talk about *your* desperation!'

He took her roughly and held her close to him, her body heaving in distress and fury. He felt her tears but he forced himself to continue. 'Baron Kurt von Zeiss,' he said.

She raged again as he said the name. 'I need you to *mark* him for me.'

She tried to break away but he held her like a vice. He knew he had to finish, give her more information and then she could decide.

'Why, why?' she cried. 'How can you make love to me and ask me to do this?'

It was a question that deserved a better answer than he was prepared to give. It would weaken his position if he told her more, if he took her through the quiet streets of Istan and told her he loved her now more than he ever had. That he would spend his days worshipping her, his Maria, his lost love. He could tell her so much, but the forest in Europe kept flashing in his mind, the tanks, the dying, the retreat, the army easing back to the sea. Time, they needed time.

'I need you to *mark* von Zeiss,' he said again. He had to persuade her, he must bend her will to his. He told her of the plight of the British army and the urgency of their gaining time to get to the coast. He told her of Charlie Peake and lastly, as the night air began to cool, he unveiled his plan and her part in it. She shivered and took his hand, leading him back into the room. She was calmer and her natural self again, controlled, poised. Her speech had returned to its warm, brown tone.

'So we have to get your scheme known to the German High Command?' she said with a wry smile. 'And the best mark is von Zeiss.'

'He's known to you and we don't have time to cultivate new territory. And what's more important he's now the silent banker for Rudolf Hess and that's the biggest break of all.'

'For how long?' Her eyes shone with excitement.

'Hess has been shifting assets out of Germany since '32,' he said. 'He's not on his own. Goering, Himmler, Bormann, Goebbels, they're all at it. Most of the stuff comes here to Spain and then on to South America, using Spanish holding companies formed by prominent Spanish citizens, like our Baron von Zeiss.'

'But Kurt is German.'

'Yes, but because of a couple of odd deals he made with the House during the Civil War he secured enough favour in the Franco government to hold a dual passport.'

There was a silence while Donna Maria gazed up at him. 'I want you to *mark* the Baron because it's through him that I get to Hess. And it's got to be quick,' he said. She returned to the sofa and slowly sat back into the cushions. Her face was white and began to twist with pain. Ronay moved to her with concern.

'I'm all right, Marcus. Don't fuss,' she said, pushing him away. 'It's just a migraine.'

A knock at the door brought the butler into the room.

'Señor, it is the Doctor. He has returned with the man Gomez.' Ronay followed him to the door.

'Will you be all right?' he asked. She waved him away. Once the door had closed she gave a deep breath and forced herself painfully from the sofa, moving slowly to the cabinet holding the gramophone. Inside the cabinet was a white enamel basin containing the hypodermic syringe and drug. She fiddled with it, her fingers shaking. The pain inside her was beginning to boil over.

'He told me you had a migraine.' She swung round to see the Doctor coming towards her, his face tight and serious.

'I *have* got a migraine,' she said.

'Like hell you have! For God's sake, Maria, let me do something.'

She inserted the needle and looked at him, half in desperation and half in defiance. 'You promised me I'd keep my mind,' she whispered as the needle pricked into her white flesh. He watched the drug disappear into the needle.

'God help you, you will.' He whispered the words. He knew the concoction of morphine and heroin was going to be enough for now, but he knew what the future held: the addiction, the total dependence on the strength of it to pass the waking hours. Then the twilight life – the half living mind waiting for death.

'See how I trust you,' she said as she gently pushed the last of the drug into her vein. Then, within seconds, her twisted face became tranquil, her eyes sparkled. The weakness within her was still apparent but the concern and the tension that dominated her lovely face had faded. Her smile returned.

'Oh, the peace!' she said as he took her into his arms. She returned his embrace, pulling him to her.

'It's just a migraine,' she said into his ear, her eyes searching the room nervously. 'That's what we tell Marcus. It's a passing pain, no more. I must have my senses. He has a lot to tell me and I must remember. I'm going to Madrid.'

The Doctor attempted to move from her grip but she held

him fast. 'I'm going to Madrid and you must not spoil it for me,' she cried.

'Who are these people, this Englishman?' he said in desperation. 'What kind of hold can such a man have – what kind of promise has he given? For God's sake, Maria, everything is happening too quickly. And you're dying, my love.' His voice shook. He pulled away and saw that her eyes were full of tears.

'In Madrid I will live,' she said, holding her head proudly. His eyes searched her face for some sign of weakness, some chink in her new-found armour that could be used to stop her plans. But he knew he couldn't fight her. 'You'll call me when you need me,' he said, as he left the room.

When Ronay saw Gomez lying on the hall table, he smothered a grin. The fat man lay like a newly prepared mummy, his face as white as the bandages on it. His torn coat and shirt were still on his body but falling open, showing the dressing around his chest and stomach. Gomez looked at the ceiling above him, his eyes wide and unmoving, oblivious to everything and everyone around him. Ronay's grin disappeared.

The Doctor came to the foot of the stairs and checked the pulse of the wounded man. 'He's hardly alive,' he said. Ronay shrugged and looked at his watch. 'We'll have to get him home. Can he travel?' He kept the question hard and his voice flat. The Doctor laughed without humour, and walked out into the drive and out of sight towards the village. It was obvious that for him the matter was closed.

Gomez made a sound from the table. Ronay went to him and put his head down to the sweaty face. 'Forgive me, señor,' the fat man gasped. Ronay mopped the cold sweat off his friend. 'You're going home soon.' He had to force the words out. It wasn't part of his plan to return to Gibraltar, it wasn't prudent to change plans in mid-stream. Detours were dangerous. And he had a time schedule, damn it!

Maria joined him at the foot of the stairs. She took his hand.

'The best laid schemes of mice and men,' he growled.

'You know he can't stay here,' she said quietly.

'How the hell am I going to get him back on the Rock? I wouldn't even get him as far as down the mountain in his state.'

Gomez lay, his eyes still fixed above him but his ears listening. He knew he was badly hurt but he couldn't believe he was as bad as Ronay was implying. He heard Maria's heels on the tiled floor come closer. She looked down on him; he saw her eyes and their sadness; he forced a smile. 'I go home soon,' he said weakly. He felt her touch. She kissed his forehead and walked back out of sight, and he heard Ronay walk after her into the night.

He thought of Conchita and the young ones and choked back a sob. He felt ridiculous lying on a table in a splendid hallway up against a tall gilt mirror. If he were dying he couldn't think of a worse way to make an exit. He was Tomas Gomez, husband of Conchita Carmen Pilar Roderiguez, daughter of merchant Miguel Luis Roderiguez of Cadiz. Their children were part British, part Gibraltarian, mostly Spanish. A fine pedigree, a fine family. This was not the place for him to die. He half turned his head away from the ceiling and caught his reflection in the mirror. God he looked ill. His hair was falling over his left ear and making the baldness very apparent. He decided this was definitely not the place.

He felt down by his side for the edge of the table and held tightly. Then he moved his legs to the edge and tensed the muscles in his back and shoulders as he slowly allowed them to slip over the side. The pain that shot around his ribs brought a cry to his lips that he fought to control, but it was a pain he would have to endure if he were to get off the table and onto his feet. With another great effort he found the floor but once his feet touched the tiles, his legs gave way, causing an agonising twist to his tormented body. As he fell to his knees he caught hold of the hall table to stop falling onto his back. Once more he faced himself in the mirror. It stared back at him, twisted and tired. He knelt there and summoned up what last strength he had, filling his aching lungs with the night air as it wafted through the open front door. He would make one more attempt to get back onto his legs and he would do it without crying out. Now!

He managed it, but the task of getting to the front door and down the front stair was even greater. He discovered that half falling down the final three steps was easier than taking them one at a time. Strangely too, he was in less pain. He lay there in the darkness of the drive, and he felt stronger. His breath was still coming in gasps but that was because of his damaged ribs and lungs and he couldn't expect miracles. But he did feel stronger and his side felt warm. He glanced down at his bandages and saw blood seeping out between the folds. He would have to move quickly if he were to get home. He dragged himself to the shadows of the grand terrace and heard Ronay and Maria above him, walking by the rail. Then he heard tables and chairs being moved. They would be dining there, on the terrace, tonight. Excellent.

He waited until he heard glasses and crockery and soft voices, then he made his move towards his car. She stood a matter of yards away from him. She looked so welcoming, her chipped paint, her torn body. They were a pair. He prayed she would have the key in her ignition. His hand shook as he pulled himself up to the open window and reached under the steering wheel; the key was there. He sat thankfully on the running board and waited for his strength to build up again. The bandages now were becoming very wet. Up above, the glow of candles came from the terrace, dinner was in process. He quietly opened the car door and, using it as a crutch, swung his body between the steering wheel and the torn seat. His fingers felt nervously around the centre of the wheel arranging the levers of the choke and mixture. Then he felt for the ignition key and prepared himself. He would have just one chance to start the engine, then one attempt at getting the car out of the drive and down the mountain. If he failed, if the engines didn't spark, he knew Ronay would be down from the terrace and he would be back on that table watching himself die in that awful mirror. After a quick prayer, he was as ready as he would ever be. He depressed the clutch and pushed the gear lever into first, then he released the hand brake, gave one last look up to the terrace and twisted the ignition key.

The engine fired, the choke raced and she complained just slightly by giving a sudden stall and a heroic backfire. Gomez heard Ronay's voice shout something from the terrace but now the car was moving between the entrance gates. His eyes were hazy, he had to concentrate on the dark road and, once out of the drive, the blackness of the night came like a sudden blindfold. His hands reached downward stretching for the headlight switch on the dashboard, the action sending pain searing across his chest. He gasped for breath from the pressure on his lungs.

The car sped into the darkness. He knew a bend was close and after that the long drop to the valley below, but he dared not stop as she might never start again. Then he found the switch and pulled hard. The lights flashed onto the road and suddenly the bend loomed before him. He pushed the car hard to the left. The front mudguard tore off on part of the mountain protruding onto the track, the near side door caved in, shattering the window, but miraculously the car didn't spin over the edge. He straightened her and disengaged the choke and mixture. She coughed and gave another backfire but she was fine now. The petrol gauge was showing enough to get him home and that gave him confidence to concentrate on just that and nothing else. Ronay was where he wanted to be and that too was good. He had done his job, he was Gomez, First Eleven, he would enjoy telling the tale to the children.

From where Ronay stood on the terrace he could see the lights of the car probing their way down the track. Maria caught her breath as the car swerved with the sound of screeching tyres. 'You could chase him in my car,' she ventured but Ronay shook his head. He knew why Gomez had made the break. And that he had to make his reappearance in Gibraltar before too many questions were asked. So there he goes, Ronay thought, risking what life he has left to keep himself and his plan in the clear. Not the kind of reaction expected of a fat slob some might say, but then Ronay knew his Gomez now. 'He knows what he's doing and he knows why. Just pray he makes it,' he said. They watched silently until long after the lights disappeared, each with their own private thoughts, each with their own prayers for the fat little man from Gibraltar.

Once down the mountain track and onto the main road, Gomez relaxed enough to become aware of his own condition. He felt much weaker now and assumed the wetness of his lower body was from loss of blood. He wound the window down to its limit to gain the full force of the night air pushing past. There was little or no traffic so he allowed himself the luxury of deep breaths and little concentration on the dark road ahead.

Eventually the lights of La Linea blinked on the horizon. As he neared the town, the dark shadow of Gibraltar seemed to float further back into the sea, slowly and silently as if hoping not to be noticed.

He turned off the coast road and onto the main Spanish street. It was quite busy. Noisy bars and cantinas opened onto the pavements, spewing forth their loud-singing, staggering, patrons, night people drinking their fill and paying their way. He slowed as the occasional, inebriated body negotiated the narrow roads. There were a few cars and an abundance of bicycles so it was a wall of death for any pedestrian and Gomez was in enough charge of his wits to realise he couldn't take chances. Gradually the crowd and the music passed, the street lights ended, and then came the frontier.

The area was bathed by a couple of high-powered arc lights. He slowed to a stop and the car gave an exhausted backfire which brought the guard from his hut at the barrier. The guard walked slowly towards the car with its bonnet rattling and its exhaust steaming. Gomez forced a weak smile as the guard looked at the bandages on his head with the seeping red blood oozing from the edges, ignored the Gomez smile and walked back to the hut where he spoke into the dusty microphone and a light shone in the small house adjoining the hut. Gomez knew it was the main station of the Guardia police. Obviously the soldier had called someone of higher rank. The situation was not looking good. At that same moment, across the causeway, he saw a collection of shapes walking into the British arc lights. For a while, they were silhouettes. Then, as he strained his eyes, he focused on Paco and the elder children. To the right the younger boys came to the wire. His heart leapt and his pulse raced.

He gave a jump. At the window two men looked at him with serious, searching faces. One was a Guardia officer, the other a man in civilian clothes. The officer poked his finger through the open window and into the head bandages. Gomez flinched with pain.

'Well what have we here?' the officer smiled. 'Gomez Casanova returning with the pox?' Gomez bared his teeth and managed a hoarse chuckle.

'Si, señor, my visit was not as expected,' he said, swallowing the saliva.

The officer poked again. 'You sit there while we search,' he said, opening the rear door and looking under the seats. He then moved to the boot and waved his torch into the darkness. Meanwhile, the civilian stood watching Gomez. The officer came back to the window, poking again at the covered head wounds. Gomez gasped but feigned weak laughter. 'Please, a horsewhip is painful enough,' he cried, praying the officer would stop his sadistic probes. The officer turned to the silent civilian.

'He says it is a horsewhipping,' he said. The civilian nodded again, saying no words but just staring at Gomez.

The officer thumped on top of the car. 'Okay, go home,' he said gruffly.

Gomez formed another tight smile and rammed the gears. The car gave a burp and crept slowly up to the red and white posts that formed the barrier to the causeway. Gomez halted, waiting for the soldier to lift the post. He summoned every particle of self-control in his body. Once the barrier was up, he would have only the causeway to encounter, just the causeway, just a few yards and then the children. He could see them more clearly now. They stood bathed in the light, watching, waiting. He would be home soon. The officer was speaking to the civilian, the barrier lifted, he engaged the gears, the civilian came to his window as the soldier waved him through. The car moved very slowly. Gomez didn't want to make any silly moves. He didn't want to do what his body ached for him to do. He would be foolish to go too fast, he would show respect to the civilian while he was on the causeway, while he was in Spain he would show respect. He would not stop, he would creep closer to the British gate, but he would not stop and he would not be foolish.

The civilian walked alongside. 'You came across with your children this afternoon yet you return alone. Is that normal for you, Señor Gomez?' he said, looking ahead and keeping astride with the car.

'It is normal when I wish to be alone,' Gomez said, not taking his eyes off the causeway ahead. The children at the gate came closer. He could see their eyes. They were smiling. They had no idea.

'Where have you been alone?' the civilian asked.

Gomez thought through his muddled brain. He had to choose a place far away from where Ronay was at that time. 'Algeciras,' he said firmly.

'Then you came from Algeciras?' The question came from the civilian.

'I did,' Gomez said.

The children began to wave, two of the younger boys

began to climb up the wire, the British guards pulled them down playfully, the civilian put his hand on the handle of the car door.

'You came from Algeciras, yet your car arrives from the direction of Estepona.' With that statement the civilian pulled open the door, the moonlight hit the interior and there in full view was the blood-soaked body of the fat man, his right foot perched limply on the side of the accelerator, his right arm hanging paralysed by his side.

'That is a lot of blood for a horsewhipping,' the civilian said, his voice louder now the tension was showing. Gomez began to panic. He forced more pressure into his right foot, the car purred and moved a little faster, just a little faster. The combination of the added pace and concern made the civilian pull at Gomez. 'Stop the car,' he shouted. The bandages in his hand came away wet and useless from Gomez's body. Gomez saw the children pushing at the wire. They began to shout, some encouraging, some with fear. The British soldiers came closer, the car revved loudly, it was impossible for Gomez to change gear. His left arm was steering for the British gates, his right arm was useless.

The civilian took the dead arm and tried to pull Gomez from the car. 'Get out of the car,' he shouted, but Gomez yelled – he did it to keep his senses more than anything else – and half fell out of the seat, his right foot jammed onto the accelerator, the engine well past its maximum. He couldn't go any faster without a gear change. Steam forced itself out of the battered bonnet, oil splattered at all angles. Gomez caught one last look at the children as the civilian jumped onto the running board and tried to take the wheel. 'Who is this man?' The question burned into Gomez as he struggled his last.

'*Mein Gott*,' the civilian yelled as the British gate loomed closer.

The German accent came like a bolt. Gomez gave a mournful cry, his whole body struck with the sudden shock of the information. He turned the wheel as hard as he could over to the right. Gomez could hear the children at the fence, the British soldiers cheering at the top of their voices. He saw the Spanish guards running towards him now. All was up; he knew it but he couldn't be taken. He couldn't have the questions that would risk Ronay, his friend.

He tried not to think of the children. Now the civilian was grabbing at the steering wheel again. The Spanish guards, their guns out, were firing into the air. Gomez aimed the car towards the water. The last sound he would hear would be the shouts of the children as he pushed the battered heap over the brick edge that separated the water below from the causeway. The front of the car hit hard, causing it to somersault in the air. For one split second it hovered, going neither one way nor the other. He heard the guns fire again. It was enough. He was Gomez, First Eleven. He had escaped. As the car hit the water, bonnet first, he gripped the civilian tightly with his one good hand. The shocked German was locked in a death grip as the cold Mediterranean gushed through the door opening. Gomez opened his mouth and let his lungs fill.

It took two hours for the combined efforts of the British and Spanish to salvage the car and the bodies from the depths. Gomez was still at the wheel. They laid him beside the wire fence of the British barrier covering him with an oily tarpaulin from one of the fishing boats moored to the dock. The children watched from the fence, the elder boys held the girls tightly, their faces stiff and drained. The younger ones cried unashamedly. Conchita held the sleeping baby and reminded them quietly that they had never met a tall Englishman and the name Ronay was unknown to them.

At first light the following morning Donna Maria gave her final instructions to the assembled staff, Ronay slipped out of the villa and into the car without fuss. The Doctor walked up the drive from the village.

'How is she?' he asked.

Ronay shrugged. 'She's fine, very happy, anxious to be leaving.'

The Doctor walked on with no more to say, enjoying the sight of Donna Maria on the front steps.

'You outshine the sun,' he said, gazing up at her. She wore a three-piece travelling costume in grey flannel with high shoulders and fashionable lapels. A masculine tie and matching stetson with snap brim only added to her absolute femininity.

'I'll be fine, Felipe, I promise.' She blew him a kiss and left him. He stood watching, helpless to do what he desperately knew was right. She shouldn't go, she shouldn't be leaving his medical protection, she shouldn't be leaving the love he had for her. Why was he so weak? He wanted to shout for the staff to stop the car and drag the Englishman from her side but the Englishman had a hold on her, some dark secret hold, and she was happy because of it.

The car crept noiselessly down the track. She changed gear and placed her hand on his knee. No word, just that action. They had planned to leave the car in Malaga, seventy kilometres away, and there they would separate and take the train to Madrid. It was important that he stayed in Spain until they made contact with their 'mark'. It was also important that he kept his head down. He had no means of identification on him and no permission to be in the country. That was as planned. From now on the less seen and heard of Marcus Ronay the better.

Donna Maria had barely entered the foyer of the Palace Hotel before she was besieged by hotel staff. She felt as though she were floating. It had been a long time since she had been in Madrid. It was the season and an ideal time of year to be seen. The way to the wrought-iron lift was cleared of lesser guests as the hotel manager insisted that life had not been the same since the last time she had graced the capital. The lift jumped before ascending. The attendant avoided the angry look of the manager and muffled an apology.

Maria smiled to herself. The lift had always jumped and it would again when it reached the top floor. It did. The manager and attendant exchanged embarrassed glances as she swept out of the lift and into the spacious corridor. Two small maids stood by the door of her suite. They bobbed and kept their eyes down, not daring to look up at her. She felt wonderful. Her reputation had preceded her and her reputation was good.

Ronay went to a tiny street off the Plaza de la Cortez. He had used the private facilities of a modest hotel there before, and had taken a gamble on its still being in business after the Civil War. Thankfully it was. No doorman and no fuss – just the pleasant clean entrance hall with a concierge and a counter. Ronay signed the register and waited for the request for his passport. It didn't come. Good. It was as before. He filed his excuses ready for another time and carried his small case up the polished stairs to the second floor and his room. It was not unlike the one in Fulham. It contained a bed, a heater and the added luxury of a shower, hand basin and lavatory. He opened the curtains and looked out onto a rear mews which served as an occasional car park and as a delivery access to the hotel and to the shops that backed onto it. It was an excellent exit in an emergency. 'Always protect your arsehole in the field.' Charlie Peake's words came again.

Ronay had arranged a collection of meeting places and times with Maria to save risky telephone calls: the Botanical Gardens, the Prado Museum, the Neptune Fountain, in that order. Tomorrow, the first full day, he would be at the Gardens from nine until ten . . . then the Museum from twelve to thirteen hours, and finally the Fountain from nineteen to twenty hours. The second day the hours would go forward, ten to eleven, thirteen to fourteen, twenty to twenty-one. It would do for a time and then they would change the venues, if necessary. But he hoped it would not take too long before she found the Baron.

He spent the rest of the evening walking the shopping

precincts. His first priority, buying a few sets of underclothes, a couple of shirts, socks and toiletries. Now, he would await the action. The thought of it instilled in him a dull ache.

He knew his Maria, her record with the Factory, her exploits in the field, her victories, her way. There was none more adept at her profession, but he had never arranged these sordid situations before. It was distasteful to him but he knew that the ache was not from distaste. It was jealousy. She was his. She loved him, yet she was about to give her body to a *mark*. The Baron was to be the innocent in the match but he would take that lovely body and do his will.

He returned to the little hotel at the Plaza, and took a warm shower, trying to dismiss Donna Maria from his mind, at least until after dinner. He dreaded the thought of the coming night with just his imagination for company.

Donna Maria replaced the telephone by her bed and eased herself back into the feather down pillows. She had placed calls to four highborn families, announcing her arrival in Madrid. Through them would come the social invitations, but as time was pressing she had to choose the invitation most likely to lead to an early meeting with the Baron. The season would ensure that he would be in circulation, but where? A discreet enquiry here and there would determine her correct acceptance. Meanwhile for a moment her whole being lay becalmed on the luxury of the bed until she trembled with the first signs of returning pain.

The dull ache was followed by a sudden twinge in the region of her liver. Her body would soon be ravaged by an uncontrollable pain and then, thank God, the needle. But she didn't move from the pillows. She would delay her dependence on the hypodermic. It was against the Doctor's wishes of course. He advocated her use of the drug freely, and merely to strengthen the dose gradually when required. But she was no fool. By pushing more and more narcotics into her system, she was gradually negating her senses. Control of her mind was most important of all. She had to know what she was doing.

The twinges came suddenly and sharply. Her liver seemed to curl up with the shock. The pain that usually followed after four hours was now coming earlier, just as the doctor had warned. She began to cry. The telephone by her head sprang into life and she snatched at the receiver, trying to control her voice. A huge whine came down the line with the unmistakable monotone of Botty Cartwright.

'Darling, I've just heard you've arrived, and what has little old Madrid done to deserve such an honour? Tell me that, you little treasure you.'

Maria laughed. She laughed loud and hard. Of all the people she hadn't expected, top of the list would have been Botty Cartwright. The American lady's drone came again.

'If you don't spika da Inglais, dear, I'm going to have to come around and you know how dangerous that can be. Remember New York when you had that dreadful chill and I'd just docked on the *Mauretania* and I spent the whole day in your room with two acres of luggage in the foyer. You slept eight hours while I talked myself hoarse and when I got downstairs again the damn luggage had been put back on the *Mauretania* and shipped off to Bermuda.'

Maria gave another joyful burst of laughter. Her pain had eased. She felt truly wonderful about Botty's being there.

'Where are you, Botty?'

'In Spain. Where else? Do I get to see you or are you ignoring the peasants this trip?'

Maria laughed again. 'Behave yourself, Botty. Are you close by or long distance?'

The monotone continued: 'When you get to my age, dear, crossing the street is like going on safari. But I'm downstairs in the foyer of this demi-paradise, avoiding the searching eyes of a dozen gigolos and hoping to get to your domain virgo intacta.'

Minutes later Botty Cartwright bundled into the suite.

Her dress sense was awful. Deliberately so. A vast collection of coloured feathers cascaded from a ridiculous skull cap that sat on the top of the blue rinsed hair. Her face was masked in a thick white base with her eyes lined in black and lashes jutting out a full inch. Her lips were orange, her neck was hidden by a python of pearls, and her stumpy body was covered in a creation of something cerise and synthetic. She held out her arms as Maria approached her.

'Don't touch and for God's sake don't kiss me,' she drawled. 'I've had three hours at the salon and so help me I'll crack up if I'm molested in any way.'

The two women just touched with the tips of their fingers. Maria's eyes shone with the pleasure of seeing the sight before her. Botty Cartwright's face stayed like her voice with no sign of life except her eyes alert and friendly.

'Darling, you look ill. You also look young. And don't say it, I'm looking fit as a fiddle and old as the hills.' She glanced at a mirror on the wall above the writing table and touched her white caked face gently with her forefinger. 'It's called Winter in Venice,' she said. 'It looks more like a panda with piles.' Maria made no comment. Botty was firing for effect and it was wonderful.

They dined later at the Briganza Grille. Botty had a lot of questions and heaps of scandal. Maria said very little apart from trying to explain her long absence from the social register. The suggestion from Botty that she had fallen in love and had become a midwife in the mountains caused much laughter, but Maria had little else to do but listen and wait her chance to get invited somewhere. The invitation came with the sorbet.

'How do you feel about the Krauts?' Botty said, licking at the ice, not wishing it to come into contact with her face. 'You know, the Germans.'

Maria shrugged. 'I have no particular reason to like or dislike them. But why the question?'

Botty gave an arid chuckle. 'I'm giving a summer *soirée* on Friday and I've made it invitation by telephone only, which means I can change the guest list by the second. Clever, eh?'

Maria smiled. She always admired this multi-coloured American.

'The problem is what with the War on and all, do I, an American living in Spain, mix openly with the antagonists?'

'Have you invited the British ambassador?' Maria asked.

Botty gave a hoarse semi-squeak. 'Darling, one *always* invites the British ambassador.'

'Well, there's your answer. You can't take sides so you have to invite the Germans.'

Botty quiffed her hair under the skull cap. 'But they're so boring, darling. All stiff and sabre cuts everywhere.'

Maria took her opportunity. 'Wasn't there a rather handsome uncut Westphalian. . . ?'

'Kurt von Zeiss.' Botty came up with the name like an automatic address system.

'Very charming, if I recall,' Maria prompted.

'Well I could ask him,' Botty said, deep in thought. 'Do you think it'll show I'm not one-sided, even if I am?'

Maria patted her gloved hand. 'It will show you to be a diplomat,' she said.

Botty gave a high-pitched whistle that drew every eye in the Grille. 'Sonofabitch,' she growled. 'I nearly smiled there, damn it.'

The next day was Thursday and Ronay arrived at the Botanical Gardens early. He hadn't had a good night and the sunshine was more inviting than his hotel room. He tried to concentrate on the beautiful flower arrangements but he was constantly allowing his gaze to wander towards the entrance, hoping for a glimpse of Donna Maria. At eleven-fifteen, he left the Gardens and made for the main shopping area, then to the Prado Museum.

He saw her as he reached the steps. She caught his eye and turned into the building, knowing he would follow. A spot close to the Inca masks was safe enough to exchange a few words. In a series of short murmured sentences, she told him of her meeting with Botty Cartwright and of the coming party. He was both relieved and disappointed. He hated the thought of leaving her. But she had a job to do. They agreed to keep to their open schedule of meetings and he dragged himself away from her and the Prado and returned to his hotel.

In spite of the sounds of the city outside, he felt lonely in the room. His feelings for Donna Maria were very much stronger than he had ever felt for her before. He was an intruder. Her thoughts would not be of him but of the Baron. The pang of jealousy swelled inside him once more and it was like being young again. He sat on the bed and dragged his concentration back to the task in hand. He would have to inform Charlie Peake that he was in Madrid. He slipped down to the reception to ask where he could send an overseas telegram. Thankfully it wasn't far. He could walk it and have lunch, then back to the hotel before going to the Neptune Fountain in the hope of seeing her again.

The town house of Botty Cartwright was at the end of a cul de sac off the Prado. A small arch led into the cobbled courtyard with the house built around it like a square horseshoe. Its windows were tall and thin, with small terraces protruding from below holding pots of falling geraniums that splashed the formal façade with dashes of colour. A warm glow came from within the house, the soft sound of a piano tinkling something by Gershwin against the collective voices of the guests.

Donna Maria checked the time. It was fifteen minutes after twenty-one hours, fifteen minutes late and just right. She had left the hotel early and instructed the cab to drive around the Neptune Fountain. She saw Ronay standing by the south corner. He didn't see her but that was as she wanted it. She enjoyed having him waiting for her, unlike the past when it was she who stood in the rain and she who sat alone by a dying fire and she who cried herself to sleep and snapped herself awake when she felt him getting into bed beside her.

The cab stopped halfway inside the arch, unable to negotiate the host of limousines parked around the courtyard. Chauffeurs in various uniforms appeared from the shadows, some extinguishing cigarettes, others blatantly puffing them with their hands in their pockets. Donna Maria alighted and swept towards the house, aware of the eyes. She paused at the front door and turned suddenly. The massed uniforms crept back into the shadows. She felt wonderful.

The Cartwright butler opened the door and bowed deeply. Botty half screamed from the sitting room opposite the hall, 'Darling, Maria,' and rushed to her with absolutely no grace and no deportment and no style. 'The dress is a decade out of date, dear, but with you in it who cares?' She gushed just loud enough for everyone to hear.

Donna Maria kissed her on both cheeks and followed into the huge room. The pianist demoted Gershwin for Rodgers and Hart as the strains of 'Funny Valentine' throbbed from the baby grand. Botty gave Donna Maria the grand tour of handshakes. She knew absolutely no one. It was quite surprising that out of some sixteen or so guests, only Botty was an acquaintance. Except for the tall grey man in the white tie and tails, Kurt von Zeiss, with a full moustache and bifocals. He beamed at her from his side of the piano. She gradually made her way to him during the last of the introductions. He held both her hands tightly.

'I want to click my heels, Maria,' he smiled.

She remembered the time she had scolded his ritual. 'I could also try to impress you by singing the lyrics to this tune,' he said, 'but the effect would damage my suit for your attentions.'

He continued pressing her hand and she smiled back, lowering her eyes just a little.

'How are you, Kurt?'

'You look quite ravishing,' he said, ignoring her question.

She squeezed his hands and pulled herself away. She felt his gaze burning into her back as she drifted towards Botty who hadn't missed a thing.

'Listen, if you could make the weight I'd back you against Joe Louis,' Botty growled. 'With the haymaker you just hit that poor man with, I could lay the world.'

Donna Maria ignored her and accepted a glass of champagne.

'But have you met him before?' Botty was pressing. The chances were she already knew the answer but that was Botty Cartwright's style. And with her you played the game.

'I met him about three years ago,' Donna Maria said. Botty's eyes widened along with her ears.

'Where? When?' she panted. 'Was he wonderful? And rough?'

Donna Maria smiled. 'He was a perfect gentleman,' she said. She blew Botty a kiss and circulated the room. At the far end a table was laid for supper, the Cartwright silver dominating the fine array of porcelain and china, especially the infamous Cincinnati Salt rising from the centre of the table. Made by American craftsmen to the design of Botty's first husband, Waldo. According to Botty, it started at the base as a totem pole, showing the beginnings of the New World, and then somewhere in the middle the Empire State building unfolded, balancing the Statue of Liberty atop its spire. Around the bottom of the effigy, the four legs holding the salt were a series of bucking broncos and cowboys fighting Indians, added by Remington to give the piece 'class'. But half a million dollars and all the goodwill in the world couldn't stop it becoming known as 'Cartwright's Cock', baptised by Botty and paraded with great honour wherever people of quality gathered to discuss the finer things of life.

Donna Maria edged around the table as if admiring the centrepiece but secretly eyeing the place cards against each napkin. It was as she feared. The Baron was seated well away from her. It was bad luck.

At the crowded end of the room, someone French began singing something French. The pianist playing yet another love song to 'Paree' had been joined by a bone-thin woman in a beautiful short-cut evening dress, blatantly revealing, disgustingly French and 'in'. She sat at the end of the long piano stool and leaned on the musician's tuxedo jacket, leaving powder and make-up on the collar. Her words were inaudible as she had neglected to remove the long ebony cigarette holder from her clenched teeth. The piano was now surrounded by singing guests. Deep within their ranks Botty Cartwright could be heard urging them on to the chorus.

Donna Maria picked up her place card and shifted around to the far end of the dining table, nonchalantly dropping it on the place next to the Baron's. The card of an unknown female vanished under the table and onto the carpet out of sight, out of mind. Tonight Donna Maria would make every effort to arrange an affair.

As the guests sought out their allotted chairs, Botty Cartwright sat at the head of the table and directed operations. The French woman with the cigarette holder prowled around the crowd three times before Donna Maria's switch became apparent. Botty was the only one who suspected. The French woman was embarking on her fourth voyage before the last empty chair became obvious. Botty chuckled as the unfortunate traveller sat down and looked towards the Baron in puzzled dismay. She then looked at Botty who shrugged and rang the silver bell, summoning the *cantaloup à la mode* – a strange concoction in any other home but here.

Donna Maria approached the lump of vanilla ice cream floating in the middle of the melon with some reservation. She felt the Baron's knee press into hers. She pressed back.

'How clever of you to choose vanilla, Frau Cartwright,' he called from across the Cincinnati Salt. 'The colour and texture match the cantaloup to perfection.'

Botty filled her mouth with the culinary combination. 'Bullshit,' she said.

The table collapsed in laughter except for the French lady who glared at everyone, especially Donna Maria. The Baron pressed knees again. No jokes. No accident. Deliberate and suggestive. Donna Maria smiled.

Throughout the meal conversation flowed across the table at all angles, on all manner of topics, but for her it was his whispered asides that made a success of the evening. Where had she been for so long, he asked. Spain was beautiful once more. Could he possibly see her again, he pleaded. Could it be soon?

The French lady reclaimed the Baron immediately after the dinner but not before Donna Maria had shyly promised that she would be at the opera the following evening and that her diary was free for the rest of the week-end. It was late when she returned to the Palace Hotel, tired but exhilarated. Botty had promised to keep a place in her box at the opera and all was well.

As the lift clawed its way to the top floor, the pain was beginning. But the needle was waiting.

The next day was the third and last of the arranged meetings with Ronay. The Botanical Gardens at eleven o'clock were crowded but he was there. He thought she looked unbearably lovely. The flowers complemented her.

'How did it go?' he said without looking at her.

'He was there and I'm seeing him tonight.'

Ronay's heart missed a beat. 'Excellent!'

He forced the word out as nonchalantly as he could.

'When shall we meet again?' she asked.

'Tomorrow,' he suggested.

She shook her head. 'That's too soon. I hope to be with him the whole week-end.'

He had to do something with his hands. He clawed some roses from a bush and turned to look at her. Her face was still, her mouth gentle and moist, her complexion white and her doe eyes telling him she loved him. He pushed the roses into her hands, roughly. The thorns pricked her skin, but she understood.

'Monday. The Fountain. I'll be there all afternoon.' His words were stiff.

'I'll try,' she said as he turned away and vanished into the crowd.

'I'll try.' He couldn't get those last words out of his mind. He walked the Prado and had a beer at the Brasserie. 'The whole week-end,' he laughed bitterly.

That evening news blazed across the front page of the late editions. German tanks were pushing on, in the wake of an Allied retreat. He felt he couldn't care less. The war and England were a lifetime away. His whole future was where she was, and she was a week-end away. He took the paper to his room and slept with it.

The dapper little man from the fashion house scuttled to and fro with Donna Maria's selection. From the bedroom of the hotel suite, the hum of a sewing machine stopped and the seamstress announced that she had finished. The small man threw a kiss to the heavens and scuttled into the bedroom. He reappeared with a long evening dress cascading from his arms and sang with pleasure in his high textured voice.

Donna Maria moved from the sofa on the terrace into the room. Evening was close and the beautifully furnished lounge was spacious and airy and cleverly lit by elegant lamplight. She stood in the middle of the room and allowed her négligé to fall to the floor, her satin underclothes catching the light. The little dress designer tried not to focus on her long slender legs, the fully fashioned stockings making an endless journey to her thighs where they clung to her suspenders. He held the dress open for her to step into. The act of easing her body into the creation surpassed most fantasies the little man had ever had. He burst into song once more as she turned and posed for him. The seamstress appeared, collapsing under the sewing machine in her arms.

She too trilled in delight. The designer clapped his little hands, scolding her, and then he followed her out of the suite, with a deep bow and just one more glimpse of Donna Maria before closing the door.

She eyed herself in the long mirror and was pleased with the image. As she moved, the soft texture of the dress brushed her body and sent excited chills through her. It was a feeling she had always had from something new and exquisite and expensive.

It was almost time. She went to the bathroom and took the hypodermic from the small vanity case. She selected a small glass of the drug from those housed in the lid and gently flicked her finger into her arm, encouraging a vein to come to the surface. There was a knock on the door of the suite.

'Just a minute,' she called as she stabbed the vein and pushed the drug into her bloodstream.

She opened the door to reveal a young man in his mid-twenties, a crop of red hair protruding from his scrubbed head and wearing a dinner jacket with the bow tied too tightly. His shirt was new, overstarched, and he was ill at ease. His eyes widened to see Donna Maria standing there, her dress gracefully hanging from her white shoulders, her hair pulled back into a smooth coil with the front teased over her forehead. She stood for a moment, gazing at him.

'Harvey Teckner, ma'am,' the young man stammered in a soft American accent. 'Aunt Botty's nephew. You may recall she had to go back to the States. Bolt from the blue.'

The look on her face showed that Botty Cartwright had not informed her. His face turned the colour of his hair.

'Huckleberry hell!' he gasped. 'She didn't call you.'

'Mister Harvey Teckner, do come in,' Donna Maria said warmly to ease his embarrassment. She offered her hand which the young American shook rather heavily.

'Are we alone, Señorita Domenquin?' he asked mysteriously.

She nodded. The young man was puzzling.

'May I be frank?'

Again she nodded. He sat down on the edge of the chair.

'God, it's so embarrassing,' he mumbled.

'What is?' She wasn't sure what to expect.

'Aunt Botty,' he said. 'Well she's not Aunt Botty. I mean she's just plain old Mrs Cartwright and we've only known her since today.'

'Who is we?' Donna Maria hid a smile. Botty hadn't changed. She guessed the answer that was coming.

'Chuck Blackwell,' Harvey blurted. 'My best friend. We're from McKeesport. That's in Pennsylvania. We're majoring in Spanish. Gee, we only got here on Thursday. Then Chuck and me met Aunt . . . I mean Mrs Cartwright just this afternoon. Next thing is Chuck is going on this trip and I'm knocking on your door. Gee, it's embarrassing.'

Donna Maria held back her laughter and ruffled his wiry, cropped hair.

'Well, I consider the whole episode a stroke of luck, Harvey. May I call you Harvey?'

The young man nodded. 'How lucky is that?' he asked naïvely.

'Lucky that I have a gentleman to escort me instead of a dragon and lucky that the gentleman is charming.'

Harvey Teckner tried to loosen his bow tie but the redness still came rushing from his neck.

'Huckleberry hell!' he said, offering her a small box with an orchid inside. She accepted it with a deep smile and gave him the flower, pointing above her left breast.

'Would you be so kind as to pin it for me?'

Harvey Teckner reddened once more. His eyes bulged to enormous saucers as he tried to push his fingers behind the top of the dress without touching the white skin below. Donna Maria looked at him calmly. He suddenly came out with a torrent of words.

'Donna Maria, if I prick myself during this task of some delicacy, I shall in all probability bleed. That act of human frailty will in all probability stain your beautiful attire. And that in all probability will ruin not only your evening but my whole life. I'd just like you to know that, ma'am.'

Donna Maria laughed. 'Harvey Teckner, you are most gallant and please call me Maria.'

He smiled, too, and offered his hand. 'In that case let's start again. I'm Harvey.'

'It's a pleasure to have you as my date, Harvey,' she laughed. 'Where are you taking me?'

'I have Mrs Cartwright's box tickets for "Don Carlos". I don't even know what it's about but I hear we have champagne and caviare during the interval.'

'Well, during the season in Madrid the opera is mostly about being seen.'

Teckner shoved his hands in his pockets and sat on the edge of the sofa, shaking his head in confusion.

'I've been in Spain two days and to be honest I don't know what the Huckleberry I'm doing. I speak real bad Spanish, I find the food weird and socially I'm not doing too well. I'm told that if I want to succeed I've got to have "class" and everyone in town is talking about you. . .'

Donna Maria floated over to the worried young man. 'Harvey Teckner, give me your arm.'

He stood and blushed gratefully. Maria hadn't forgotten the Baron and the importance of the evening, but she felt sympathetic towards the young American. Besides, he would serve as a pleasant smoke screen and be easily disposed of later.

'All you need to know for tonight is that "Don Carlos" is by Verdi and that it's loud and long. The champagne and caviare will help us survive. But you and I will have every eye in Madrid on us, and that, I believe, is what they call "class".'

She glided out of the suite with Harvey Teckner in close attendance. He followed like a red setter, spirited and ready to obey.

The foyer of the Teatro Della Zarzuela was small but here, before the performance on the stage, a performance of the social graces was given with an art practised over the centuries. The style and the elegance were pure 'class'. The various groups were from all parts of the world, a truly cosmopolitan crowd.

The heads of the people nearest the entrance turned as Donna Maria Domenquin floated in with Harvey Teckner close beside her.

Her appearance was a subject for immediate discussion. The women looked with a touch of scandal in their eyes; the men, as one, were captivated.

'Together we stand, divided we fall,' she whispered.

'McKeesport was never like this,' he whispered back.

As Donna Maria glided amongst the crowds, the resentment of many of the women was apparent. The men paid her hesitant court and as she encountered old friends and acquaintances, Maria returned their greetings warmly. Eventually, she saw the one face she had been looking for. He stood with three other men; one of them, an ambassador, wore a small badge depicting a black swastika on a white/pink background. The other two were high-ranking German officers. Knowing where he was, Donna Maria relaxed immediately.

The auditorium below the box was a mass of colour. Diamonds flashed from an array of tiaras, necklaces and rings. The grand clothes of the patrons blended with the regal gold, blue and red of the decor. Deep within the moat of the pit, the variations of a perfect 'A' rang from the waiting orchestra. Maria saw the Baron enter a box in the opposite tier. He scanned the area below with his opera glasses. She waited for his head to tilt to her level, knowing his eyes were seeking her. He had her promise to see him that night and she felt a perfect prize. The Baron hastily returned his gaze to the scene below him. Harvey touched her shoulder.

'My God, did you see that,' he said indignantly. 'That old guy gave you the once over.'

'I didn't notice,' she replied.

Then the lights fell and all was still. Donna Maria searched for Harvey's hand in the darkness and squeezed it.

'I've never felt so classy in my life,' she whispered.

After the performance Harvey was anxious to have her join him for a late supper. She declined a dozen times, feigning tiredness. But he insisted on taking her back to her hotel. She paused at the door to the suite and offered him the key to open it. He did so and gallantly returned the key to her gloved hand. She stroked his cheek and kissed him fully on the mouth.

'Huckleberry hell!' he gasped.

'Goodnight, my good knight,' she smiled, and began to close the door.

He blurted out, 'May I see you again please?'

'Call me any afternoon,' she smiled.

'Real soon?'

'Real soon.' The door clicked closed. Passing the foyer, Harvey Teckner froze at the revolving doors. Baron Kurt von Zeiss was walking towards the reception telephones. The American turned in his tracks and approached the Baron.

'Excuse me, sir,' Harvey said.

The Baron replaced the receiver and frowned.

'My name is Teckner. I was at the opera tonight with a lady.'

The Baron stood silently, offering no reply.

'I just hope you aren't about to bother her again.'

The Baron gave a bow. 'Your anger escapes me, sir,' he said.

'Well she ain't no race horse. Stick that in your binoculars,' the young lion growled.

The Baron glanced around the foyer. The boy's voice was becoming too loud for comfort. 'Goodnight, sir,' he said and left the hotel. Harvey watched a while before leaving. Then, his appetite gone, he took a taxi to his lodgings.

She sat there for much longer than she had intended. Her eyes had become weary. The room was in darkness save for the light of the Iberian full moon giving a glow resembling the limelight of an elderly theatre. The suggestion of blue in its throw was both mysterious and restful. If the telephone didn't ring soon she would have failed. The signs had all been good but why hadn't the Baron called? She hoped the morning would bring an explanation.

She slipped out of her dress and prepared to run her bath; then a knock came to the door. Harvey again. She was going to have trouble with that boy. She slipped on a soft négligé and went to the door. She opened it an inch. Kurt von Zeiss was standing there. He half bowed and shrugged.

'I couldn't telephone. Your American eagle is too protective.'

'Surely he isn't still in the hotel?' she said.

'I think not, but one can never tell with the young.'

She stood leaning against the closed door, watching him stalk across the darkened room to the window overlooking the terrace.

'It is most beautiful, your Spain,' he said without taking his gaze from the view. 'Like you, my dear, it stays unchanged, its beauty eternal, its magnetism stronger than the stoutest heart.'

She didn't reply. He looked at her standing there, her lithe body emphasised in the soft moonlight. He moved towards her, two or three steps, a test. Would she falter from that seductive pose or would she hold it? She knew the signs and made a slight graceful movement that would appear hesitant yet accessible. As he stepped closer, she lifted her hands as if to touch her hair in half defence. He reached out.

'Let me do it,' he said firmly.

She made a mock attempt to stop him.

'Kurt, it's late.'

The words came gentle, not scolding, a half apology. She felt his body stiffen, then shake. Then suddenly he pulled her hair half free of the ribbon. She gave a soft whimper of pain. He panted loudly and dragged her across the room. She fell to her knees, her hair completely free now and falling over her face. As she slid over the tiles she tried desperately to keep control of the situation. The ferocity of the Baron was totally unexpected, and yet the last thing she could do was to discourage him. She had to stay and play whatever game he chose.

He stood over her, breathing heavily. Slowly he removed his spectacles and placed them carefully in his jacket pocket, and then he began to undress. She tried to stand but he pushed her back to her knees and she fell heavily. She felt even more alarmed; this was in no way what she had planned. She made no more sound, no move, merely lay there watching him strip naked, her head bowed, her arms by her side.

He bent down, she thought to lift her up, but he took the fringes of her négligé and tore them apart in one movement, still smiling. She knelt there waiting. He took her breasts in his huge hands and pinched hard into her nipples, all the while kissing her hungrily. She must try to take the lead. It was her only hope. She put her arms around his neck and pushed her tongue into his mouth, hoping he might relax his grip, but he bit deeply into her tongue. She gave a muffled scream and pushed him away. He tore the négligé off her shoulders, pinning her arms to her side like a straitjacket. She tried to struggle. He laughed.

'Make me do it, make me,' he cried, ripping her satin pants from her thighs and pushing his head roughly between them. She screamed in agony as he bit deep into her. Her legs tried to kick out but he held on to them in an agonising vice. She couldn't tell how long he had her there. Some of the time she was half conscious, but at last he had finished. He collapsed on her heavily, kissing her clumsily.

'Forgive me, my dearest,' he mumbled, 'forgive me.'

She felt angry, defiled. The pain between her legs and over the rest of her body was intense but she knew she couldn't ruin the opportunity. She had made her mark and determined to secure her victim.

'Untie me and kiss me,' she said softly.

He loosened the négligé around her arms.

'I'm spent, my love. Empty,' he sighed.

She sat up carefully and took a deep breath. He watched her guiltily as she went into the bathroom. The sight in her full length mirror made her sick. Apart from her tangled hair, her face was bruised, her neck a mass of love bites seeping blood. Her breasts were bleeding and the agony between her legs was unbearable. This man was a sadist and she had not bargained for that. She sprinkled oils into the bath and gently eased her torn body into the hot water. The cuts smarted, bringing tears to her eyes. She leaned back onto the edge of the bath and allowed herself to cry. First a sob and then a flood of tears. He came in with champagne. She half caught her sobs but he saw and his face was grey with concern. She forced a smile.

'I don't know what you must think of me,' she said.

The lie came easily, neatly screening her true thoughts. He knelt by the bath and stroked her face, his fingers cold from the champagne glass. The effect put her on guard.

'And I don't make a habit of loving a man on a first date,' she sobbed, accompanying the statement with effective shyness.

He filled his hands with the foam of the soap and gently massaged the full cream into her skin.

'I would like to assure you that if I hurt you I . . .'

She darted a look at him. She must attack now and secure her position in the relationship. Her face clouded into synthetic anger.

'Do not apologise for giving me what I wanted,' she interrupted. 'Just accept that for once in my life I surrendered to a man too early for my good name.'

She paused, letting the statement sink in. 'But then we did promise each other a long time ago. Remember?'

He leaned back on the tiled wall and closed his eyes. His face was open and relaxed, 'God, that song.'

She began to hum. He half sang the first line with her. '*Bei mir bist du schön.*'

He suddenly stopped and stood up nervously. 'This isn't another brief one-night meeting, is it?' he said. His hands were fidgeting. 'I couldn't take that, Maria. Not again. Not now.'

She shook her head. The heat of the water had taken its toll on her. Sweat covered her face and breasts, running down into the water.

'Leave me your telephone number,' she said. 'I'll come to you this time. I can't have you using the Palace as a bordello.'

He went to her, taking her wet hips in his hands and pulling her to him.

Her body, red and oiled from the luxury of the soap, held sensually in his fingers. He kissed the sweat from her breasts.

'Go now,' she said. 'Go home. I'll call. I'll come soon.'

He turned and left without a further look. She heard the outer door click shut. Once more she looked at herself in the long mirror. The welts and bruises were still there, along with the hurt and the memory of the night. But Marcus will be pleased, she thought. She had the fox in her lair.

Sunday presented itself to Ronay with the distant peal of the first church in the city to get to a bell. Soon a cacophony of ringing tones swelled from the warm morning and totally shattered his rest. Thankfully, he decided, for his dreams had not been of good things. It was of nightmare doings, involving him and shadows and sex and tears, and her.

For a while he missed Mrs Baylis. On such a day the aroma of bacon or kipper would be rising from the kitchen below and a pot of tea would be awaiting the shock of boiling water to bring it to life. His mouth watered.

His choice of clothes for such a day was the same as the day before. He'd a change of underwear – his last, but with luck he wouldn't be in Madrid after tomorrow. Then, at the Neptune Fountain, he would see her and all would be over, the Baron in his place and Donna Maria back in Ronay's arms, back where she should be, where she wanted to be. Unless the charms of von Zeiss were such that any possibility of her leaving him would be unthinkable. Ronay dug a comb in his hair and deliberately tugged it, but he couldn't shake the thought. He threw on the rest of his clothes, lying in all parts of the room. Without a shave, or even a wash, he hit the warming pavements of the city and headed towards anywhere.

The traffic had been replaced by pedestrians, children dressed beautifully for their Sunday walk, proud parents with bunches of flowers and holy books. The most Catholic of countries celebrated the day in the true tradition of the faith. Ronay watched the bright happiness as it moved in all directions. He envied them their peace, their trust, their safety; but then they had already had their war, the bitter civil combat. Fascist and communist, brother and son, had faced each other's wrath and now, with the dead buried, only a memory of the conflict was left. They needed their day of rest and their children and their bells to assure them the Almighty was here, promising them peace.

He bought a newspaper and a large red apple. Crunching into its tight skin, the juice stung his palate. He looked ahead and there it was, the Palace Hotel. True, she was ever on his mind. Yes, he did want to see her. But he hadn't come here deliberately.

Finally committing himself, he tossed the core of the apple into the gutter and sat on a low parapet. He looked up at the hotel and tried to guess which would be her floor and then her window, her terrace. Perhaps he may even see her. Or him. They could both be there, both watching him and laughing. To hell with them, he decided. So, his pride well protected, he sat there in the sun with the song birds competing with the bells and the children arguing and playing and singing.

Donna Maria's feet glided along the gravel drive of the country estate. The high trees in full leaf and the rolling hills of lawn had none of the trappings of the city yet the location was no more than thirty minutes from the Palace Hotel. Kurt von Zeiss had finished instructing the elderly groom about his hunter and came to meet her at the end of the stable yard. She took his arm with both hands as he steered her towards the great house on the brow of the rise. He walked without speaking and the gravel sang beneath their riding boots. She was pensive and unsure, half dreading the next hour. They would make love soon and then she would have to begin the last move of the game. This was a fish of cold waters. She would warm him and settle him before offering the bait.

The high tea prepared in the summer house by the swimming pool was delicate and delicious. The staff appeared as if from nowhere to serve, then vanished in the same way.

Maria knew he was becoming anxious. His nervous way of rubbing his hands and avoiding her eyes warned her. She waited just long enough before rising and holding her arm out to him. He took her into a firm embrace that became firmer. She gave a gasp of enjoyable hurt as he crushed her into him.

'Take me to bed,' she cried.

He pulled away and silently led her to the terrace steps. He watched her undress, his eyes like a fox darting from one part of her body to another. At last she stood there, her firm figure throbbing. She slid beneath the sheets and in her turn watched him prepare.

Once more there was his long intense stare at her, and then the ritual of removing his spectacles and breathing on them before placing them in his jacket pocket. Suddenly a sharp pain ran through her, her body gave a jerk and she bit back a cry. He continued undressing, unaware of her distress. Her fist clenched around the edge of the pillow as the pain hit home again and she felt her head swim. Her focus blurred and the room went into shadow.

She saw his dark shape loom nearer, his arm lifted high.

Her eyes gave her only a shadowy impression. Then the arm came down swiftly. She felt the whip of leather across her breasts. She caught her breath in surprise and hurt as he lashed her again. Once more her head swam, the sheets were dragged from her twisting legs, his belt laid across her in a succession of violent blows, and she could no longer determine the exact source of her pain. It was all one. She screamed.

The sound of her added to his excitement. He grabbed her, his shaking fingers tearing into her flesh, as he turned her over. With a brutal hand he held her head into the pillows while the other whipped the belt across her buttocks. She could hardly breathe. His hand had a vice-like grip on the back of her neck. She tried to turn her head to get more air. She could allow herself to black out which would be a blessed relief but there was the risk of suffocation. Again she dragged her chin to one side; again the belt fell in a succession of penal strokes. She pulled her knees up to her breasts. He roared his excitement. Then he let her knees free and allowed her to crawl up to the head of the bed. She pulled herself up and gasped. Her position was one of complete submission, total surrender. A tight smile twisted his mouth.

He fell onto her, thrusting himself into her, moaning his pleasure into her ringing ears. She tried to concentrate on something, anything to take her away from this terrible agony. Then she thought of the needle and the peace it possessed. She would persevere. The pain was bearable now, with the needle close, just a few steps to the handbag by the dressing table.

'It's wonderful, Kurt,' she whispered hoarsely into his ear. 'Finish it, finish it, my love.'

He obeyed with a high, breathless cry, and then at last he rolled off her. She waited a while, lying there listening to his apologies and then, kissing him gently on his wet forehead, she rose painfully from the bed and forced herself to the handbag. Slowly she made the interminable journey to the bathroom and locked it before falling to her knees, her last strength spent. She stayed there, fumbling with the hypodermic until at long last the drug entered her system and she lay back on the tiled floor, preparing herself to act the most important part in her life.

She made the first move during cocktails that night in the library. She spoke very little and on most occasions when he looked at her, she drew her eyes away. He became more aware of her performance during dinner and, when the staff had cleared the table, and left them with the coffee and liqueurs, he watched her avoiding him.

'Would you care to discuss it?' he asked.

She shook her head and allowed herself to cry a little. He left her to herself for a moment, walking out onto the lawn that rolled from the tall windows of the dining room. She knew his thoughts would be racing; he would be concerned for her and soon he would press her for an explanation. But first she would shock him.

'I have to leave Madrid very soon,' she said.

He heard her but made no effort to answer.

'I'm sorry, Kurt, but it's something very urgent.'

Again he stood silent. She left the window and went to the bedroom. She had most of her belongings together when he came in and he watched her finish packing the small case.

'Is it me?'

The question came in a sad, sullen voice. He was visibly affected. She sat at the dressing table and played with her hair.

'No, it's not you my love.'

'But why now? What could be so urgent that it takes you away so quickly,' he said. He threw his hands up in despair. She allowed her tears to come again.

'You remember Barcelona. Our first meeting and the two men from Berlin and the House.'

He remembered and waited for her to continue. She paused deliberately, and then spoke very slowly, allowing every syllable to sink into his brain.

'The House has contacted me. Today, at the Hotel. They called. They need me.'

He went to her and knelt, taking her hands and watching the tears fall from her lovely eyes.

'You can't go, Maria. Not to the House. Not now. They can't just call you and expect you to go.'

She looked down at him and pushed her hands through his silvering hair.

'But they can and they have, my darling. I still have a cause, Kurt. The communist threat is as strong as ever in my country and now, with the war in Europe, it is getting stronger still.'

He fell silent for a while, his brain searching for words. 'Can you tell me what you have to do?' he asked. 'Is it like before? Can it hurt you?'

She laughed softly. 'I hardly think so, my love. All I can tell you is that what's about to happen is quite wonderful.'

'How much more wonderful can anything be than this moment?' he murmured.

'This terrible war between Germany and the Allies could end as quickly as it began,' she said. 'The House has information that contact through secret channels is desired between England and Germany, using Spain as the springboard.'

The Baron froze; she could almost hear his brain sorting through the possibilities.

'How do you fit into this plan?' he asked.

'I know the person bringing the outlines of the peace offer,' she said. 'I'm to help him contact German agents in Spain. There's no time to lose. The whole basis of the plan is governed by the state of the British forces fighting in France. I have to see him tomorrow.'

'And then?' he snapped. His question had the fire of a hunter. He was on the scent and running.

'Then Barcelona perhaps. Wherever the House decides to make the first moves.'

'Why do the British want to deal through the Secret Service? What's wrong with diplomatic channels?'

She thought for a moment before delivering the final thrust. 'They think that what they have to offer is something too important for simple diplomacy.'

'And you have to be part of it?'

'I do. Please understand,' she cried.

He pulled her head up to his and kissed her. She looked up at him, her eyes alight with excitement.

'The House wouldn't know,' she said, 'and even if they did, I wouldn't care. Wouldn't you like to come with me tomorrow and meet the British agent here in Madrid?'

The Baron's mouth was wide with surprise. 'Why on earth would I do that?' he asked.

'Because it's Marcus,' she said giggling like a schoolgirl.

His solemn face lit up. 'Ronay? Here in Madrid. Tomorrow?' And then, as suddenly as it had come, the smile vanished. She feared she might have gone too far, too soon. He was silent, deep in thought. She decided to risk an interruption.

'If you'd rather not, it doesn't matter darling. I just thought it might be fun, that's all. Come, I must fly.'

He picked up her suitcase and then said, 'I'd hate to offer my hand to him and have it bitten. We are enemies, don't forget, he and I.'

She smiled and kissed him sweetly. 'My dear, darling Kurt,' she said, 'I'll meet you in the foyer at eleven o'clock tomorrow morning and when Marcus sees you he'll be the happiest man in the world.'

As the car pulled away from the house, the Baron waved her away, unaware of the neatly woven web left in her wake.

'Monday!' Ronay spoke the word at the bare ceiling above his head as he lay in bed at the hotel. He had two hours before the meeting at eleven o'clock and they would go soon enough. There must be no sign of the strain or the jealousies he had been going through over the past few days. He sprang from the bed and went to the shower, turning it on to its coldest, then a brisk rub with an abrasive towel. He retrieved his trousers from under the mattress and they came out stiff and sharp at the crease. A smile of satisfaction came across his face. His shoes had a grey film of dust over them but a vigorous massage with his bath towel gave them a sort of sheen.

'England expects . . .' he grinned.

At ten-fifteen, Ronay presented himself in the foyer. The concierge eyed the New Look as he pushed over a buff envelope along with the bill. Ronay settled the account and left his case at the reception desk. He would collect it later.

He crossed the street to the small café opposite and ordered a croissant and black coffee. The buff envelope revealed a Swiss passport with his photograph and particulars in the name of Otto Hellier, and an air ticket for London that night. Charlie Peake had prepared his exit neatly.

Ronay's excitement was mounting with each minute as the meeting came closer. At ten-fifty he tossed a handful of pesetas onto the table and rid himself of the rattle in his pockets. He looked forward to the half-crowns and farthings of England, and the Fountain, and Maria.

He saw them from a good hundred yards away. The Baron saw him too but Ronay ignored his wave. He waited until they were within hailing distance.

'Marcus, Marcus, over here,' the Baron shouted.

Ronay's instinct was to give an enormous cheer, seeing the *mark* waiting to be led to the next step of the scenario. But instead he feinted an absent-minded gaze in their direction. Then, as if seeing them for the first time, he broke into a slow run and a wide smile. He took the Baron's outstretched hand and at the same time gazed down at Maria. He was impressed by her appearance as always. The beauty was there but she had a look in her eyes that was strangely frightening, as if she were in some sort of terror. She was pale and he thought thinner. She stepped between the two men and they all fell together in a loud, laughing clinch.

After the kisses and backslaps had subsided, Ronay asked for silence.

'I believe you know a quiet house in the City?' he said in a tone of mock intrigue. Maria touched her breasts with her hands. 'Is nothing sacred?' she cried, pretending to cover them. The Baron fell against the wall of the Fountain and allowed the spray to fall lightly on his head.

'*Bei mir bist du schön*,' he sang with the slur of a drunk. Again the trio rocked with uninhibited laughter.

That was the way it was through their walk down the Prado and well into their second drink at the Braganza. Between times they swapped their stories of the years apart, Maria's tranquillity in Istan, the Baron's travels between Germany and his beloved Spain, and Ronay's lies of heading a Government secret office free of espionage and counter intelligence but full of the excitement of seeing through Government policies on the national front – 'watching for the Reds and the anarchists within the ranks of the growing unionism and docile democracy of the country.'

The Baron received the lie well, anxious to press for more details but aware of the barrier between them due to the War. Ronay decided to bait the trap during the dessert course.

'I must congratulate you on the Ardennes offensive,' he said to the Baron. The words hit von Zeiss like a bolt. He fussed with his spectacles and coughed.

'I would thank you for the compliment,' he said eventually, 'but, my dear friend, it grieves me to acknowledge such an accolade.'

Ronay reached across the table and laid his hands on the Baron's warmly.

'Soon, soon my friend, we'll be one again.'

Maria's hand joined them. She cried softly. Just enough, always just enough.

'Please God,' she said. 'Please God, it will be soon.'

Again the Baron poised for a question, but again he bit back his curiosity. A silence followed.

'Look, are you two together? I mean, well you know, together?' Ronay said with the perfect touch of naïvety.

'Yes, we are together,' Maria said, looking lovingly into the Baron's eyes.

Ronay fought to conceal his jealousy. 'Then you must have told him why I'm here,' he said, quietly.

She shifted in her seat, pushing the Baron's knee with hers under the table. 'I told him of your visit. Not why,' she cooed.

Ronay grinned at von Zeiss. 'She lies beautifully,' he said. 'I'm quite sure that anything I tell you, my lovely lady,' he addressed Maria, 'will find its way via the pillow to my fine friend and enemy here, so what the hell.'

He ordered more coffee and some brandy. The three huddled closer and Ronay's voice lowered.

'I've been sent over to await contact with Germany through the Spanish House.'

The Baron nodded.

'Well, you know that much then,' Ronay grinned. The Baron stammered. Maria signalled again with her knee under the table. Ronay noticed but continued.

'Since our two armies began battle in France, Winston Churchill has assumed the leadership in Britain. I take it you know that much as well?' The Baron nodded along with Maria. Ronay had their undivided attention.

'Churchill never has believed Germany to be our natural enemy. He has spoken from the back benches for years about the real threat to world peace. He has written countless articles too, but until now no one has listened. Now he is PM, they will. Russia! That's his worry. That's our worry. There isn't a non-aggression pact in Christendom that will stop the red flag walking over a hundred borders.'

The Baron nodded again. Every word rang with authority and good sense. Ronay continued.

'But now, with Chamberlain and his appeasers out of power, Churchill can force the British Parliament to look at the eastern threat. And as they look we can present his ultimate plan for the free Western countries. A European Parliament.'

The Baron sighed, but didn't interrupt.

'All the great countries of Europe with one dream, one goal, with strength to withstand American wealth and a combined will to stop Stalin in his tracks.'

The Baron ached now to add his sentiments but Ronay wasn't finished. 'I have with me certain points for discussion direct from London. For *secret* consideration only. If the Spanish House can find me a powerful ear, I'm to arrange a meeting of certain principals. But it has to be soon before our two countries annihilate our chances on the fields of France.' He paused, 'I hoped Maria could assist.'

Maria gave a nervous laugh. 'I've yet to receive instructions from the House, but I'm sure they'll know how to make contact,' she said breathlessly.

Again the table fell silent. Ronay had gone as far as he dared. The Baron had to take the lead now. The bill came at Ronay's request, but the Baron insisted on taking it and ordered three more brandies. He obviously wanted to stay longer at the table. An encouraging sign. Then it came; the signal that the bait had been taken.

'I think I might be able to help,' he said.

Ronay frowned as though expressing slight doubt. The Baron continued, 'But would you be prepared to name your principals in such a parley and give me a résumé of the Churchill proposals?'

He was a clever man but he was hooked. Ronay waited. He sat, his face grim, weighing non-existent pros and cons for the Baron's clever brain. Then he took a sheet of paper from his pocket and opened it.

'I can let you have this,' he said, 'but, if I may, I'll read it to you first. Then you can consider your next action.'

The Baron eased closer. 'If you believe it warrants your assistance, I'll pass it over to your safe keeping.'

The Baron agreed solemnly. Ronay, his voice grave, began. 'Point one,' he read. 'The British Government will recall his Royal Highness, King Edward VIII, Duke of Windsor, to his rightful throne. The present King will vacate the Crown honourably and willingly. Point two. Germany will recognise King Edward VIII and offer the crown of Hanover to its rightful heir. Three, the new King will call upon the governments of Great Britain and Germany to form a European Parliament. Four, France, Italy and the lowland countries will follow suit. Five, the Führer will be called upon to become President of the European Parliament with Churchill as Prime Minister. Six, a constitution will be agreed and war declared on the Soviet Union.'

Ronay slowly offered the paper over to the Baron. Even Maria sat dumbfounded. The Baron rose to his feet. His ashen features were tight with emotion. 'Even now we may be too late,' he said. 'A great dream for our two peoples may have escaped our grasp but, if I may, I shall take this document home with all speed.'

Ronay stood also. 'I too must ask you for *your* principals in this. You must understand that, Kurt.'

The Baron nodded and took the paper. 'I speak for Rudolf Hess, Deputy Führer of the Third Reich, a dear friend, and one who will embrace such dreams with passion.'

Ronay waited for just a split second before releasing the paper with a nod of agreement. The two men embraced emotionally and then the Baron broke away to address Maria. She was still sitting in a state of wide-eyed amazement. She had had no idea of the nature of the bait.

'Darling, I must return to Germany. I need your strength and your prayers,' the Baron said to her.

She rose from the table and took his arm. Ronay longed for her to stay but knew he could not ask.

'Where are you going from here?' she asked Ronay.

'Back to England to wait,' he replied.

'And how do we advise you of progress?' the Baron said.

Ronay gave him his card with the Fulham address. 'My

cover. Remember there must be nothing official. Not until we're ready.'

The Baron understood and led Maria out of the Grille. Ronay watched them go. He would have cherished a last moment with her, alone, but it was not to be. And somehow the chain of events outweighed his deep feelings for her, his triumph overshadowed his jealousy. He sat at the empty table, his mind on edge, his heart pounding. Contact was made. Now he would return to London and find a chameleon.

Book IV

The Chameleon

Charlie Peake had sat in the Chief Whip's office for most of the morning, his stomach growling with hunger pangs. He pulled his heavy overcoat around him. The hallowed halls of the Houses of Parliament were chilly.

He had been summoned by Lord Beaverbrook that morning. Ronay had arrived back from Madrid the previous night and Peake had de-briefed him before allowing him home to the flat in Fulham. Charlie ran through his checklist once more: the contact with Hess had been made favourably, the points of discussion would now be in Berlin. Ronay expected a positive contact from von Zeiss so it was now urgent for him to allow Ronay to put the rest of the plan into action.

Code name: 'The Final Run'. He tried to concentrate on its merits once more, but he fell asleep. Charlie was no longer a young man.

Elsewhere in the building, Winston Churchill was presiding at his second Cabinet Meeting that morning. During the night, Beaverbrook had told him of Ronay's successful contact with the Baron and the promised contact with Hess. Churchill had said he would give the matter some attention but, with the present day's news from France, all that would seem to have been placed elsewhere on the agenda. The

Cabinet spoke in low grey tones and Beaverbrook was sitting silently on the perimeter of the table.

At one forty-five, the Cabinet rose. The room appeared to float beneath a fog of dense smoke and the eyes of everyone blinked with nerves and lack of sleep. Two male secretaries cleared a pile of paper from Churchill's place. His short arms lay stiffly before him, his podgy fingers entwined as if in prayer. Beaverbrook moved to remind the man of his presence. Churchill fixed him with bright eyes.

'How is it going over there?' Beaverbrook asked quietly.

'I need a general who runs well – in reverse,' the Prime Minister growled. 'The Expeditionary Force is at Pilar, thirty miles from the French coast. Three hundred thousand men are going to hit a beach somewhere in Normandy in less than a week.'

Beaverbrook took the offered map and glanced at the host of dots above towns and villages with names which meant nothing to him. He shook his head helplessly and laid the map back in front of Churchill. He wanted to mention Charlie Peake again but decided against it.

A secretary approached the table. 'Admiral Ramsay, sir.' Churchill waved the secretary to bring him in. The Admiral emerged from the ante room of the Cabinet office, his gold braid and coloured ribbons dazzling. Churchill peered over his glasses as the Admiral sat at the table.

'You've heard the latest position?' he questioned. The Admiral nodded.

'The reaction of my Cabinet colleagues is no antidote to such bad news.' Churchill crashed his podgy fist into the table. Beaverbrook shifted uneasily in his seat. Ramsay sat unmoved by the sudden outburst.

Churchill continued. 'The words "stop" and "delay" and "capitulation", gentlemen, are unpalatable, unspeakable and unacceptable to the British people.'

He rose slowly from the chair. 'We have our army rushing north. Three hundred thousand men. But they run with method because they know they are running home.'

Ramsay made a move as if to speak. Churchill stopped him.

'They hit water in less than a week, Mr Ramsay. What do you suggest?' The Admiral sat stiffly in his chair and spread his arms onto the table. He spoke slowly and deliberately.

'As of this moment, subject to tides and depth advisements, I am preparing what I would like to call "Operation Dynamo".'

'But where do we send them?' Churchill stabbed the question.

'Dunkirk,' Ramsay murmured. 'Dunkirk, to the east of Calais. It's lightly fortified but it has the best chance to mount an embarkation.' Ramsay referred again to the map before him. 'And as it is lightly fortified, the army would have to fight a rearguard action without heavy guns.'

'How about naval guns?' Churchill ventured. Ramsay shook his head.

'I don't have the water to bring in anything much bigger than a destroyer and even then I can't guarantee the range. Not at this moment. The time factor is crucial. That's the basis of the whole plan. How much time *do* we have?'

Churchill peered over his spectacles at Beaverbrook. 'Is your man still around?' he asked. Beaverbrook nodded.

'Bring him in.'

A heavy snore came from the Chief Whip's office. Beaverbrook shook the sleeping Peake and brought the old one back from hibernation. His small eyes blinked only once before he was fully alert and on guard.

'It looks like your plan's on,' Beaverbrook said. Charlie registered only the slightest reaction by grunting and rising slowly from the chair.

'He wants to see you.'

Charlie nodded as he padded alongside the news baron. His mind was busy. If Churchill was waiting, it meant the army was following along the lines of the Alex Villiers theory, which meant they were going for the sea, which meant he would have to allow Ronay to continue with the next move of The Final Run.

As they neared the Cabinet Room, Churchill was standing in the middle of the corridor.

'Charlie Peake,' Churchill boomed. 'I'm told you can give me time.'

The words reverberated from Churchill into the bronze and marble of other statesmen posed stiff and still, their lifeless eyes awaiting the answer. The old one sucked his teeth and approached the war horse.

'Yes sir, I can give you time.'

Ronay didn't stay in the Fulham house longer than to greet Mrs Baylis and to use her bath. Then he was out and by first dark was in the claustrophobic streets of Soho. Because of the hostilities, the infamous area was not as bright and garish as in the past but there were still the shadows of the shop fronts and half-opened doors and soft music – the streets of a thousand promises were still working although somehow subdued. Ronay paused at a small Italian café, the aroma of fresh coffee beans tweaked his nose. He sat at one of the tables on the open pavement and looked across to the building on the other side of the street; he felt that he could almost touch it.

A soft samba came throbbing from one of the upper windows and he could see figures drinking by the open frame. By the time Ronay had finished his third coffee, the person he had been waiting for emerged from a taxi. He was a short man, past sixty, and accompanied by two young boys. Ronay was across the road in two strides. The man saw him and beamed.

'Run along chickens,' he cooed in a high effeminate voice. 'Auntie's here.'

The two boys moved into the building, unsmiling. Ronay tried unsuccessfully to keep a brave face.

'You're glad to see me, aren't you?' Blanche Wells said, pushing at his perfectly coiffured grey hair. Ronay grunted and walked back to the Italian coffee shop. Blanche Wells, his small, plump frame forced into a tight waistcoat and an elegant jacket, bounced after him. He sat opposite Ronay at the table, his darting inquisitive eyes teasing.

'The boys seem younger than ever,' Ronay said.

'Yes, it's a shame isn't it?' Blanche Wells examined his polished nails. 'But we aim to please.'

'I need a chameleon,' Ronay said.

Blanche Wells nodded, the gaiety gone.

'When?' he asked.

'Soon.'

'How soon?'

'Now.'

Blanche Wells rose from the table. 'Excuse me, darling, I've left the gas on,' he smiled and made to walk away.

Ronay pulled him back. Blanche Wells knew that look of Marcus Ronay – there was a time when it excited him, but now he didn't relish the threat.

'There's one we know – you know – I mean you *knew*. He's looking at a bank in the city.'

'When do we meet?'

'Soon. I'll deliver him soon.' Blanche Wells felt the sweat roll down the back of his ears.

Then Ronay was gone. The two boys called from the building opposite. But Blanche had other things to do. He had to find a chameleon.

The branch of Lloyds Bank in Leadenhall Street was preparing for the last hour of business. From two to three every Thursday its ledgers and calculating brains were tried to their limits. With the weekend looming, the settlers, hoarders and depositors descended upon the windows to add to their tallies. The Chameleon stood by the doorway giving the interior of the bank one last check. His small eyes shifted to and fro and in an instant his calculations were made. There was no one here that posed a threat to him – a last glance at his reflection in the window and he was ready. He looked perfect for the part – Josiah Bingley, citizen exemplary. He pushed open the doors and made his entrance.

A huge, fat man, he waddled along the aisle of the bank towards the chief cashier's window. In his sixties with thin hair and long sideburns and angry bushy eyebrows, he was wearing a homburg hat and a three-piece suit with a pattern of checks that positively blazed with life. His trousers, well cut, and spats presented him as a rather prosperous penguin. He used a walking stick as a threat, slamming it into the floor as he walked. He rapped impatiently at the polished wood of the chief cashier's window with his stick. The clerk behind the desk jumped with fright, and then closed the giant ledger in his hands in silent anger. The Chameleon spoke with a heavy northern accent, the words flowing into each other without pause for breath. He had begun the charade.

'Bingley's the name, Josiah Bingley,' he barked. 'I'll see him if he's in, and he is in isn't he?'

'The Manager, sir?'

'You know damn well who lad. I've been coming here this past damn month, same time, same damn day, so stop the bloody dithering and tell him Bingley's here. Mr Josiah Bingley.'

The rest of the staff at the bank gave each other knowing looks as they watched. Mr Jays, the Manager, a tall bespectacled man in striped trousers and a wing collar, came to the door of the far office. His face was a picture of pain and silent suffering. He forced a smile and waved the fat man into his area of the bank. Bingley glared at the clerk by the window.

'Well am I coming in or do I stand here like a monk on a custard powder?' he fumed. The clerk fumbled with the wooden flap of the counter and helped Bingley to push through the small opening. He cleared it with an agonising roar.

Once inside the Manager's office, Bingley took off his homburg and placed it unceremoniously on the desk. He then pulled off his coat, revealing the full splendour of his double breasted waistcoat, from the pocket of which he took a thick gold chain with a thick gold watch with an even thicker golden sovereign hanging from the fob. Without a word, Bingley then removed the waistcoat. Under an ample stomach, a wide brown belt held up the checked trousers aided by the added security of a pair of red braces. Mr Jays sat transfixed while Bingley continued the striptease. The belt, the braces, came away followed by the trousers, followed by the shirt, followed by the string vest and then his longjohns. He stood there stark naked apart from a huge money belt half hidden by his fleshy stomach. Bingley took a deep breath and then painfully bent over to retrieve his waistcoat from the pile of clothes on the floor. He fiddled with one of the pockets and took a small key from one of them. He turned to Mr Jays, who was now aghast.

'Be a good lad and undo the bloody thing. I feel sick,' he moaned. Mr Jays unlocked the belt, allowing the fat man to fall back into the chair with a gasp of relief.

'It's Chinese torture, that's what it is,' he gritted. 'Is it worth it I ask myself? I say, is it bloody worth it?' Mr Jays laid the belt on his desk and sat opposite Bingley, awaiting the worst.

'You'll find a thousand pounds there Mr Jays,' he said looking at the belt. 'I say . . .' It wasn't the effrontery and rudeness of the man that gave Mr Jays a peptic ulcer. It was his annoying habit of repeating every statement as if everyone listening to him were stone deaf.

'Yes, Mr Bingley, one thousand,' Jays interrupted impatiently.

'As per usual.'

'As per usual.'

Bingley bent low again, gingerly removing a tiny diary from his jacket pocket. From the binding he took a small pencil which he wet in his mouth and began to scrawl on the pages.

'That, to my reckoning, is five thousand pounds to the

penny as of this visit,' he said. Mr Jays nodded and began to count the five pound notes out of the money belt. Bingley proceeded to re-dress, talking in his dull monotone as he went.

'Now I've come by a bit of business in this last week Mr Jays and I'll be calling on the services of your good offices to assist. I say. . .'

'Mr Bingley, you have my undivided attention. What can we do?' Jays retorted, finishing the count and pushing the empty belt towards Bingley.

'I've had the occasion to come to an arrangement with a business man from Germany of the Jewish persuasion you understand, a refugee. It's terrible the goings-on over there you know. Any road, he's in industrial diamonds and wishes to dispose of them. I hope you're getting all this because I'll not be going over it all again. . .' Jays nodded patiently. Bingley went on.

'Industrial diamonds as I say. We have agreed a sum of five thousand pounds for these goods and you will oblige me by having that sum prepared in cash tomorrow, Friday. I say, we have agreed. . .' Mr Jays gave a resigned sigh. 'Now comes the most important part, Mr Jays, now this chap (called Bloom by the by), this chap is a mite cautious. I can't say as I blame the poor bugger.' Jays coughed loudly. 'Any road, at this moment in time he doesn't want to tell me where we're to meet to exchange diamonds and money. I know it's this Friday and I know it's at three o'clock sharp. . .'

'I can see no problems this end, Mr Bingley,' Mr Jays ventured, hoping for an end to the lecture.

'I've not done yet,' Bingley said. 'This man Bloom, to my mind, is a valuable business associate and I don't want him upset by anything that might give him the impression that I'm not a man of substance and standing. . .'

Mr Jays muttered something to put Bingley back on course. 'So listen here, he's to pick me up this bloody Friday afternoon to take me to the exact location of our exchange.

I've said here, in the City, because I'm not traipsing about over all bloody London. But *where* in the City I don't know till he picks me up. But it's not that big a place is it? Now, here's my instructions. Once I know *where* in the City, I go to the nearest branch of this bank because to my reckoning you have five branches in this here area. I say you have five. . .'

'Five!' Mr Jays forgot his trained composure and yelled the number at Bingley, who appeared to miss the outburst completely.

'And there you'll have arranged for me to cash a cheque for five thousand pounds.'

Mr Jays ached to bury his head in his hands to block out the torture and Bingley started to hop angrily around his chair. The huge man had talked himself into a masochistic panic. 'I don't want me standing there in that bank with a prospective client waiting for some dozy pen pusher to check and doublecheck some bloody memo or other and I don't want signatures and counter-signatures and I don't want to look like I've come cap in hand looking for loans because I'm a business man of some standing so I walk in and I sign my cheque and the cash comes over damn quick. If he's got the stones I've got the brass and I'll have no why's or wherefore's!' The outburst over, Bingley reached for the back of his chair exhausted.

Mr Jays relaxed his grip on the side of his desk and allowed the blood to return to his brain. He poured himself and Bingley a glass of water.

'My dear Mr Bingley, there really is no problem,' he sang. 'I shall give the direction to expect you at any of our branches here in the City tomorrow. Your cheque will be honoured immediately. No delay. No questions.' Mr Jays wrote out the directions to the sister banks and made a mental note to arrange for a brother manager to take over the Bingley account.

The Chameleon watched his *mark* react to his performance. He enjoyed playing this Bingley – it would be a shame to lose the character after tomorrow. He forced himself back into the performance.

'I expect to complete between three and three-fifteen, Mr Jays.'

The next day was humid and threatening rain, and soon after two that afternoon it came. A sudden flash of light, followed by a crash of thunder and then by sheets of rain. The streets were approaching the rush hour and with this extra bonus the rush was truly on. People scuttled under canopies and into doorways to escape the wet. From the confusion came the Chameleon.

Mr Josiah Bingley, business man and scourge of bankers, paused only to straighten his homburg in the window of the St Paul's branch of Lloyds Bank before entering. His stick rapped a passage through the soaking customers. No one argued as he beat his way to the front of the longest line. The clerk serving concentrated on the next customer. He saw Bingley but attempted to ignore the red, fuming face glaring over the counter at him.

'Bingley. Mister Josiah Bingley.'

The name pumped across the desk made no impression on the clerk. But the stick pushing the giant inkwell into his lap brought him leaping out of his high chair.

'Don't dally with me! Cash this and quick about it!'

The Bingley cheque floated onto the polished counter. The surprised clerk hissed at the chief cashier, who left his window.

'I've never been so insulted in my life,' Bingley bashed the table with the stick again. The customers at the back of the line pushed forward for a closer look at the disturbance. The chief cashier gave both the crowd and the cheque a fast look before remembering the dreaded name of Bingley. He dived into the money drawer and counted out five thousand pounds. Bingley watched every note flip by and repeated each count with his own.

Eventually half the line of customers was counting too.

Then finally the last elastic band snapped over the last thousand and the Chameleon was on his way out of the bank and into the rain. He braved the elements for a hundred yards before turning off the main thoroughfare and into a side street. He signalled the waiting taxi and bundled himself into it.

The taxi ploughed through the deepening puddles and eventually edged itself into the packed confines of Cambridge Circus. The Chameleon alighted outside the Palace Theatre and paid off the driver. From the canopy of the Theatre he looked across at the roundabout in the middle of the Circus. There, standing like an oasis, was the Gentlemen's lavatory, its regulation green iron railings glistening in the downpour. A sign hung over the gates.

'Closed,' it read.

Bingley stood there until, at last, he saw another taxi stop at the junction of Charing Cross Road and the Circus. From it came another check-suited person of huge proportions sporting a homburg, and spats and cane. He, too, looked across at the Gentlemen's WC before waddling between the traffic towards it. The Chameleon gave a sigh and watched his double ignore the sign over the gates and disappear down the steps. Ten more minutes he stood there until three more Bingleys had alighted from three more taxis, all of them disappearing into the depths of the convenience. He then made his move over the road and down the stairs.

With the rain bucketing down the stairwell, he hastened to get to the bottom. His spats filled with water from the sodden steps as his heavy frame thumped home on the iron stairs. Below, Blanche Wells crept from the inner sanctuary of the convenience. He had heard the sound of the footsteps and prayed it would be the Chameleon. If it weren't, he would simply die, but even that threat did not stop him from teasing his coiffured hair in the mirror. He crossed his fingers and stepped out into the rain. He gave a high-pitched shriek when he saw the Chameleon.

'Filch!' he screamed with delight.

The Chameleon paused and looked back at the sheltering pedestrians. The rain stung his eyes but apparently no one had heard his name being called. He didn't like it – not in costume.

'George Filch, you clever cow you.' Again the shriek from below. The Chameleon hurled his frame the last few feet and pushed past Blanche into the comparative safety of the lavatory. Inside four men were facing the long mirror above the wash basins; some washing, others removing wigs and make-up. Along the wide expanse of ablutions, the checked suits, together with the rest of the Bingley trappings, hung from the communal clothes hooks. Blanche Wells came mincing in with a swagger, his tight white working jacket soaked through and his neat hair-do falling limply over his ears.

'Isn't it wondrous, dear heart,' he cried. The others acknowledged George Filch, the Chameleon's, arrival with applause, except for the youngest man at the far sink who calmly removed a wad of tight padding from the inside of his cheeks and pulled the false wax nose from the bridge of his own. He watched Blanche fussing around Filch and gritted his teeth angrily. Eventually Filch joined the younger man at the sink. He began to pull at his own false eyebrows and then the balding wig came free, revealing a shock of black hair greying at the temples. A few vigorous rubs with cream and astringent and Bingley had vanished. George Filch dabbed his sore face and beamed.

'Any problems?' he asked, his soft educated accent far removed from the brash northern of Josiah Bingley.

The others shook their heads. Blanche Wells turned his attention to the pile of money on the centre table, thrust his hand into it and threw it into the air.

'I'll never be hungry again,' he said, looking melodramatically to the heavens.

Filch looked at the clock on the white tiled wall. It read three-forty.

'How long for safety, Blanche?' he asked.

'Yonks, ducky,' Blanche mused. 'I told you this is the quietest cottage in the city. Till five, then it's watch your cocks!' The young man sneered as Blanche rattled on with his high voice and exaggerated mannerisms. He was in his early thirties and, after pulling the mass of adhesive tape away from his flattened hair, a host of blond curls fell free. Blanche clicked his teeth.

'I see Mary Pickford rides again,' he teased.

'He did bloody well,' Filch said goodnaturedly. 'You all did bloody well. You've left all the costumes and props?' They all nodded.

'You can leave this one behind for me,' Blanche said, nodding at the young man, who snarled, 'Take the piss out of me once more, you old queen, and I'll kick your arse in.'

'Paulie Telfer, wash your mouth out,' Blanche scolded. Filch stepped between them before Paul could carry out his threat.

'Blanche behave,' Filch said firmly. The little man gave a curtsey and bobbed out of the room, up into the street. Three of the bogus Bingleys came out of the darkness and dispersed in different directions. Filch and Paul Telfer came next. The young man pushed past Blanche and walked across the road alone.

'Very deep that one, darling, deep as the bleeding ocean,' Blanche said, watching as Paul dodged the traffic.

'I've left the coats and hats for you Blanche,' Filch said. 'Keep what you get for them and I've left a couple of hundred on the table. Buy yourself a twin-set and tweeds.'

'Tweeds! There's nothing dikey about me, darling,' the little man warbled. 'There's a bloody war on and I'm getting more sailors down here than the Ark Royal, so I'm investing in a few gallons of rum, dearie. There'll be fifteen men on this dead man's chest if it kills me and it will, please God!'

Filch smiled and gave Blanche a little kiss on the cheek. 'Now she tells me,' Blanche cooed. 'See you in court.'

Filch didn't hear the last words. He was moving quickly across the road to catch up with Telfer. Blanche stepped aside to allow a young guardsman into the lavatory, looking to the heavens and following him down the stairs into Shangri-la.

It took Filch some time to draw level with Telfer. The young man ignored him and pushed on through the rain. It was obvious to Filch that his lover was upset. After their five years together, he knew that the slightest thing could bring about this state. He fell into his usual role when such moods prevailed, staying within vision and saying nothing, showing Telfer that he would always be there, ever present, ever available, safe, strong, loving.

'When you mix with old queens like Blanche Wells you drag yourself down to their level,' Telfer said eventually. The anger was still in his eyes but the voice had softened.

'And how *down* is the level of an old queen?' Filch said after a pause.

'You tell me,' Telfer said. That statement hurt but it was all part of the pattern.

'How about dinner at the Ivy and a revue to celebrate?' Filch said, changing the subject, but the shiver in his voice betrayed him and gave his lover the opportunity to strike again.

'Dinner! That's all I need. An evening with you crowing about how wonderful you were. No thank you very much!' Filch stopped, the rain pelting his tight, sad face.

'If I didn't know better, I'd swear you were jealous Paulie,' he half murmured. Telfer stopped angrily and grabbed him by the collar.

'Now understand this. For five years I've had to endure your roof and your abominable body,' he gritted. 'I've had to suffer your friends, your pathetic nothing friends from the age of Oscar Wilde and the Brighton Dome. They're sickening. They keep you old. All their twee and bitchy asides. Don't you see that?'

'They're my friends, Paulie. You take away my friends, you take away my life.'

'What about me then?'

'I love you, Paulie, and that's more important. You know that.'

'You know I don't want to be seen with that crowd. I don't want my friends to think I've anything in common with them!'

'You don't want your friends to think you've anything in common with me is what you mean. Perhaps you're afraid you're getting old too.'

The hard slap of Telfer's hand against his face made Filch's ear ring and he felt a warm trickle which might be blood creeping from the side of his mouth. He was deeply hurt.

'I'm old. I was old when you were a chicken,' he cried. 'I've always been old to you, but we have love and that's wonderful.'

'*You* have a love that's wonderful. I have a habit,' Telfer snapped. The statement came out clear, concise and as cool as he intended. He waited for the full effect to take its toll and then moved across the road, leaving Filch to the driving rain and the bitter sadness.

The imposing building of 14 Wilhelmstrasse sat squat, safe and secure, the strength of German architecture ramming home its message. Here were the unbending foundations, the harsh lines of the neo-Gothic style coupled with the glory that was Rome. The façade was of heavy concrete. The windows were wide and expansive, the entrance high and intimidating all but the stoutest hearts who walked below the giant eagle. The swastika above dominated everything. Below, at each side of the entrance doors, stood two unmoving guards. The black uniforms of the SS were stark against the white of the walls. Their caps, with the death's head motif of the SS spitting out its warning from above the peaks, hid their eyes from the world.

The Mercedes limousine stopped outside and a grey uniformed chauffeur escorted Baron Kurt von Zeiss to the entrance. The guards made no move.

The Baron reached into his pocket and pulled free his permit, flashing it in the air as he passed between the sentries. Once past the portals, the building opened out into a vast marble hall, reaching up to a giant ceiling, glistening with expensive stone which echoed every sound. To the right of the hall there was a long line of individual desks. A clerk sat at each, with a telephone, an intercom and an SS guard. On the left, long wooden forms were crammed with people, civil and military, who sat quietly, waiting to be summoned to the desks. At regular ten-yard intervals, huge oak doors stood closed and menacing. 14 Wilhelmstrasse was the centre of the party machine.

For the Baron, the walk through the hall chilled his soul. He ached for his warm Spain. Double doors dominated the annexe at the end, and here the Baron halted. He was expected. One of the guards knocked at the door and pushed it gently open to reveal a heavily panelled room. At the furthest end, a small man sat huddled over a large desk. Behind him, the flags of the Nazi party and Germany hung from gilded staves and a portrait of Adolf Hitler glared down from the wall. The only sound in the room came from the scratching of the pen of Rudolf Hess, the Deputy Reich Führer. With perfect timing, he glanced up from his paperwork and smiled as von Zeiss reached the desk. His eyes were black and sharp and hooded, his brows heavy and black as his hair. His jowls seemed unshaven.

'Can you verify this, Kurt?' he tapped the paper in his hand.

'I can.' The Baron's voice was slightly tentative. Hess pushed a button on his intercom.

'Come!'

A weedy clerk slid silently into the office.

'I want a private meeting with the Führer today.' Hess did not look at the man. 'Top priority. Go personally. No memo, no telephone. Go!'

Hess walked over to the Baron and his eyes were moist. 'My dear Kurt. We have a chance here to join our great nation with others of equal stature.' He pulled the Baron into an embrace.

'Germany and Great Britain leading Europe against the Soviet Union. With communism defeated we have an alliance that dwarfs even the Americans. Think on that. A united Europe with communism crushed. What a dream.'

'The structure of this united Europe,' the Baron mused. 'That's the difficulty.'

Hess threw his arms wide, and strutted theatrically around the room. 'At this very moment the British and French are running to the Channel. They are defeated.'

He stopped beneath Hitler's portrait, gazing at it in fanatical adoration. 'Our Führer will decide the structure. But this outline tells us the shape of the alliance. Its form is quite excellent. With the faith and vision of our Führer this opportunity will not be ignored, I promise you.'

As the intercom buzzed loudly, Hess took the receiver and clicked to attention.

'Yes, *mein Führer*, I understand.' The eyes of the Deputy Reich Führer were wide with enormous dreams.

Swinging the Gate, the revue at the Ambassador's Theatre, ended at nine-twenty sharp. The Friday evening audience, delighted with the antics of Hermione Gingold, the West End's new favourite, spilled out onto the pavements. The evening was warm and humid.

George Filch and Blanche Wells paused by the telephone booth at the corner of Newport Street and St Martin's Lane and waited for it to become free.

'Is it really worth ruining the perfect evening?' Blanche said. He was sure Filch had put the day's tiff out of his mind. The revue had been a joy and the promise of dinner imminent. Filch ignored him and peered again at his watch in the half-light.

Two soldiers finished their call and bundled out of the booth. Blanche struck a promiscuous pose. 'Want a naughty girl?' he vamped. The two soldiers gave a unanimous wolf whistle and marched off to another promised land, ignoring the offer of the little man.

Filch glared disapprovingly at him and entered the booth. He dialled Telfer's number five times before giving up. Blanche took his arm and led him towards the Ivy.

The theatre restaurant was softly lit, a small trio played in the foyer, waiters resplendent in white tie and tails swept along at all angles. The 'in' establishment was crowded as usual at that time of night. Blanche Wells straightened his velvet jacket and ruffled his shirt closely around his coloured scarf. The head waiter ignored him and bowed to Filch.

'Mr George,' he beamed. 'I've got an excellent table, sir.'

Filch followed, with Blanche dancing at the rear, and accepted the leather bound menus. Blanche glanced over at his sad friend and dropped his menu in despair.

'You resemble a beached whale, my dear,' he said. 'Paul's all too much for you these days, isn't he? I don't know why you put yourself through it. He's not worth wetting your knickers over. Deep as the ocean, I've always said, deep as the ocean.'

Filch shook his head. 'Shut up Blanche, do,' he begged.

'When you're on heat, there's no getting through,' Blanche said picking up his menu again.

Filch suddenly burst out angrily. 'It's always the same bloody performance with him. First the need for more bloody money. Then when the appetite's satisfied, the chick spits from the nest. It's sickening.'

Blanche took his friend's hand and searched his face. 'Look, take some of the spoils, buy yourself that little boarding place in the Lake District and stop torturing yourself. Find yourself a nice bit of yokel trade and settle your feathers. I would, given half the chance.'

'There's one thing to be said for the relationship between Paulie and me – he never could improvise,' Filch said sadly. 'Always the same. First he gets me a little upset, then he flies out in tears, then I wait. A week. Ten days. Back comes

Dorian Gray and the painting in the attic gains another scar.'

'So what's divine about that?' Blanche said.

'He comes back.'

'Great. I didn't think of that,' Blanche said sarcastically. 'Look, come to the Embankment with me tonight. A little cruise will bring the sparkle back.'

'You're lovely, Blanche,' Filch smiled. 'But you know me. Lumpy but loyal.'

Blanche stood up and sighed deeply. 'Well you can tell the rent boy that he missed a lovely show and that he's ruined my evening.'

Filch rose from the table but Blanche pushed him back into his chair.

'Courage Camille, courage,' he said and, wishing his friend *bon appetit*, he made for the exit. As he edged past the crowded tables he paused by the entrance foyer and looked at Marcus Ronay sitting by the hat check desk. He gave a nod towards the interior of the restaurant. Ronay shook Charlie Peake, who was fast asleep at his elbow.

Charlie Peake wiped his mouth and with a huge effort removed himself from the deep sponge sofa. The two men negotiated the busy salon and made for the lone figure at the far end of the restaurant. Filch saw Ronay before Charlie Peake came into his view. 'Christ!' he exclaimed. 'What's this, Marcus? Coincidence or con?'

Ronay shrugged. 'You've met my friend I believe?' Charlie Peake hovered closer.

Filch sat back in his chair and eyed the two men carefully.

'I thought the old chap was dead,' Filch said. 'And you were dumped years ago.'

Ronay grinned. 'I thought the same about you till Lloyds had a run on their branches recently.'

Filch looked at him with the innocence of a babe.

Ronay switched on the lights of the dingy apartment and led Filch and Charlie Peake through the small corridor into the untidy room. Filch made for the solitary window and tugged it open. He looked around the room. 'It's in the same state it was the last time I was dragged in.'

'Suits me. It's like a comfortable shoe,' Ronay grunted.

Filch started to pick up odd bits of clothes lying over the floor. 'It's more like an old trench boot,' he said, undoing his bow tie.

Charlie Peake sank into the warm armchair and watched him remove his dinner jacket.

'Now don't get any amorous ideas, Charlie. Just tell me what you're up to while I fuss about a bit,' Filch smiled. With that he took a large chipped enamel basin, filled it with water and then with a pile of dirty cups and plates from the sideboard.

'We would like your special talents for a little job we've got on the boil,' Ronay said slowly. 'It's quite a risky business but there's no one I know who could pull it off better than you.'

Filch gave a dry humourless laugh. 'Compliments, too. It's my night, isn't it?' he said, patting Charlie Peake on his parchment cheeks.

Charlie sucked his teeth. 'Show him the brief and let's get it over with,' he snarled angrily. He wasn't comfortable with Filch and he never had been.

Filch continued with the washing up. He betrayed no interest as Ronay pinned a sheet onto one of the walls of the flat, but just a little curiosity when a film projector was assembled and the celluloid clicked into the jaws of the machine. Ronay started the projector.

The images thrown onto the makeshift screen were grainy and in soft focus, but clear enough for Filch to distinguish that the subject was Winston Churchill. Then a flash of numbers, cutting to another set of candid shots. This time the central figure was the Duke of Windsor.

The projector finally ran out of film.

'Don't tell me you're pinching the crown jewels,' Filch said. 'We can get hung for that.'

Charlie Peake stirred in the sofa. 'Can you handle it?' he said with his tired gravel tone. 'Winston Churchill and the Duke of Windsor?'

Filch giggled. 'How about Blanche Wells for the Duchess?'

Charlie Peake rolled out of his lair and fell onto Filch. 'We want a Churchill and a Duke so stop fucking around, you degenerate, and make a noise like a volunteer,' he snarled violently.

Filch pulled himself away from the gnarled fingers. 'I'd have to know the job you've got in mind,' he said uneasily.

'It's abroad,' Ronay said, not looking at him, as he unpinned the sheet.

'Oh lovely. Miami? West Indies?'

'Germany.'

'You can forget it,' Filch said, flouncing angrily about the room. 'He's got to think I'm demented, you know that? Bleedin' Germany. There's a war on. I've done some tricks in my time but trolling with that bunch of queens takes the bloody biscuit. I'm good! But I'm not about to find out if I'm *that* good. Getting up at dawn for the Nurse Cavell bit is definitely not me.'

'It's important,' Ronay said.

'It's *always* important,' Filch steamed.

Ronay pushed him into a chair. 'We've done good and bad tricks in the past, George. I guarantee this one is the cream. We couldn't play for higher stakes. I'm going into Germany with a Churchill and a Duke of Windsor, and we're coming out with a good chance of Britain winning the War.'

Filch's eyes widened. 'That big, eh?' he mused.

'The biggest ever,' Ronay said.

'Terms?'

Ronay shrugged. 'No proceedings *vis à vis* the last job and perhaps a little bonus on completion.'

'A damehood?'

'None of this is official,' Charlie Peake interrupted tersely. 'We're off the cuff.'

'Oh, so we're going into the eagle's lair with no official nod, no bonus, and no bloody brains. That's wondrous.'

'The big is only for the best, George,' Ronay said.

Filch thought for a moment and then walked over to the telephone. He listened to the unanswered ring for a full minute. His vision of Paul Telfer at the other end sent a cold shiver down his spine. He replaced the receiver and started to put on his evening jacket.

'With this figure and the right drag,' he said, 'I'm a dead ringer for Winnie, so I'll do it. And as for your Duke, well there's a man . . . I don't think you've met him but he deserves a little treat. Something to get the stars out of his eyes. I'll be back in the morning, Marcus,' he said. 'Remember me to Charlie.'

Ronay turned to see Charlie Peake fast asleep on the sofa. The door to the flat clicked shut and Filch was gone.

Grease Mews was one of those pleasant retreats from the noisy shopping precincts of Knightsbridge – not yet the more expensive side of the park but bordering on the affluence of the Royal Borough of Kensington and just becoming a noble address before the outbreak of war.

The mews was a one-sided affair. On one side the small Georgian houses sat atop their foundation of large stables, and facing them on the other side were stark brick walls. The street was cobbled and still lit before the blackout by gas from Victorian lamps.

George Filch walked to the third of eight mews houses and looked up above the polished yellow front door to the small windows. The curtains were drawn tightly but the tiniest chink of light was visible in one corner. It would have escaped an air-raid warden's eye but not Filch's. He fumbled nervously in his pockets for his keys, before he unlocked the door. He glanced once more at the chink of light and bit his lip. It was the sign, the rotten sign, their sign, his and Paul's.

The agreement had been struck at the Salisbury in St Martin's Lane five short years before. George and Paul, the fiery young actor, had been playing the Feydeau farce for over a hundred performances. It was Paul's first break in the West End and during the second week of rehearsals Filch had befriended him. The frightened look behind the young man's eyes brought out a protective instinct in him. During the out of town try-outs the friendship had grown. Their affair began in Manchester.

It was the last night before returning to London for the big opening. The play had been received enthusiastically in the provinces and the new young actor was added to the lists of 'future stardom'. That night in the Midland Hotel, Paul knocked at Filch's door and apologised for the late hour. The boy was a bundle of nerves, his eyes burned with tiredness and fatigue, his speech faltered, his hands shook. Filch poured a brandy and bathed him with kindness and good counsel. Even now, after so long, Filch couldn't remember whether it was he or Paul who drew the first kiss.

In the good moments, the times when they were together and ecstatic, Filch would know that it was Paul who gently took his face that night and kissed it without a word. But when the hurt came, when love foundered, in those moments it would be he who took the first chance in that place, that wonderful warm place. Would he and Paul ever experience such a night together again?

Filch gazed at the curtains above the yellow door, begging them to open, but they remained closed. He was about to use the telephone box at the far end of the mews when the door opened. He threw himself into the shadow of the wall just before Paul Telfer came out with another man. They talked for a while in soft low tones before shaking hands warmly. The man waved from the other end of the mews and disappeared into the night. Telfer re-entered the house and closed the yellow door behind him. Filch fought to control himself, a thousand permutations running through his mind. He could chase after the stranger and threaten, warn, or perhaps even beg him to stay away.

He decided, as usual, to allow Paul time to straighten out the rooms. There would be no embarrassment then for either of them. Finally the chink of light went out and the curtains opened. Filch came from the shadows and quietly entered. A small staircase barely wide enough to accommodate his frame led from the door to the landing above. To the left of the landing were the bathroom and bedroom, to the right the lounge and kitchen. Filch crept over the carpeted floor and into the kitchen. He put on the kettle.

The bedroom was in darkness but Filch knew Paul would be watching. He took the tea tray to his own side of the bed and gently laid it on the wine cooler that served as a side-table. He poured his tea and sat on the bed. The hot liquid burned into his throat. He felt a little calmer now; he felt Paul stir.

'You've got perfect timing, George.'

The statement came with a taste of bitterness.

'Would you like a cup?' George asked.

Paul stirred again. 'I didn't mean the damn tea and you know it,' he rasped.

Filch began to undress.

'I don't know how you do it,' Paul taunted. 'How you calmly get into this bed without commenting on the buzz beneath the sheets, the warmth, the reek of pleasure that is beyond your comprehension.'

Filch lay back on the pillow and mentally rehearsed his opening line. Paul pulled on the covers and settled himself for a sleep that Filch knew he would not be enjoying for many long hours yet.

'I met two men this evening,' he began.

'Good for you,' Paul rapped.

'It appears our little action today in the City has been rumbled.'

He felt Paul's body jump in the dark. The lights flashed

on, as the events of the day were discussed between the couple living in the third mews house on the left above the yellow door.

The next morning started for Ronay with Mrs Baylis thumping on his flat door.

'Yes?' he called through a haze of half-sleep.

'Two gentlemen downstairs. They say as you're expecting.'

Ronay glanced at his watch. 'It's six o'clock in the morning, Mrs B.'

He heard no answer. The landlady hadn't waited for his response. He hurriedly threw on his overcoat and made his way down to the front door. George Filch stood there with Paul Telfer, both in a dishevelled state and both in need of a shave.

'May I present Mr Marcus Ronay,' Filch said to Telfer. 'Mr Ronay, this is Edward, Duke of Windsor.'

From Mrs Baylis's rooms there came a crash of crockery. She must have been eavesdropping. Ronay shook Paul Telfer's hand and led the two men up the stairs.

'You know the time, I suppose,' Ronay said gruffly.

'Listen, dear heart, we've been up all night worrying over this little charade of yours so why should *you* miss all the fun.' Filch puffed the words as he dragged behind.

'George tells me you have knowledge of our little trip yesterday,' Telfer said as the three of them took what seating was available in the small space.

Ronay nodded curtly, 'You hit five banks all at approximately three o'clock yesterday afternoon and got £25,000.'

Telfer slapped his hands on his knees in frustration. 'To have that information as quickly as you did, means you have had knowledge about it *before* we did it.'

'I did,' Ronay said simply.

Telfer looked at Filch, who shrugged his shoulders.

'Who the hell are you, anyway?' Telfer asked sharply. 'Just who the hell are you?'

Filch motioned Telfer to relax. 'I told you. I've known him for a long time. Take it easy and listen.'

Telfer snorted and then sat stiffly in the chair with his arms folded.

Ronay began. 'Ten days ago,' he said, 'the German army invaded Belgium, Holland and France, taking the British army and our allies completely by surprise. They are now retreating and heading towards the French coast. In a matter of days, that force of over three hundred thousand men will hit the beaches at a place called Dunkirk.

'We have a plan,' Ronay said. 'Churchill has made it known to the Third Reich that it would be more prudent for us to fight the Russians than each other. To strengthen the bond between us, he has suggested that His Royal Highness, the Duke of Windsor, might be invited to reign as King of Germany and Great Britain. A European Parliament would be formed and, as one giant force, Britain, Germany, Italy, France, Holland, Belgium and the rest of the low-land countries would declare war on Russia.'

'And the men at Dunkirk?' Filch asked.

'If the Germans agree to a dialogue, it follows that we'll have a cessation of hostilities. That's where we come in. We have to go through the motions while the boats make ready.'

'Boats?' Filch asked.

'Yes, we're going to get the boys home in boats,' Ronay said. The answer came simply as though a matter of fact.

Telfer tried to say something but choked on the words. His face was a picture of disbelief. Finally he rushed out of the room. They heard the front door downstairs slam, and then the room and the house were quiet again. Filch and Ronay sat looking at each other.

'He'll be fine, Marcus,' Filch said. 'He's a bit concerned, naturally. He hasn't played any of the big parts yet, but he shows great promise. I've got a collection of reviews to confirm it.'

Ronay grinned. He knew Telfer was coming back. His

only worry was whether the man had the guts to go the whole way.

Filch walked over to the picture of Cheney and picked it up from the mantelpiece. 'I met her once. Remember? You'd just come back from a long time in Spain. You came to see me at the Lane. She was so sweet and so good for you.'

Ronay took the picture from Filch and placed it back on the mantelpiece – Cheney's eyes smiled at him. As if she knew about Maria, as if she always knew. And understood.

The backs of Donna Maria Domenquin's hands sang with a bouquet of aromas. They had been sprayed from the array of scent bottles assembled on the long glass counter of Las Brisas. The famous perfumery housed the top labels, and the luxurious atmosphere was a heavenly alternative to the hot, busy streets of Madrid. The last few days had been spent sitting by the telephone in her suite waiting for news, wondering whether the Germans had taken the bait and, if they had, whether or not Ronay had been contacted.

Maria eventually chose a small, unknown brand of toilet water, the suggestion of lemon in its base was cool. The sales girl made a mental note to put the rest of the shipment to one side. If Donna Maria Domenquin had given it her blessing, then there would be others wishing to walk the same cloud.

Maria checked herself in the long mirror in the shop before venturing back into the streets and tipped her cream beret more to the right side of her head. Her hair was pulled into its neat coil, her cream suit featured her favourite high shoulders, the *crêpe-de-chine* blouse broke away from her long neck, its cream colour blending with her marble skin and dark eyes. She tipped each of her snake skin shoes onto its toes, satisfying herself on the seams of her fully fashioned stockings. The picture was attractive; she was satisfied, and walked out into the street.

As she walked, her head became light and she felt no weight in her legs. Her shoes appeared to float above the pavement and she had the impression she could walk miles without taking breath. This was a new feeling. It was an elation, a euphoric weightlessness. Then all at once she seemed to slow. The glorious brightness in her seemed to be burning out at an alarming speed. Her head began to swim as she fought for breath. Sharp flashes of colour blinded her eyes – reds, greens, blues – then white, only white. Bright, flat light. Her heart began to pound. She knew her knees were losing their strength and she fought against falling but couldn't stop herself.

The hard pavement met her thighs as she collapsed. She heard voices and saw silhouettes and then the white became black. A silence followed and she lay within a vacuum, a nothingness. She couldn't move, she couldn't talk. Then she felt her body being turned and examined in her darkness. She couldn't determine what the voices were saying. There was just a steady beat of sounds throbbing from the region of her head. Her eyes flickered open, the light came painfully. Heads peered down into her face. One face came into focus. One face she knew.

'The ambulance won't be long,' Harvey Teckner said, gently stroking her forehead.

She forced herself to make words. 'No ambulance!' she gasped. 'No ambu . . .' She fell back onto his hands, her strength gone.

'No ambulance?' Harvey asked, mystified. Donna Maria pleaded with him, her eyes filled with sheer panic, and he understood. He asked for a taxi and when it came, he put her into it. They drove away, passing the screaming ambulance as it sped towards them.

Donna Maria relaxed, safe for the moment. Then an enormous pain jolted into her side. She felt herself gasp and then came that same whiteness. She knew the black would follow soon, but the pain came again and then again. Harvey's arms held her to him and, with that to comfort her, she surrendered to the blackness.

Her vacuum had no memories in it. However long she lay within its grasp she had no idea but, when she finally came to her senses, the pain had subsided and she felt warm and comfortable. She was tucked up to her chin in soft sheets and heavy blankets in a huge brass bed. Not ten feet from her, an enormous fire crackled. The flames gave forth the only light, a rosy flickering.

It was night and she could see the moon through the leaded windows. She sensed a movement on the other side of the room where Harvey Teckner was lying on a sofa, his long legs uncomfortably dangling from one end, his neck twisted to an impossible angle at the other.

'Harvey!' she called hoarsely.

His legs swung at all angles, but he finally scrambled to his feet.

'Oh thank God!' he cried. 'Thank the good Lord!'

He made to go to her, but then rushed over to a small stove and lit the gas under a saucepan.

'It's soup,' he called. 'You've been unconscious since yesterday afternoon. The guy in the drugstore said you were to eat, on account of your being out so long. So I figured soup. Y'know, good, old-fashioned, beat-it-all, soup. Huckleberry hell! I'm so glad you didn't die.'

She smiled, the mere sound of his excitement was like a tonic. He left the stove and leaned over her.

'Do you feel like soup?' he asked hopefully. She nodded. He gently eased her up to the extra pillows and laid a cloth neatly beneath her chin. He stepped back and admired the picture.

'You look like a little girl, so vulnerable,' he said in some wonderment. 'I know you're not, but what I mean is, you look so. . .' The saucepan began to sizzle.

'Hell!' he exclaimed and dived towards it.

He fed her slowly and she managed to drink most of the liquid. He sat on the bed holding her hand.

'What do you think of the place?' he said, looking round the friendly, untidy attic room. 'It's not the Palace but the bit about the ambulance kind of scared me, your being sick and all. So I brought you home. OK, by you?'

She blew him a kiss with her full lips.

'Most gallant,' she smiled.

He looked at his watch and whistled.

'Wow! It's nearly morning. You get some more sleep. And don't worry, I'll be close by.'

She lay watching the shadows of the fire dance on the ceiling above her head. 'Do you believe in chance?' she murmured.

'Sometimes. Why?'

'I was thinking how lucky I was that you were there in the street.'

He didn't answer. She could hear him shift about uncomfortably.

'Don't you think it was lucky?' she asked.

'No, I don't think so,' he mumbled.

'I didn't hear that,' she said curiously.

'I said I didn't think it was lucky. My being there I mean.' His reply was clipped and tentative. She lay there silently, trying to figure out the young American's answer. Again he moved from the sofa and came over to her, his face red.

'Hell Maria, I followed you from the hotel. I waited for you outside the shop and I saw you collapse.'

She opened her lips, about to speak, but he stopped her by sitting on the bed and taking her in his arms.

'Forgive me, darling Maria, but I've been outside that hotel at all hours. Every day. I can't forget you. Not for a moment. I know it was wrong and crazy, but you don't know how it is to feel like I do.'

She hushed him and kissed his cheek.

'I'm just so glad to be here,' she whispered.

He looked down into her hungry eyes and kissed her, and she kissed him back. He risked putting the tip of his tongue into her mouth only to receive hers, long and hot. The texture, sensuous and wet, stabbed his throat. She eased him away gently, but firmly.

'I do love you, Maria,' he said, as he went back to the sofa. She closed her eyes. Her thoughts were of Marcus.

The flat in Fulham was in a state of chaos. A sheet still hung from one wall, the other held a collection of photographs pinned by their corners already curling from the constant steam of a thousand cups of tea. In the middle of the room, the one table housed the warm projector and a wide mirror. The light bulb hanging from the middle of the ceiling hovered at the end of an extension flex which brought it down level with the mirror. Its naked bulb poised like a sword of Damocles. Paul Telfer sat at the table making notes. George Filch was bent over a large suitcase. Telfer left the table and checked his notes against what Filch had placed in the suitcase.

'My wardrobe *still* isn't complete,' Telfer snapped.

'We're not going for a month,' Ronay said patiently.

'I've got to be covered for every eventuality you know. I'm playing a bloody king and I've got to look it at all times, thank you very much.'

Filch interrupted, 'Wigs! I've got make-up, padding, props, but the wigs are a real teaser.'

'Christ! I thought we *had* the bloody things,' Telfer shouted. 'I tried mine on yesterday.'

'I didn't like the lace frontings,' Filch said. 'They were OK for stage and film, but a close look at them could show the lace. That's the bit we glue to our forehead and temples, Marcus my dear. So I've asked for as little lace as possible. I sent them back for re-doing. Don't worry, they'll look wonderful.'

'And we pray someone doesn't sneeze within a fifty mile radius when we've got them on,' Telfer said sarcastically.

Filch pinched his cheek playfully. 'Look dear heart, when I'm working I like to concentrate on what I'm doing and not on what another chap is looking at.' He smiled wickedly.

Telfer grabbed him by his open shirt. 'If you've frigged up my bloody wig, I'll choke you with it,' he raved.

Filch dragged himself away. 'He's so insecure, dear,' he hummed to Ronay.

Ronay pushed past them. It was becoming too much for

him, this constant bickering, and it could all still be for nothing. Charles Peake had called by that morning to inspect the make-up. He hadn't said much, which was a boon, but he too had been on edge at the lack of news.

Ronay decided on a walk. Anything to clear his head of the quarrels and frustrations of waiting. He reached the end of the street and turned towards Putney Bridge. As he crossed the road, a loud hoot brought a taxi rattling alongside him.

'Taxi, sir?' The driver touched his cap and leant out to open the passenger door.

Ronay shrugged. He got in and eased back into the comfortable seat. 'Wimbledon,' he said tiredly. He didn't know why, but Wimbledon had a quietness about it.

The cabbie pulled open the communicating window between them and shouted over his shoulder. 'A right mess over in France, eh Guv?' he shouted. 'I can't understand how them Germans could have got away with it. So I said to my missus, I said how did they get away with it, I said. She said, parachutes. Parachutes! You can't parachute a bleedin' tank down can you? I mean the sky ain't big enough is it?'

Ronay grunted. 'If you ask me,' the cabbie shouted on, 'I think they've took a right bleedin' liberty them Germans. Course it don't say a lot for our mob, does it?'

Ronay rapped the communicating window. He'd had enough. 'I'll get out here,' he said. He pulled some coins from his pocket and offered them through the window. Instead of taking them, the cabbie caught Ronay firmly by the hand.

'Thought you'd never come out, Mr Ronay. Been waiting, I have.'

His voice had lost its cheerfulness, his face had hardened. Ronay forced a calm 'Yes?'

'I have an urgent message from Berlin,' the cabbie rapped. 'A meeting is agreed. The place is the Ritz Hotel in Paris. The time is two o'clock. Afternoon this Friday. Agreed?'

Ronay looked thoughtful and there was a long silence. 'Agreed,' he said finally.

'Any changes since you last contacted us?' the cabbie asked.

'No,' Ronay said. 'Everything is still according to my last instructions.'

'We'll see you in Paris in two days then,' the cabbie turned and beamed at an old lady, as she staggered towards his cab.

'All aboard the Skylark, lady,' his happy voice returned. 'Ready to take you anywhere but France. So I said to my missus, I said . . .'

The cab pulled away. Ronay felt shaken. How long had they been watching his flat? He quickly retraced in his mind what they could have seen. Nothing to alarm them, cause suspicion, of that he could be certain. His two chameleons had been kept well out of sight – to avoid the prying eye of the law. That was an ironic bit of luck. And the curiosity of Mrs Baylis.

Charlie Peake had only made one appearance and that old fossil was officially on the slagheap. No danger there. But Ronay hadn't been fox-alert. And he should have been. He'd been lucky. He hoped that was a good sign. He believed it was. But from here on, no more reliance on Lady Luck.

Ronay turned and walked back towards the flat in Fulham. His plan had come to life; the characters were taking their destined places. His pace quickened. The feuding twosome would have to prepare. Could his plan possibly succeed? He started to run. The questions were too late, the doubts were too late. Paris in two days! The Ritz! The domicile of the exiled Duke. The Germans had done their homework well. He had to reach Charlie Peake. He ran faster. Fulham seemed an age away and Paris was only two short days.

Before the daylight had time to settle on the attic garret of Harvey Teckner, Donna Maria's body had turned into a torture chamber. She gave a soft whimper from the bed then, as if ravaged, the whimper became a plaintive cry for help. Harvey was immediately by her side. As he rubbed her hands and arms in a vain attempt to comfort her, he saw the small wounds from countless hypodermic needles on the upper arms and wrists. He knew the meaning of them.

'Do you need an injection?' he whispered as she turned and tossed in the bed.

'Yes! Yes!' she cried. 'Please, yes. The hotel. The handbag. The black handbag in the bathroom. Please hurry!'

She started to convulse and he found that he couldn't think straight. He wouldn't leave her; he couldn't bear the thought of her going through these torments alone. But as her distress became swiftly more and more evident, he ran to the window of the attic and looked down to the street below. There was no miraculous answer there.

She fell from the bed and began to rub her hands over her body as if she were on fire. Teckner had to struggle with her to force her back under the sheets.

'Please help me!' she pleaded, her eyes wild and not focusing on him as she whispered the words. Her plea wasn't really directed at him, it was to whatever hell she was travelling through, something out there beyond his vision.

'Please! please!'

He made a decision. He pulled the sheets from her and tore them into strips, then took her kicking, naked legs and arms and tied them to each corner of the bed. He knew it wasn't as awful for her as it was for him. She was beyond knowing what was happening to her, but he couldn't bear to look at her like that for long. Taking her room keys from her purse, he ran out of the attic room and into the street.

The journey to the Palace Hotel was second nature for Teckner. He would be there soon and back in minutes. He couldn't bear to think of her tied like that. He couldn't bear to think of the agony she must be enduring. And worse, she could die. Donna Maria Domenquin could die in his bed and he, not knowing one thing more about her, would not be there. That must not happen.

Baron Kurt von Zeiss had telephoned Donna Maria's suite for most of the morning and half the night. The unvarying answer from the hall porter that she was out had now become unacceptable. She had to be there. He had news, important news. Nobody, least of all his beautiful mistress, would ever risk being unavailable for that.

Von Zeiss threw down the telephone angrily and rang for his car. He had twenty-four hours before returning to Germany, before Ronay would be arriving in Paris, before the plan would be in motion. She had to be there to share it. He rasped his order to the chauffeur.

'The Palace.'

The car burst along the tree-lined drive, past the tall gates and, without pause, exploded into the road to the city.

Harvey Teckner climbed to Donna Maria's suite by way of the stairs. Once inside, the luxurious aroma of the woman filled his senses, and once more she became a mystery.

Teckner's first visit to the suite had given him the impression it was large but now it appeared quite small. He went to look in the drawers of the writing desk, anxious to discover more secrets about the lady in his attic, but her agonised cry for help kept echoing through his head. He would search later. With the hypodermic and drugs safely found and on his person, he could spend perhaps a few fast seconds satisfying his curiosity.

He found the needle and accessories where she had said. He felt strangely ashamed for her, that someone of such quality, of such excellence, should be a slave to the false moments given by these small glass bottles.

He went back to the writing desk. As he sifted through the drawers, the doors of the suite suddenly clicked open. Teckner felt a flood of guilt which made him rush for the long curtains of the terrace windows and stand behind them. Someone, somewhere in the room was standing near. He could hear breathing. He held his own breath, listening for every move, then footsteps, doors opening and closing. Then silence. The breathing was there again. Was it someone else or was it in fact his own lungs? He took one more deep breath and listened more intently.

It came like a battering ram, sinking into his solar plexus. A nerve-jarring blow with no warning. As Teckner fell to his knees, another punch followed into his eyes and the added terror of the curtains falling around his head like a hood made him vomit. A succession of kicks into his ribs made him roll in agony. The curtains were snatched from him and, as he lay there cowering, his attacker knelt and grasped him by the throat.

'Where is she?' The question rang into his ears. The grip around his larynx tightened. 'Tell me where she is or I'll kill you.'

Harvey Teckner felt his last breath vanishing as the aggressive fingers choked him. He couldn't bear the thought of more pain and knew he would have to tell the truth. He pushed his hands limply into the air in a signal of submission. He was beginning to lose consciousness.

'For God's sake let me breathe.' He forced the hoarse words through his contracted voice box. The death-hold relaxed and Teckner fell flat and exhausted at the feet of Kurt von Zeiss. The Baron was white with anger. But there was panic there, too, Harvey sensed.

He swallowed and felt the awful dryness leave his throat. Another kick into his side jolted him back to his own predicament.

'Where is she?'

The halting explanation began with the crowd in the street and Donna Maria Domenquin's not wishing to be in an ambulance. The Baron sat there listening to the story. More than once he removed his spectacles and polished them absentmindedly as he contemplated beating this youth, making him whimper, making him pay for being close to her. But it was more important to find out what the young man knew. He knew so much, perhaps more than he was telling. There was the feeling that there was more.

The Baron's message from Berlin and Hess was of the highest importance. There was a new dramatic plan for the European war theatre and here in the shape of a weak, frightened American college boy was a threat to it all. It seemed so ridiculous. Was there an antidote? He had his pistol. In the attic garret, he would decide. Solitary, dark, out of sight, out of mind, he could if he wished finish it there.

'Take me to her,' the Baron demanded.

Harvey Teckner dragged himself to his feet and led the way out of the suite, anxious to get away from the hotel. Once in the attic, he would have his revenge. His body ached with the sadistic attack of the pig. He would bide his time in the attic and then make the swine pay.

The sight of Donna Maria lying there was a shock for both of them. Her hair, matted with drying sweat, was spread across her pain-stricken face. What they could see of her eyes were dark pools set in the hollow caves of their sockets. Harvey was relieved to see that her convulsions had waned. The only sign of life was concentrated around her mouth. She mumbled strange noises which sounded foreign, and the unrelated words poured out in long unintelligible sentences, then sometimes in short phrases or odd words. She had no inkling of their presence.

The two men stood there, looking at her wide-eyed. The Baron saw the bonds around her ankles and wrists. They had bitten deep into her skin leaving red, angry welts beneath the knots. Harvey knew what the Baron would be thinking. He wasn't given the opportunity to explain. A heavy blow struck his mouth. Once more he fell, once again he felt the hardness of the floor and the degradation of being at this man's feet. His eyes glassed over. He was in a semi-conscious state for the second time that day.

The Baron had removed the last of the cloth manacles and was talking to her, trying to get her attention, when Teckner staggered to his feet. Donna Maria was still somewhere inside herself, suffering her own private nightmare. Harvey Teckner could feel the hypodermic in his pocket. He knew that her short salvation was there. The Baron was shaking her, seemingly totally unaware of her need. Harvey went to the other side of the bed and took out the needle and the small glass bottle.

'She needs this,' he said.

The elder man sneered at him, as if he were an idiot unworthy of attention.

'She really does need it.'

The Baron studied her as if looking for a cleaner, simpler cure. One more cry from her brought him to his feet. 'Do you have any idea of the dose?' he asked, taking the hypodermic from the American.

Harvey shook his head. 'I guess each bottle is a whole treatment,' he said reluctantly.

The Baron took her arm and felt into her soft skin. 'We have to find a vein, I believe.' He saw the host of other needle wounds he had never noticed before. She couldn't be an addict, not Donna Maria. He would have known. She must be diabetic. Of course. Poor, wonderful, Maria. He would save her. Thank God he was here in time to save her.

'She's suffering from sugar diabetes,' he said. Harvey nodded in mock agreement.

He watched the needle enter her. 'You could have killed her,' the Baron murmured. 'Tying her up like that. You are a fool.' He was trying to talk himself into believing his own diagnosis of her state and the verbal attack on Harvey Teckner was a salve to his conscience. Again Harvey accepted with a mock nod.

Donna Maria began to react to the drug. She gave a small hoarse cry and her eyes came to life. Whatever torment she had been in, was now releasing its hold and soon she was sitting up against the pillows, rubbing her sore wrists with some cream Harvey had given her. The Baron sat by her feet, massaging them with tenderness.

Harvey felt his concern for her relax. He had more small bottles of the drug for her, so she would be protected for a time. He allowed full rein to his anger for the man at her feet, this cruel punisher, this Svengali. Did he think he could fool anyone with that story of diabetes. This was heroin or some such heavy drug and she was a prisoner to it. And introduced to its temptation by this monster no doubt.

Seeing the two of them there together gave rise to another thought in Teckner's mind. There must be something more between them than he had as yet brought to light. But in time he would be privy to it. He was sure of that.

First, however, Teckner would have to negate the Baron's present power. The gun was in the jacket on the floor at the foot of the bed. He had seen it when the Baron threw it down there. He would have to get that gun.

Teckner edged around the foot of the bed and bent as if to look under it. As he did so, he pulled the jacket. He felt the cold steel of the barrel and searched for the safety catch. It released with a soft snap. As he raised himself from the floor, Donna Maria saw his look and then she saw the gun.

'Harvey, don't be silly.' Her control of herself was total. Her voice, authoritative and steady. Teckner paused, the gun levelled at the Baron.

'I tell you, no,' she snapped. She sounded angry.

The Baron turned from her feet and his eyes bulged as he faced the barrel. 'That is quite ridiculous, Mr Teckner,' he said.

'Harvey, if you shoot this man you will never forgive yourself,' Donna Maria said, half-pleading. All the plans of Marcus Ronay, the hopes all flashed through her mind. One young, foolish, love-torn American with one false move could end everything. Harvey had still not relented.

'This man is very important to me,' she said gently, looking at the Baron who was beginning to sweat profusely. 'You must not harm him.'

Harvey controlled his excitement. He was about to hear something to satisfy his curiosity, he was sure of it. If the Baron stayed there close to her, no moves, no sudden move, then she would keep talking. But he must hear more. 'He hurt me,' he gritted.

'I was worried for Donna Maria,' the Baron said in his own defence.

'That's crap.'

'No, it's true,' Donna Maria cried. 'We have something we must do together. Something important.'

The Baron took her hand. He frowned a warning. She ignored him. She was sure the boy was serious and would shoot. 'We have an arrangement.'

Harvey's grip on the gun tightened. The Baron saw it. 'I have come from my home in Germany to take her back with me,' he said, beginning to feel real concern for his own safety.

Donna Maria thrilled to what he had said. The dialogue with Berlin must have been accepted. She squeezed his hand, and for that brief moment forgot the gun. 'You've heard then?' she asked.

'I'm to go back. We meet in two days. I want you there with me, my darling.'

She kissed him. Donna Maria saw Harvey's reaction and laughed. 'Harvey, you lovely boy, put that away,' she cried. 'Everything is so good. Don't spoil it.'

He knew he was no longer considered a threat and that suited him very well. 'Well, whatever's going on I'm keeping the gun with me,' he said, pocketing the weapon.

'Look, we have something to discuss,' Donna Maria said to him. 'Be a dear and get something to drink. Go and buy something for us. To celebrate.'

'Celebrate what?' Harvey growled.

'Look at me,' she smiled. 'I'm well, I'm myself, I'm happy and I'm with two wonderful friends. I wish to celebrate that. Please Harvey, we do have something private to discuss, so get something delicious, sparkling and very expensive.'

The Baron took a wad of notes from his pocket and tossed them over to the American.

'I'm sorry for hurting you. I misunderstood and acted rashly, because I was most anxious about our Madonna here.' He smiled, holding Donna Maria to him.

Harvey muttered as he left the room. He listened outside the door for a moment but he could hear only their low voices and not their words. He decided to go for the wine and try to find some answer to his questions later.

'But what do we do about our young Sir Galahad?' the Baron said finally.

'You must not hurt the boy. You know that, don't you?' she said.

The Baron walked around the room. 'He has my gun which keeps him safe,' he said.

'He's not to be harmed,' she insisted. She knew it wasn't Harvey's well-being that concerned her. It was the fact that if the boy were to be frightened or put on guard, he could go to his Consul or to any kind of official body. Then what? Anything! Worst of all, was the risk to Marcus.

'We'll take him with us,' she said firmly.

'We'll do no such damn ridiculous thing,' the Baron fumed. 'That pouting child in Germany with us, with me, with them? You don't know what you're saying, Maria.'

'I *do* know Kurt. I know he can't be here, loose in Madrid, for the next few days and I know he can't be harmed, so he comes with us.' She went to the cracked mirror by the sink and turned on the rusty tap. The cold water hit her wrists. All was clear, all was back under her control. She saw her reflection in the glass and she did not look well. She thought she could detect a suggestion of grey at her temples and there was a line here and there on her face which she hadn't noticed before. It must be the light in the attic, she thought, for surely in the short time she had been there it wasn't possible to suffer such change. But the main thing was, she was in control.

'We'll invite him for a short trip. A few days in another world. He'll behave and stay out of the way. He's a good boy.'

Harvey Teckner waited outside for the silence after Maria's words and then fiddled with the door handle to announce his return. A trip to Germany would be very welcome, he thought. Eventful too, he wagered as he caught sight of the Baron's smile and Maria's beckoning hand.

Since the shock of the meeting with the taxi driver, Ronay had become paranoid about the plan being discovered. The Germans having their men in London was part of the game – he accepted the fact and would keep his head down. And the heads of his chameleons firmly down too.

Charlie Peake was to be kept away, Ronay decided, and the telephone used very carefully. Filch and Telfer hadn't been back to their mews house since the contact had been made and that was the way it would stay.

The atmosphere in the flat was a strange chemistry. It blew hot and cold. Sometimes arguments would flare for no reason, and flow like steam released through the eye of a needle. And then there would be times of long quiet. The men would be thinking of the challenges of the task ahead. And the risks.

On the morning of May 23rd, Ronay took the steps up to the flat two at a time. He burst into the room, surprising Filch at the ironing board and disturbing Telfer's lie-in. He stood at the door grinning, flushed from the run and tense with the excitement of it all.

'It's done! It's done,' he said. 'Christ, we're in luck, George.' He sat at the table pushing away a pile of clothes and opening out a book of notes.

'We've had contact with Fruity Metcalfe in Paris,' he began. 'Metcalfe is private aide to His Royal Highness, the Duke of Windsor.' He read from his notes. 'His Royal Highness, not being privy to the reasons for your request, has graciously agreed under certain circumstances to act in your best interests.'

Filch gave a whistle and spat onto the hot iron.

Ronay went on. 'At twelve o'clock on the afternoon of May 24th, the royal party will take lunch in their private rooms at the Ritz Hotel. They will confine themselves to their rooms incommunicado. All future meals will be served by their staff in private. They will follow this procedure until notification that the Final Run is safely cleared from Germany.'

Filch snorted. 'Funny, isn't it? Who'd have believed I'd have a king of England jumping through hoops at my every whim.' Telfer glared at him. Filch winked and returned to his ironing.

Ronay was elated. The royal party had agreed to stay confined in their rooms on the seventh floor. Charlie Peake had arranged for a 'Ghost Room' on the sixth floor where Filch and Telfer would wait. The 'switch' had been used on other jobs before. Once the time was right, Filch and Telfer in their disguises would leave the 'Ghost Room' and go to the seventh floor by the stairs. Once there, they'd call the lift so that any spectator would accept that they had come from the royal suite.

'It's tonight. We go to Paris tonight,' Ronay said. He looked young, eager and confident. 'Dishy, isn't he?' Filch murmured to no one in particular as he pushed the point of the iron across the polka-dotted bow tie of Churchill.

'There's about four more miles of conifers before the valley,' the Baron called to her over the din of the diesel engine. The huge SS staff car negotiated the mountain pass without effort. The uniformed Waffen SS driver and his sergeant occupied the front seat whilst the Baron sat with Donna Maria and Harvey Teckner in the rear, braving the flying dust of the early summer. They were covered to the waists by a heavy, itching army blanket.

They'd been on German soil for five hours. It was early

evening on the twenty-third of May and the cool mountain air was blowing. Harvey Teckner used the excuse to snuggle closer to Donna Maria and smiled, his face as red as his hair. 'When do we see this Berchtesgaden?' he called.

'We don't see it, Mr Teckner,' the Baron snapped. 'It is here in the mountains but we will not see it. We go below. There, do you see the green valley? The hunting lodge? We are going there.' The Baron felt beneath the blanket for her hand and squeezed it hard. 'Isn't it magnificent.' He didn't attempt to hide his excitement.

She kissed his shoulder. 'Kurt, anyone would think you had never seen it before.'

'It is a shrine,' he shouted, his voice echoing in the mountains. 'It's a shrine to you and love.' The hunting lodge of the von Zeiss family gave the impression of growing out of the ground like the forests surrounding it. The tall, evergreen foliage provided a backdrop of grandeur and depth. The car stopped at the foot of the rustic stairs leading to the double-fronted doors. A platoon of Waffen SS clattered down the steps to assist with the luggage.

Donna Maria listened in surprise as the Baron barked commands with great authority. She had never heard him speak in his German tongue. The harsh, gutteral sounds were those of a stranger.

He spoke with an SS officer and then eventually he escorted her up the stairs and into the lodge. The main floor consisted of a huge room dominated on one side by an enormous window that ran the length of the structure and overlooked a lake lying as still as a mirror. The reflection of the green trees at its banks gave the impression of a giant paperweight, never changing, ever there.

The Baron led the way up the narrow staircase to the only other floor of the lodge. Around an open area was a gallery which gave on to the bedrooms – one master suite and four others for guests. He showed Harvey Teckner to his room, and then led Maria to theirs, the master bedroom. It was a magnificent room with polished wood of a honey colour which gave the walls and furniture a rich glow. The four-poster bed with its high pillows and multi-coloured quilt invited all manner of ritual. The gloss floor was decorated with the skin of a brown bear and a huge window looked out onto the lake. One could smell the deer roaming through the far green hills.

Donna Maria went to the window and strained her eyes for some movement on the water. She found the lodge itself, and the view, quite breathtaking. The Baron pressed her close.

'Look to the north. Those high trees, there by the cedars. Do you see the mountain?'

She strained her eyes past the lake and the first bank of trees in the direction he was pointing. 'Yes,' she said.

'Berchtesgaden!' he murmured. 'Hidden by the shadows, the retreat of our Führer. In twenty-four hours, my darling, you will be there, on the mountain. We will be there.'

Donna Maria took his arm. She felt his emotion, his pride. 'The British will be here tomorrow,' he said, without taking his eyes from the lake. 'You and I as hosts here at the lodge will be expected to see our guests are safe and relaxed before we dine at the retreat. After dinner they will have their dialogue with the Führer and then return with us here to the lodge. On the morning of the twenty-fifth they will return to Paris with a new world at their feet.'

He pulled his gaze away from the lake and looked at her. 'The rest will be history, my dearest love. History!'

Maria smiled and kissed him. His excitement, his passion, was built on clay, but she had her part to play. And Marcus would be with her soon.

Book V

The Final Run

Folkestone seemed strange and ghostly at such a late hour. They had driven past the Leas just before two o'clock, the splendid Edwardian hotels standing proud in the moonlight, a breeze stirring the tamarisk trees. Charlie Peake snored next to Ronay in the army coach. In front were Telfer and Filch, the younger man fidgeting, unable to relax. The coach clattered up and out of the town and then along the quiet coast past a martello tower hiding in the sea mist.

A discreet torch flashed from the next part of the coast that appeared around a small bay. The transport slowed and, by the time it had stopped, the occupants were wide awake, clutching their cases and anxious for action. Charlie Peake was first to the door and onto the damp grass verge. The hooded torch loomed closer and became a fisherman.

'Name of Peake?' he asked through a heavy black beard that made his head almost invisible in the night.

Charlie grunted. The bearded man flashed his beam back towards the bay and another light answered from the water. The bearded man beckoned the party to follow off the grass onto the stones; then the shale, cracking under their shoes, became without warning soft, silent sand.

'Stand fast, and identify,' a voice called from the water.

'Final Run,' Charlie Peake growled.

It was all very boring, he thought. The sooner the party was off the land and into the Channel the better. This red tape was always unnecessary and unproductive. 'Advance Final Run,' the voice said, followed by a sharp electrical buzz and an explosion of engines.

As they neared the sound, the dark shape of a motor torpedo boat floated into focus, its motors growling under the surface of the water. A naval officer jumped from the bow of the vessel and landed in the shallow inches of the sea, his heavy sea boots shooting a curtain of spray over Filch and Telfer, who were nearest. Telfer swore as he attempted to wipe the wet salt from his face and suit; Filch whistled 'all the nice girls love a sailor' as the officer helped him up on to the bobbing craft. The fisherman with the black beard joined them, waving his colleagues goodbye, and they in their turn disappeared off the beach across the shale and beyond the grass verge. Then there were just Ronay and Peake left on the beach. Ronay could just make out the glasses and cheeks of the old one.

'It's past your bedtime, Charlie,' he smiled.

Charlie Peake shook his hand. 'I'd just like you to know I think you're a bloody lunatic,' he muttered. 'And don't deviate, Marcus. Don't adlib, and don't invent.' His brusque voice continued, 'No more contact, no more help.'

'I just hope we get the chance to have a go, that's all,' Ronay said as he stepped firmly into the water towards the boat.

'You're a bloody lunatic, Ronay,' Charlie Peake called again from the night.

The motor torpedo boat throbbed into reverse, its engines drowning out any more comment from the beach. It paused for a split second then, in full thrust, its bow lifted, its timber shook amidships and, in a garland of white illuminated foam, it powered towards France.

The bearded fisherman stood with the officer at the shoulder of the naval rating steering the boat. At various intervals he would shout an order into the rating's ear.

'Starboard a touch,' and the boat would dip to the right in answer to the order. 'Come a'port easy like.'

Ronay sat at the side of the small bridge and allowed the spray to hit his head. He was tingling from the vibration of the engines and his own exhilaration. They were off and running. He felt ten feet tall.

A sound like distant thunder came from the east. Then, as they closed to the French coast, the sound became a series of separate sounds and crunches. Krump! Krump! In the moonlight, what looked like another planet appeared off the port bow. It had a black, moving cloud of spent explosive hanging over it. Flashes came from within its darkness.

'Dunkirk,' the officer yelled to Ronay.

Filch pushed himself close to Telfer, shoving his hand into his friend's raincoat pocket and relaxing with the warmth of it. Again the distant thunder came; the black cloud seemed a little too close.

'Christ! How much bloody nearer?' Filch shouted at Ronay. Telfer felt the panic too and staggered over the dancing deck to the officer and the bearded fisherman – 'You're too fucking close,' he yelled.

The officer shook his head grimly. 'We're well away from it,' he shouted. 'It's about twenty miles east of here. It's the smoke that's coming to us.'

For another ten minutes the blackness loomed ever nearer and then there seemed to be a break in the rhythm of the thumps and crunches that came from it. Then there were no more explosions. It was eerie.

Ronay gestured to the officer. The bearded fisherman came to the side and listened. Filch and Telfer looked at each other, neither speaking.

'Stop both engines,' the officer called. The rating obeyed and the MTB settled immediately. With one gentle splash her wake caught her up and pushed her playfully. The blackness still prevailed around them but there was silence from Dunkirk. The occupants of the MTB stretched their necks, their ears seeking anything that might answer the nagging question 'Why?' The radio transmitter crackled from below the conn. The officer reached under and pulled free the microphone and ear piece.

'Final Run', he said urgently. 'Final Run.' He pressed the earphone into his hair and listened intently, scratching the radio pad with short, scrawling words. 'Message for Final Run,' he called to the men at the boat's side. 'German assault on Dunkirk has stopped. Your journey very necessary. Signed, Peake. Message ends.'

Once more the MTB rose from the water and powered towards the grey coast ahead. The bearded fisherman pulled himself to the bow and peered at the nearing land. It was apparent he knew the water here as well as at Folkestone, Ronay thought, as the big man signalled with his massive arms to the officer on the small bridge. Left, right, one point, two points. France was now clearly visible. The nearness of the land with the coming dawn made it possible to make out first the high ground, then the small inlets and then contours and roads and now buildings. Small, squat dwellings with no lights, no smoke, no people, everyone asleep.

The naval officer shouted to the bearded fisherman still standing at the bow.

'We'll hug close,' he yelled.

The MTB listed hard to starboard and powered on. Ronay checked his watch as Filch swayed over to him.

'Why don't we get off here?' he said.

Ronay pointed ahead, 'We go to the west, to Le Tréport. There we can make our way undetected. Be patient. Another couple of hours and we'll be in Paris.'

Le Tréport was an unassuming little haven. The white buildings of the fishing village glistened in the early morning light. The MTB dipped low and allowed the incoming waves to ease her ever closer to the beach. At first it seemed this place, too, was asleep. But up beyond the small houses a figure signalled. Their French contact.

Ronay shook hands with the crew and led Filch and Telfer onto the foreign sand. They passed the houses silently without seeing another soul, but, by the time they had greeted their contact and driver, the sudden roar of the MTB had acted as an alarm. A dim light appeared in the house nearest the car. A window rapped open and a French voice called testily. The MTB roared once more into forward thrust. No one in Le Tréport could have noticed the little whine of the Citroën saloon as it crept out of the village. To anyone awake that morning it was only the noisy vessel showing the white ensign of the British Navy that had their attention.

The road to Paris was quite beautiful, clean and well shaped with clipped hedges marking neat fields. The contact said nothing, concentrating and doing his job. But when they came to the approach road to Beauvais the picture changed considerably. From the north east a line of military vehicles came in a single cloud of dust. Filch grabbed Telfer in panic – he thought they must be German panzers pushing through to Paris. But it became clearer as they neared the town that the machines were French and Belgian. Caked with mud and dust, they were filled with grim-faced soldiers, their heads bowed, their helmets hiding their eyes. This was the other flank of the retreat from the Ardennes.

Ronay nudged the driver fiercely. '*Allez*! *Allez*!' he cried.

The contact eased the car in and around the slower military traffic. There were no plans for these retreating men. The tired soldiers were merely making blindly for the comparative safety of Paris.

'*Vite*!' Ronay banged the rear of the contact's seat. The last thing he wanted was for them to be bogged down in the middle of a full retreat. He had to get them away from here; he had to get them into Paris before noon. A black cloud began to creep up from the north behind the ever-coming column. Ronay banged his fist again into the seat. Telfer too, and Filch joined in, shouting at the driver.

'*Vite! Vite*!'

The car horn joined in the general hubbub but the little Citroën wasn't the only vehicle anxious to move on.

Just after eleven a.m., two men wandered into the Ritz Hotel, enquired for the head waiter and asked if they could take morning coffee. A table was prepared for them in the small alcove off the public rooms. From their vantage point, they had an uninterrupted view of the foyer. They ordered small sandwiches with their drinks and settled with their copies of *Le Figaro*.

A great army truck dragged its silent cargo of soldiers slowly up the hill for what seemed an eternity to the occupants of the small Citroën following behind. Eventually, it reached the brow. The Citroën changed gear and sped past. Ronay checked his watch again. The Paris rendezvous was for noon and with all the will in the world he wasn't going to make it. Filch and Telfer dozed against each other.

At twelve forty-five Paris paraded its wares. Long, wide expansive avenues with their ant-like traffic promised a faster passage through to the hotel. As they came near the Place Vendôme, Ronay placed his hands on the contact's shoulders. 'Slow down at the next intersection,' he said.

The Citroën slowed and stopped. Filch and Telfer looked at Ronay expectantly.

'I'm getting out here,' he muttered. 'You proceed as directed.'

Filch pulled the door shut as Ronay alighted and the car purred away, leaving him standing on the pavement. At twelve fifty the little Citroën deposited Telfer at the corner immediately behind the hotel. Filch drove on to the front entrance and walked in, mingling with the throng. He made his way to the lift and ascended to the sixth floor. And the 'ghost room'. The key was in the lock and a 'Do Not Disturb' sign hung from the door handle. He went in. The dressing table in the bedroom had two large lamps on it. He removed the shades.

Telfer was next to negotiate the foyer. The two men in the alcove continued their vigil. So far no one had entered the hotel that interested them.

Telfer, as planned, walked past the lift to the main staircase, up to the sixth floor and into the 'ghost room'. Without a word he nodded to Filch and together they began to undress. The adrenalin was pumping wildly. They opened their cases and took out make-up, wigs and clothes which they laid out ceremoniously on the single beds. Filch ran the shower and the two men walked under its hot spray, glad to wash the dirt and dust away and anxious to begin the play.

In the cramped lavatory of the Brasserie Rouge, Ronay slipped the safety razor back into his case and wiped the excess soap off his tingling face. His new suit hung on the back of the door with less creases than he had expected. He dressed quickly, and then paused to study the figure in the mirror. He looked taller, leaner. His eyes gazed back at him with a light in them that had not been there for some time. He grinned. He pulled the comb through his hair and the roots bounced back with a youthful spring. The pumping of his heart and the excitement thrilling through his limbs added to a memorable moment.

Ronay closed the suitcase with the soiled clothes and walked back into the Brasserie. His minute steak arrived and he blessed the meal with a half bottle of house red.

At thirteen fifty he settled the bill and walked towards the Ritz. He arrived at the reception desk at fourteen hours exactly. The two men in the alcove left their newspapers and came close to the desk as Ronay gave his name to the concierge.

'Marcus Ronay. I'm expected by His Royal Highness.'

The concierge picked up the telephone to announce him. The taller of the two men brushed Ronay's sleeve.

'Good afternoon, Mr Ronay,' he whispered. 'I hope you had a safe journey.' He spoke in English but his accent was unmistakably Germanic.

'I trust my travels are just beginning,' Ronay grinned.

'Would you go right up, Monsieur. The seventh floor, if you please,' the concierge directed.

The two men walked just behind as Ronay made for the lift and pressed the call button.

He said softly, 'If you will wait here please.' The two men watched him enter the lift and, without a word or sign of acknowledgement, they followed him into it, waiting for him to press the button. Ronay's heart raced. Why this sudden change? It was not part of the plan that these two should accompany him. He pulled close the iron gates and pressed the seventh floor button. The lift slowly ascended. Did they suspect? Was there distrust in Berlin? And what now? On the seventh floor he couldn't go to the Duke's suite where he wasn't in fact expected. Charlie Peake had made the arrangement with the concierge and Fruity Metcalfe: Ronay would ring the royal rooms just to put up a bona fide front. He had expected a welcoming party, of course, but these two uncomfortable leeches he did not need.

The lift was past the fourth floor and Ronay's imagination schemed through ideas. Once they reached the seventh floor he would certainly have to do something. He couldn't disengage from his companions without arousing their suspicions.

He couldn't attack them; they were to be his guides, and without them he had no idea where to go.

The lift eased into the seventh floor and he swung back the gates. They waited for him to leave. He did and strode towards the door where a footman sat outside, his legs splayed across the corridor. Ronay came level with the man who looked up at him without a sign of expectancy or interest.

The footman still sat staring up at him while the Germans stood in silence. Anger boiled up in Ronay, anger, that the plan had failed before it had even begun. Or had it?

He suddenly snorted and slapped the footman hard across the face. The man toppled off his chair and crashed into the corridor. The Germans stepped back and waited.

Ronay pulled the footman up and followed his instincts.

'How dare you ignore me,' he snarled.

The footman struggled for some reply. He looked bewildered.

The door to the royal suite swung open. A tall, broad man in a morning suit stepped into the corridor and glanced at Ronay. 'Would you mind putting Marcel back on his feet,' he said with no sign of alarm.

Ronay released the footman. 'Please accept my heartfelt apologies,' he said as he did so. 'I've a foul temper, and in such delicate matters as ours, it tends to snap.'

'So do one's footmen, it appears,' the man in the morning suit said with the suggestion of a grin.

Ronay referred to the two Germans. 'These gentlemen are here to assist us as "*gooseberries*",' he said. He daren't underline the word more than he did, but he prayed the man would have the quickness to understand the situation. Gooseberries! It fell into his speech quite well and the Germans appeared to be still at ease. As did the man in the morning suit.

'Yes, well that's a good show,' he said. 'But the arrangement was for you to go to the sixth floor surely.'

Ronay's back stiffened. He could imagine the looks on the two German faces behind him, and the question on their lips, but he dared not turn and face them.

The broad man raised his shoulders, 'I am Major Metcalfe, aide to His Royal Highness.'

Ronay knew the man all right. Fruity Metcalfe late of the Indian Army, presently aide and confidant to the Duke of Windsor and his American lady. Things were getting more and more out of control.

'Perhaps I could explain this situation privately,' Ronay said tensely.

'No, no, dear fellow!' the Major insisted. 'You were to telephone but not actually come to these rooms. *We're* on the seventh and *you* were supposed to go to the sixth.'

There wasn't much more Ronay could do. He wanted to

take the Major by the scruff of his neck and yell the truth into his cloth ears. The two Germans came into vision. He didn't look at them. He simply glared at Metcalfe, silently cursing him.

'This was arranged all too quickly in my opinion,' the Major said, addressing the three of them now. 'HRH is not one to slip easily into these situations of intrigue, and perhaps I may have misunderstood the arrangements.'

'We too may have misunderstood,' the tall German said, slanting a suspicious glance to his colleague.

The Major clasped his hands behind his back. 'Anyway, least said soonest mended,' he beamed. 'Now you two chaps are . . . ?' He cocked his head, waiting for them to answer. Ronay stiffened. The situation was becoming macabre but there was nothing he could do, so he leaned back as casually as he could against the nearest wall and waited. The tall German reached into his pocket and showed the Major a small folded card. The aide read it and nodded.

'Oh I see. You are German reception. That's capital. But surely you were supposed to be waiting downstairs?' the Major said, his delivery that of a headmaster, condescending and gently reprimanding. 'It's quite impossible you see,' he quickly continued, preventing any interruption. 'We have our Royal party on two floors and we can't have all and sundry roaming around, can we? One must be organised, otherwise one can't tell the difference between the sheep and the dogs, can one? *Verstehen*?' The Major hit the German word in a patronising tone, as if he had total command of the language but chose to release just one clue to his knowledge.

'You do *verstehen*, don't you?' he said. The Germans did. 'That's capital, now be good chaps and wait downstairs whilst Mr Ronay and I form up our ranks.'

Ronay could have applauded this buffoon, this protector of the Raj, this Metcalfe. All of a sudden the whole terrible mess was dissolving into nothing more than a typical upper-class embarrassment. The man was a genius. The Germans bowed in apology and began walking back to the lift.

'Which entrance do we meet?' Ronay asked.

'To the south, at the side,' the tall German said. 'We wait south side trade entrance. How soon?'

'Ten minutes,' Ronay said. 'We must not rush the Duke. *Verstehen*?'

'We understand Mr Ronay,' the small German spoke for the first time. 'It appears it is *you* who do not *verstehen*. We have wasted much time. We have to be at the rendezvous for the aircraft. Please hurry.' Ronay bowed and watched them descend.

'I apologise for this misunderstanding,' he called, but there was no answer from the disappearing lift. He put both arms onto the gates and exhaled with relief. What other surprises were in store?

He felt a gentle touch on his shoulder and swung around. The Major's vacuous expression had gone. He looked at Ronay with a more serious face. 'It appears our "gooseberries" have returned to the bush,' he said. 'But I didn't appreciate that little moment, Mr Ronay. We have our arrangements and these enforced deviations can be trying and dangerous, and one must not endanger His Royal Highness.'

Ronay turned from the corridor, stepping through the staff door leading to the service stairs. The Major followed him down to the sixth floor.

'Will you have any problems staying out of sight for the next few days?' Ronay asked.

'No, we're well prepared. HRH has taken care of all the details. He's been bloody terrific.'

They walked from the service area into the sixth floor corridor and along to the 'ghost room'.

'Please give him our thanks,' Ronay said as he rapped twice on the door.

'Winston Churchill' came through the portal followed by the 'Duke of Windsor'. The Major gasped. Then he started to applaud. Filch winked at him as he passed. Telfer paused and practised his most vulnerable royal smile.

'Will I do?' he asked, knowing all the while that his make-up was perfect. The Major bowed.

'Then take this,' Telfer said grandly, and shoved his suitcase into the aide's hands.

Ronay signalled from the service stairs and the Royal party followed, with Metcalfe stunned and seemingly unable to believe the evidence of his own eyes.

The service stairs led to the kitchen below the hotel. There was pandemonium, head chefs, commis chefs, maîtres d'hôtel, assistant porters, waiters – all yelling, all demanding and all sweating in the heat of a hundred dishes. None of them paid any attention as Ronay pushed hurriedly through the throng with the others close behind. Ahead of them blazed the bright lights of the south service area.

As they stepped into the comparative calm of the fresh air, the two Germans sidled up from the shadows. They ignored Ronay and even Churchill. For them Telfer, the jaunty young man in the pin striped suit, was the focal point. The small German came to an enormous heel click and a swift sudden clipped bow from the nape of his neck. The tall one followed a split second behind, like an echo.

'Your Majesty, it is with great . . .'

The Major stepped between them and shoved Telfer's suitcase into the little German's hands. 'Be a good chap and see this doesn't get lost,' he said, dismissing him in style. The German gave another bow and led the Royal party out of the quiet south entrance into the transport.

Donna Maria held the long white satin dress up to her skin. She had followed the ritual at least a dozen times that afternoon. She loved it, the fall of the material, the cut, the line. She envisaged how her hair would be at dinner that night in the retreat, and her make-up. How she would appear to the leaders of the Third Reich and to Marcus. She saw herself walking among them, tantalising him and tempting more than one of the gathered guests with the promise of a night to remember.

She felt the nipples of her breasts harden under the bodice and she dropped the creation onto the polished floor, her body tingling with energy. She ran her fingers down from her shoulders around her breasts and then felt her muscles quiver as she caressed the insides of her thighs. She began to sweat. She saw Marcus in a haze of dreams kneeling by her feet, looking up at her, helping her. Her knees trembled as she searched with her fingers. The thought of her Englishman coming to her filled her with ecstasy. It was a moment to cherish, standing there. She wouldn't let it pass. She would enjoy her dream and she floated to the bed, dragging the dress behind her. She lay on top of the covers and eased the soft satin over her. It was ice cold . . . sensual.

Something suddenly loomed over her. She sat up, holding the dress to her, dizzy with the thought and shock of discovery. The Baron stood looking down at her.

'Rudolf Hess, the Deputy Reich Führer, is on his way over from Berchtesgaden. Can I rely on you to be ready?' he said. She wasn't sure if he had seen. He had a way of hiding his feelings.

'Yes, I'll come now,' she said breathlessly.

'In something a little more than you have on at the moment, I hope,' he said half smiling and left her.

She fell back, her eyes welled up and tears began to fall. She sobbed with shame and the need to have completed her dream.

She heard the jack-boots of the guard assembling outside the lodge and, remembering her position in the Baron's household, she went to the wardrobe and took a plain simple dress from the hanger. She pushed her long hair up and pinned it loosely. From the distance the drone of cars came towards the lodge. She was downstairs and prepared by the Baron's side, as the SS guard presented arms to the swaggering strut of Hess as he approached the entrance.

'My dear von Zeiss,' he laughed, 'the day is beautiful and so, if I may say, is this vision.' He bowed gracefully to Donna Maria.

'May I present my hostess, Donna Maria Domenquin,' the Baron said proudly. Hess kissed her hand and stepped past her into the main room.

'This is exquisite,' he cried, looking at the panoramic view of the lake, his legs astride, his hands on his hips. 'The view of kings,' he said grandly.

'Would the Deputy Reich Führer care for some refreshment?' Donna Maria asked. He waved his hands without turning from the view.

'No, no, my dear. I'll drink this intoxicating Fatherland until our guests arrive.'

Donna Maria wondered if his speech was always so over-expressive. 'May I ask how soon they will be here, sir? I have much to do.'

Hess broke away from the scene and signalled to an officer standing stiffly at the door. 'How soon?' he rapped.

The officer consulted his watch. 'They drove from Paris at approximately fourteen ten, sir. I would estimate an hour to the rendezvous and not more than a few minutes to board the 'plane. E.T.A. here, another fifty minutes.' The officer clicked his heels and stepped back to the door. Hess rubbed his hands with pleasure. He took Donna Maria's hand and pulled her gently close to his side. He gazed into her eyes.

'Treat them well, my dear. Tend to their every need. The Führer depends on it.'

Donna Maria smiled and gave a small curtsey. Marcus. Soon he would be here. She would treat him well. Oh yes, she would tend to his every need.

When Ronay saw her standing between the Baron and Hess, he could hardly suppress his surprise and his anger. But by the time he had reached the bottom of the steps of the lodge, ahead of his VIPs, his feeling had changed to one of sadness for her and for him. Her presence could hinder things. And the danger! He didn't want Maria to be part of that.

'You know Donna Maria, of course,' the Baron said. Ronay forced a smile and returned his attention to the

'Duke' and 'Churchill'. By sheer force of personality and talent, Filch had gained more of the audience than Telfer. His gruffness, his personality shone like a light in gloom. From somewhere he had found himself a host of selected speeches, his slur of words and affected stutter a trifle overplayed, but making an impression, especially on Hess. The swarthy politician hung on the actor's every word.

'Perhaps Mr Churchill, tonight, after the dialogue, we may talk of other times?' he suggested. Churchill studied the Nazi over his spectacles and puffed heavily on his cigar.

'Other times, sir? You have me at a disadvantage,' he said. Hess gave a nervous cough.

'I am an admirer of your Boer War communiqués, sir.'

Churchill fidgeted on his chair and scratched the top of his head. 'They were the writings of a boy desirous of fame. A little fact with much imagination to inspire the reader. I was always a better writer than a hero, Mr Hess.'

The Deputy Führer was thrilled by the conversation. He pressed on enthusiastically. 'And on writing, sir, have you read the Leader's *Mein Kampf*?'

Churchill thought for a moment. 'Yes,' he said finally. 'Only the English version, alas! I fear it lost its point in translation.'

Hess shook his head. 'I beg to assure you, sir, the English translation was quite excellent,' he said. Once more Churchill fidgeted.

'Well, my copy must have had a few pages missing,' he said testily, tapping the ash from the cigar and reaching for another match.

Elsewhere in the vast space of the room the Duke of Windsor was holding court. Donna Maria sat by his side admiring the actor under the disguise. 'Did you ever see Balmoral?' the Duke said in his honey-soft voice. 'Now there you have such a sight as this, only perhaps a little better, depending on the day and the company.'

He tapped a fresh cigarette on a solid silver case and

accepted a light from a high-ranking officer. 'But one must say the lake here is magnificent. The Duchess would be furious if she knew.'

Harvey Teckner, who had been aching to become part of this illustrious conversation, could hold himself back no longer.

'Excuse me, sir, but isn't the Duchess an American?' he said. The Duke gave a lopsided grin.

'No. The Duchess is a Duchess,' he said, dismissing the question and destroying the boy. Harvey slowly eased himself back among the officers and felt as if he were disappearing into the woodwork.

'If you'll excuse me, your Royal Highness, I'll prepare some tea,' Donna Maria said, rising from the sofa.

'Hot and sweet would be most acceptable,' the Duke grinned.

'I'll just have brandy, if you can provide,' Churchill said gruffly, from across the room.

Donna Maria walked gracefully out with the Baron and Harvey in close attendance. As they left, Hess marched to the middle of the room and came to attention, formally clicking his heels.

'On behalf of the Führer,' he said pompously, 'I am to inform Your Royal Highness that as of first light today the forces of the Third Reich have stopped their advance twelve kilometres from the port of Dunkirk.'

The Duke nodded approval from the sofa. Churchill fidgeted once more and made some gruff remark.

'It is the wish of the Führer,' Hess continued, 'that you accept this as evidence of the good faith and deep hope of the German peoples.'

'Would you convey to Herr Hitler our grateful recognition of his actions and tell him our hopes, too, are high,' the Duke said.

'I look forward to this evening at dinner when our discussion may bear the fruits of friendship,' Hess continued.

‘Let’s hope the dinner is better than our lunch in Paris,’ Churchill again interrupted. ‘French chefs are like their generals. They talk a better meal than they cook.’

Hess danced with laughter, the officers applauded, even the Duke muffled a grin. Filch was perhaps going a little too far.

‘Have you discussed the protocol for this evening, sir?’ Ronay interrupted. He wasn’t going to allow the Chameleons to take over the proceedings. There were matters of vital importance to be discussed. Hess nodded enthusiastically to the question, snapped his fingers for the folder an officer was holding, and from it took out a blue-print of Berchtesgaden. The area was marked with coloured tapes and markers, an exquisite example of German thoroughness.

‘You will kindly leave at twenty twenty this evening, sir,’ Hess began. ‘The royal car will arrive at Berchtesgaden gates at twenty thirty. Upon alighting from the car, Your Highness will kindly walk the carpet way to the flag stand.’ He pointed to the blueprint. ‘The massed bands will strike up the anthems and, at your request, sir, there will be a royal inspection of the Waffen SS guard, during which the *Horst Wessel* song will be played. At this exact time the Führer and his party will assemble on the grand balcony of the retreat which is here, above the parade ground.’

Again Hess indicated the blue-print and the Duke leaned forward to look. Churchill ignored them. Ronay listened carefully to everything the Deputy Führer said.

‘The anthems will take approximately five minutes,’ Hess continued. ‘Then you will be accompanied to the tunnel here, leading to the elevator and from there up to the retreat on the mountain. I have a list of the German contingent and you, sir, with permission, will sit on the Führer’s right hand with . . .’

The Baron watched the dignitaries from the alcove of the kitchen area while Donna Maria and Harvey prepared the refreshments. ‘It’s at a time like this that I wish I had grandchildren to tell the story to,' he said, his voice hoarse with emotion.

'Yes, my love, I understand,' Donna Maria whispered.

Harvey Teckner was like a caged lion. 'My God, Donna Maria, that's the King of England in there,' he said. 'The guy that threw it all away, and there's Churchill – Winston Churchill! Son of Lord Randolph. My God, Maria, they're just a whisper away. But who's the other guy? The silent one, the tall guy. The Englishman.'

'His name is Marcus Ronay,' Maria said.

'I've never heard of him. Is he a politician or a royal?' Harvey said.

'He's neither. He worked for a government department years ago and I suppose he's here as an official adviser or something,' she said vaguely, hoping for an end to the conversation.

'On what?' Harvey pressed.

'I'm sure I don't know, but he's here so he must be of some importance,' she replied.

'Do you know him?' he asked.

'I know him quite well, but why all the questions?'

'Huckleberry hell! I've got a hundred relatives in Pennsylvania who ask a darn sight more questions than I do. I've just got to get it right, that's all. It's an old American custom.'

As tea was brought in, Hess indicated his departure. 'Your Royal Highness, Mr Prime Minister, friends, I look forward to this evening,' he said, pausing by the door and giving a final flamboyant salute. The Duke of Windsor stood up from the sofa, as did Churchill.

'Till tonight,' the Duke said.

'Tonight,' Hess replied.

The group of officers bowed and left with him. The roar of their vehicles reverberated around the lodge and then there was quiet. Donna Maria, the Baron and Harvey served the tea to the Duke and Churchill, whilst Ronay studied the blue-print of Berchtesgaden.

Ronay traced the coming night's journey from the lodge to the mountain retreat, through the pine forest, an expanse of trees which formed a first line of defence against any intruder, then the heavily guarded gates leading to the open area. Ronay estimated this area to be about the size of two rugby pitches. According to the blue-print it was here that the formal reception would take place. To the west was the tunnel. He had heard about this structure. Twenty or thirty metres of man-made cave biting into the mountain and leading to the lift, a small copper car ascending to the retreat; the only known access to the top of the mountain. He gave it all one last careful thought before making his decision.

He pushed the blue-print to one side and stretched himself up from his chair.

'I'm feeling a bit shattered,' he said quietly. 'If you don't mind I'll have a rest before dressing.'

The Duke ignored him and remained at the window. Churchill stirred on the sofa.

Ronay got no more than half-way up the stairs before he gave a sudden lurch onto the rail, then into the wall, and finally, with a loud gasp, he fell backwards down the stairs into a crumpled heap at the bottom.

Harvey Teckner was first at his side. 'Are you okay, Mr Ronay?' he said, trying to lift the tall man.

'My heart,' Ronay said in a barely audible whisper. 'My heart . . . pocket . . . side pocket . . . bottle . . . please.'

Harvey dived into the pocket of the fallen man and at the third attempt he found a small bottle. 'Please . . . must drink,' Ronay wheezed, fighting for breath, his face red. Harvey looked up to the worried faces gathered around him.

'It beats me what it is. But I guess I give it to him?'

Donna Maria grabbed the bottle, eased it to the edge of Ronay's lips and helped him swallow the contents. His eyes flickered but suddenly he stopped breathing.

'Oh, dear Lord,' she cried, and helped Harvey tear the tie

and collar away from the Englishman's neck. Soon he began to suck in air.

'Don't we get him into bed or something?' Harvey said. The Baron and the Duke lifted him and gradually, step by step, Ronay was carried to the landing, into his room and onto his bed.

'Do we ring for a doctor, Maria?' the Baron asked, his voice concerned. Donna Maria shook her head and ushered the men out.

'I'll make him comfortable. Perhaps later,' she said and re-entered Ronay's room, closing the door behind her.

She went to the bathroom and put a small towel under the cold water tap, her hand shaking. There was no knowing how serious Marcus's condition was, but it seemed certain that he would be immobile for the coming night. That meant she, Churchill and the Duke would be at the mercy of their own devices. She decided to worry about that nearer the hour. In any case, they were probably experienced Factory men, perhaps outranking her Englishman, and would have the situation well in hand. With the towel quite wet and cold, she went to Ronay's side and gently applied it to his forehead. His eyes opened wide, angry and sharp.

'What the hell are you doing here in Germany?' he hissed.

Donna Maria dropped the towel and stepped away from him. 'Dear God, Marcus, I thought you were dying.'

'Just tell me why,' he said, gripping her wrist, insisting on an answer.

'He asked me. Kurt asked me. And there were complications.'

'Such as?' he snapped.

'The young American for one.'

'What about the young American?'

'Marcus, I'm here. And I suppose I wanted to be, if you want the truth. But what about you? Are you really sick?'

'Am I hell,' he rasped, getting up from the bed and moving over to the door in a few strides. He listened for a moment for any sound outside. 'Tell Kurt and everyone else here, that I will not be going to Berchtesgaden tonight,' he said softly. She didn't have to ask any more. She walked away from him and left the room without another word.

The Baron looked up from his writing desk as she came into the bedroom. 'Is it serious?' he asked. She shook her head and began to undress. 'Your face tells me it must be serious. I'd like to know how he is?'

'He's fine, Kurt. He's sleeping. He'll be fine.'

'Will he be accompanying us tonight?' he asked.

She looked out towards the dense forest. 'No. He wanted to, but his health isn't good. He'd like you to give his apologies to His Royal Highness and Mr Churchill.'

The Baron shrugged and left the room. She stood transfixed. She didn't want to think any more, no deliberations, no conclusions. What would be, would be. She must clear her mind. Make it blank and unquestioning.

She gave a start as the Baron re-entered the room. 'I have informed the others of Ronay's wishes,' he grunted. 'It is nearly time and the escort will be here before my lover is ready to intoxicate the Third Reich.'

She went to the bathroom. Von Zeiss prepared his clothes and joined her. She sat by her draining bath and carefully combed through her long, wet hair. He went into the shower and pulled across the waterproof curtain. His shadow played on it like a cartoon.

'Have you ever soon one of our VIP occasions?' he called from the hissing waters.

'I can't say I have, my darling,' she said, not really interested. Her mind was on Marcus. What was he planning?

'Well it will be loud and impressive, knowing Dr Goebbels. The Führer likes pomp and circumstance, you know. Brass bands and lots of strong young soldiers.'

She sat, lost in thought. The bathroom door was half open. She saw Marcus Ronay almost as soon as he entered the bedroom. He fixed her with his eyes, sharp eyes, unflinching certain eyes, no questions, eyes that defied argument. Killing eyes.

The Baron began to sing from the shower. '*Bei mir bist du schön.*' She buried her head in her hands, pushing the towel into her mouth, wanting to shut out the inevitable, but unable to. She watched Marcus touch the shower curtain.

'*Bei mir bist du schön*, I love . . .'

Then in one step, the Englishman was behind it. A sudden gasp from von Zeiss was followed by the gurgle of water flooding a human larynx. Two struggling shadows played on the curtain. The shower suddenly stopped and all was quiet. Ronay stepped from it and sat on the edge of the bath, his hair hanging limply over his eyes, his clothes soaked, his hands raw.

'Go to our Mr Churchill and tell him it's done,' he said without looking at her. She said nothing. There was nothing she could do but obey. She tightened the belt of her gown and left.

Minutes later, Filch and Telfer placed the small case on the bed and helped Ronay dry his hair, then with grips and tight elastic bands they flattened the hair close to his head and eased on a wig. It was a perfect replica of the hair of the man lying on the bathroom floor. They warmed a cake of mortician's wax and applied it to the bridge of Ronay's nose, kneading it with expert care until that, too, was the Baron's nose. Ronay pushed wads of padding into his cheeks and his top lip before the moustache was stuck fast. Donna Maria dressed in silence.

'Now tell me, señora,' Filch warbled as he stepped back from the finished job, 'Would you know the difference?' Ronay took the bifocals from the side table. Filch had eased out the lenses and gently snapped in plain glass. Ronay polished them. She choked a cry. It was Kurt von Zeiss resurrected and as hateful as ever.

Just before twenty hours, Donna Maria walked into the corridor and checked that the area was clear. The three men stepped from the Baron's room and into Ronay's, carrying the body which they placed in the bed and covered with sheets.

'This room must not be disturbed for the rest of the evening. That must be understood,' Ronay said to Maria as they prepared to return to the Baron's room.

'There's only Harvey,' she said. 'I'll see he stays away. Don't worry.'

'I do worry. Fix it that he understands.' The snap and staccato of Ronay's voice made her wince.

'Don't talk to me like that, Marcus.' Her eyes flashed.

'If you had stayed in Spain, I wouldn't have to.'

'Well, I didn't. I'm here. I'll talk to the American and there's an end to it, but don't take that disguise too seriously. A wig and greasepaint are not the seeds of nobility.' She hit back at him with words, her only weapon. Ronay stared at her and then went back to the Baron's room without uttering a word.

Donna Maria knocked on Harvey Teckner's room at the far end of the corridor. She returned to Ronay soon after. He had dressed in the Baron's clothes and was sitting calmly at the writing desk. She closed the door and watched him. It was uncanny, the sight of him there, so like Kurt and yet so different. Inside was Marcus, her tall Englishman. Then her anger was gone, but the memory of the heat of the moment was still there and she felt elated by the feeling.

He glanced up from the desk and looked at her, without saying a word. She shifted softly across the room and laid out the silk evening gown on the bed. The touch of it made her tingle and then throb as she ran her hands through it. She needed to put it on, to have it caress her. She threw off her bathrobe, standing naked, and the muscles of her back shimmered in sensual movement. As he watched her step into the gown, he thought of the years lost between them and how lovely she was, how infuriating she could be, but how lovely she was, how painfully lovely. She eased the satin up slowly past her ankles and stopped just beneath her navel, leaving the gown draped like a primitive sarong. He crossed to her and gripped her warm body. Their eyes met. Both pretended no interest, both pretended there was no commitment, but equally each was unable to shake free from the other's power. He spoke first.

'You look lovely,' he murmured. She put her hands on her hips where the dress met the bareness.

'At last, a welcome word,' she whispered.

He grinned. 'I could show you how welcome, lady,' he said, 'but it's close to dinner.'

'There was a time,' she teased.

'The escort will be here in fifteen minutes,' he said nearing her, undoing his white bow and pulling the stiff shirt front from the studs.

'Like I said, there was a time . . .' she teased again. He touched her breasts. She gave a sudden start. The face before her was the Baron's. Her skin flinched, expecting abuse.

'Welcome home,' he said. Her head hung back to the sound of his voice. The blood ran to her brain; the touch, his hands, not hard hands, not hurting hands, but *his* hands; warm and sensual. She felt down to his waist and with the nervousness of an anxious bride fought to pull free his shirt. To feel his nakedness. He stopped her.

'What could I possibly do in fifteen minutes?' he whispered.

'Miracles!' she cried.

He began to pull her dress away from her hips, but she caught his hands. 'Leave it on,' she insisted, 'please, Marcus, I want it on.' She pulled the satin gown above her breasts and attached the thin silver straps to her broad shoulders. He stood watching her, his shirt and waistcoat dishevelled and his tuxedo trousers lying at his feet. As she fell across the bed, she thought of the moment when the Baron had intruded on her private dream, and she lifted her skirt high above her thighs. 'Now, now my darling,' she gasped, 'make me a miracle.'

At twenty twenty sharp, the roar of the vehicles forming the escort of the Royal party could be heard approaching along the lake. Clouds of dust shot from within the trees and wafted across the evening waters. Ducks scattered from their havens to all parts of the sky. Donna Maria and the Baron came downstairs together. Churchill and the Duke were pacing nervously across the lounge.

Harvey Teckner looked over the stair rail. 'Is everything okay with Mr Ronay?' he called down.

The Baron didn't answer, but Donna Maria looked up and hushed him quiet.

'Please remember and don't disturb him. We won't be late. There's supper in the cold box.'

'Yes, milady,' the American laughed and leant on the rail, his hands under his chin, looking at her and her well-dressed escort. 'Huckleberry!' he sighed, 'I guess they ain't never gonna believe this in McKeesport, Pennsylvania.'

Donna Maria touched her lips in a signal of fond good-night and pleading with Harvey to hold his tongue. He watched them leave the lodge. Outside the escort had halted. A high ranking SS general, in full evening dress, came to the foot of the steps. Donna Maria acknowledged his heel-clicking and his bow. The guard jumped to attention as the Duke came to the top of the stairs. Churchill followed, puffing his cigar into the cool clean night. The last to appear at the steps was the Baron. The outriders, with machine gunners in sidecars, watched for the general's signal to move off. Harvey Teckner watched from the first floor window.

'Have fun,' he yelled over the simultaneous roar of the engines as the escort disappeared into its own dust towards the retreat and the waiting Führer.

The huge area of parade ground was bathed in arc lights. Moving like ants below the high mountain retreat, the soldiers prepared to welcome the Royal guests. At twenty twenty-nine, the whistles sounded and what had been a mass of movement became a silent, stiff parade of crack Waffen SS with their black uniforms and silver flashes, polished boots and moulded faces. One thousand troops crunched to attention at twenty thirty. Harsh, clipped calls commanded them to present arms, and another to eyes right as the grand gates of Berchtesgaden swung slowly open to reveal the escort entering from the forest. Sentries at the gates came to attention as their Alsatian dogs strained at the leash. Ahead and to the left was a podium, carpeted and decorated with the two huge flags of Germany and Great Britain. The cars stopped and from the shadows came uniforms, pulling the doors open but staring rigidly ahead, not daring to face the alighting guests. The Duke of Windsor came out of the first car and the massed bands crashed into 'God Save the King' as he and his party stepped onto the podium.

Ronay moved his eyes from the dogs at the gates. He considered that there was no danger there. He looked across to the podium. Around it and behind it were high-ranking staff officers. There were no menacing plain-clothed figures in sight, no suspicious faces. Ahead of him the vast lines of SS soldiers were also safely engrossed in other things.

Donna Maria swayed towards him and looked into his face. She was nervous, he could tell. Her face was white. She really has lost a lot of weight, he thought. Yet how beautiful she was and how he loved her. But he had to put such idle thoughts, such vain desires, out of his mind. Anyhow he wished she hadn't come to this place.

Churchill and the Duke were splendid. Churchill had his hands behind his back, clutching the cigar. He saw Ronay's look and grinned outrageously like a bloated seal. Ronay hoped he'd keep control of himself, but it was too late for lectures. The Duke, on the other hand, was both behaving well and enjoying himself. As the German anthem rang out, Ronay checked the rest of the area. Immediately behind the podium and the bank of officers was the main wall, its base shadowed by the arc lights hitting the vast arena of parade ground. Along the wall, at about fifty paces, was the entrance to the tunnel into the mountain. It was the way into the lift. At the tunnel entrance two guards stood. But how many more were inside? Impossible to guess.

Suddenly the band stopped, the podium relaxed for a single moment, then a hundred drums began to roll, a deafening sinister sound. High above them was the Retreat and onto this another set of arc lights coughed into life. Ronay's heart leapt at the sight: theatrical in the extreme, impressive, breathtaking. There in the beam of light, gathered on the edge of the lair, were the senior members of the Third Reich. Some were in uniform, others in well-cut evening wear, Goering, Goebbels, Himmler, Hess and Ribbentrop – every face was known to Ronay, but for him it was the man, Hitler, the small man at the head of the crowd. The face was ashen white. The black of his hair and moustache stood out dramatically on such a face. He wore a light brown jacket with a red and white swastika on the left arm, and even high above him as he was, Ronay could see the eyes of the man: bright, hypnotic, vital eyes boring down onto the arena below.

Churchill stepped back and whispered, 'Very camp, darling. Flo Ziegfeld has a lot to answer for.'

Ronay stood, unsmiling. Around them, on the high rising banks, massive bonfires were being lit. The band crashed into the *Horst Wessel* song, the anthem of the Nazi party. This was the signal for the Duke to inspect the troops.

The party on the high Retreat stood stiffly as the band played and the Duke left the podium in the company of the general and Churchill to walk the lines. Donna Maria looked at her tall Englishman with the Baron's face. He was watching bonfires. All around, black silhouettes dodged, refuelling the flames. The side of the mountain was a masque of black, dancing shadows with the dogs barking at the distant spectres.

The band played.

Ronay thought of the warmth of the fires, the music, the

splendour. Then he saw the sand and the faces of the soldiers waiting at Dunkirk, the panzers preparing for the signal to attack. He thought of Emily Villiers and Mad Pelluw and Gomez, the slob. 'To be Quixote, señor, takes a little imagination and a little madness too.' The dribbled words of the fat man came unsolicited and vivid.

Ronay gave a final look at Donna Maria. It was time to make his move. She didn't know, but then, how could she? He watched Churchill and the Duke turn into the next line of troops and guessed that Filch would be enjoying himself studying the local form. But then, Filch didn't know either. Only he, Ronay, and Charlie Peak knew how vulnerable they would all be, once out of the shadows of the parade ground. Once in that lift and up there with the gang, make-up and courage would be useless. It was certain that at least one of the Nazis would see through their charade – Hitler himself had met the Duke before and what of Churchill? Filch would be found lacking and he, Ronay, would be a farce as the Baron. And Maria would be caught in the trap. As a complete plan, this little play was doomed – its only success was *now*. Like a golden key, the characters and the 'great European idea' had opened the gates of Berchtesgaden. He was inside – now for the real Final Run – the real reason – the real chance to destroy the Nazi threat. He would make his move. Now.

Ronay stepped back off the podium and as she saw him go, Maria made to question him, but then saw his eyes. There would be no questions. He vanished easily, past the first line of officers into the shadows of the mountain wall. The first guard at the tunnel stiffened when he saw the Baron, as did the other. But both hesitated to take action. They weren't sure. Ronay lifted his hand in the Nazi salute and went into the tunnel.

Here the band was magnified, here in the confined space every beat and belt of the brass echoed into a cacophony. He walked on towards the lift. After forty yards, he stopped. He was there. No other hazards, just the lift, his way to the

Retreat above him. He pressed the call button.

Back at the tunnel's entrance, one of the two guards broke from his post and followed Ronay suspiciously along the tunnel. He saw him standing by the lift. The door to the lift opened and the guard stepped closer. Ronay saw his shadow on the tunnel wall before him, turned and motioned the guard to come closer.

Harvey Teckner stood by the open window. He could see the distant glow behind the forest. Like an early dawn it sent its light up into the night sky. The faint tones of the band made his heart jump. Here was the tranquillity of the lake and the lodge; over there another world. He dragged himself away from the window and picked up the tray, the soup still steaming.

The fires burned higher. The Royal party was now approaching the penultimate line of troops. Donna Maria was tense and anxious, her mind wildly exploring the reasons for Ronay's disappearance.

Harvey Teckner hummed the tune still audible from the top of the lodge. He envied them being there on the mountain. He balanced the tray on one hand and tapped gently on Marcus Ronay's door. A little soup and a little chat would be welcome surely. Besides he needed to know more about the Englishman. He tapped again, louder this time . . .

The lift jolted to a stop. Ronay stayed in the car for a moment. There could be a reception committee. But there was no one. He gently opened the lift door and found he was on a plateau. The Retreat was opposite him, on a small rise, with trees surrounding it like a moat of leaves. To the right of the lift was a high wall and the glow of the fires came from below it. The band swelled up, approaching its crescendo. Two guards stood by the wall, stretching their necks for a view of the proceedings below. Ronay let the door of the lift return quietly to its lock and pushed himself into the wall. Foot by foot he neared the first of the guards. The stiletto came alive with the touch of a button.

The band played.

The Duke of Windsor was halfway along the last line of soldiers, Winston Churchill puffing at his rear. He was becoming just a little bored with constant blonds and fanatical faces. Donna Maria heard the dogs at the gate start to bark ferociously as sentries rushed to open them. Then Harvey Teckner raced into view, his face as red as his hair. He fell from the bicycle and ran blindly towards the podium. Only once was he stopped as an officer barred his way. But they exchanged no more than a dozen words. Harvey came closer, his eyes on Donna Maria. He came level with her. She couldn't believe that he had left the lodge, the brashness of this young American. He glared at her, his face twisted with shock.

'Where is he?' he demanded.

She frowned. He shouted louder. 'The Englishman, Ronay, where is he?' Behind Harvey, the officers grouped, their power supporting him. 'Answer the question!' he demanded again.

And then she knew. She saw Churchill and the Duke returning as the last bars were played; she heard the Waffen SS being ordered to stand at ease. She saw the dying fires and she saw the Retreat with the Nazi group preparing to receive the Royal party to 'begin the new Parliament'. She saw Hitler. Now she knew. So did Harvey Teckner. He followed her eyes to the high lair and rushed towards the tunnel.

Ronay was halfway around the moat of the Retreat. He reached a clump of fir trees and looked above him. There, thirty feet away, high on the flat terrace of the lair, were the Nazi leaders, only their upper torsos in view, their shoulders swaying slightly to the dying bars of the party song. He took the Browning 9mm from the holster deep in his side and checked the bullets. The high velocity shells shone out of the dark cavity of the chamber. He snapped it shut and pushed his left shoulder hard into the trunk of a fir tree.

Below in the tunnel, the sight of the guard sprawled by the side of the lift confirmed Harvey Teckner's suspicions. The man's back had been broken and his legs were at odd angles from his head. Like a marionette he lay there, his eyes wide like glass marbles, his mouth twisted in shock. The lift came. Harvey pushed the button for the Retreat impatiently.

The band was playing its last chords. Ronay aimed the gun's sights over the swaying heads above him. Past Goering and Goebbels, down through Hess and Ribbentrop. Then the head he sought came into the centre of the view finder. The white face with the dark eyes, the moustache and hair falling to one side, shifting in the high breeze. Ronay checked his distance and steadied himself.

The lift opened at the plateau. Harvey Teckner fell over the first guard, his lifeless body hidden by the shadows. As he picked himself up he looked at the Retreat. Which way should he go? Then, there, to the right, up against the first of the trees, he saw the second guard. He ran closer. The guard's throat had been cut so deep that his head was almost severed. Harvey looked beyond, towards the moat of trees. There, Ronay would be there. He ran towards him.

Ronay took a deep breath. Charlie Peake had said that sending the air deep into the lungs and slowly exhaling was the ideal preparation for delivering a 'death shot'.

There in the centre of the view finder was the target and Ronay began to breathe out.

The band stopped.

He squeezed the trigger. It was uncanny. That split second as he sent the bullet towards the target he felt a jolt in his chest as though the shell had gone in reverse. Then he knew something strange, something unexpected, had happened. His head swam, his eyes began to water, he felt the pain, a dull throbbing pain. Somehow he couldn't stand on his legs. They buckled under him and he slid uncontrollably down the trunk of the tree and onto the ground. His arms fell limply by his side and he saw Harvey Teckner looking down at him, a pistol in his hands. Ronay smiled weakly. In that instant he knew his enemy.

'Good shot, Mr Teckner,' he murmured, 'but I hope not better than mine.'

A crowd of guards came storming along the tree moat. Harvey commanded in staccato German, 'Don't move this man. You two, stay here. You others, come with me.'

Up on the Retreat, the Nazi hierarchy was gathered around the fallen body of their leader. The scene was a bitter one for Harvey Teckner. Rudolf Hess moved from the group as Teckner approached him. 'Is it bad, sir?' Harvey asked solemnly.

'Who are you?' Hess demanded.

The young man clicked to attention. 'Grauber, Herr Deputy. Gestapo.'

Hess looked back as the limp body of Adolf Hitler was lovingly raised and carried past him into the warmth of the Retreat.

Ronay was thrown into the truck last. He landed with a groan at the feet of a grey-faced Filch. Telfer fell to his knees and took Ronay by the lapels of his evening suit. 'What the fuck have you done, you bastard,' he cried. Filch attempted to pull him away, but the younger man was hysterical.

Donna Maria knelt at Ronay's side and took hold of Telfer's shaking hands. 'Let him go, if you please,' she said softly. 'If you please. . .' Telfer dropped his hands and sobbed. Filch took his head into his lap and soothed him.

Donna Maria felt under Ronay's dress shirt and her hand came away covered in blood. Ronay forced a grin. 'The first time I ever got caught,' he said. 'Christ it's sore.' She took a handkerchief from her evening purse and folded it into the wound.

'I don't suppose they have hospitals where we're going,' she said. He felt her hand and moved it up towards his lips.

'It had to be done, my love. You know that, you were the way in,' he said. She took out the wig pins, tightly holding his sweating hair, and gently ran her fingers through it. He looked more like her Englishman now. His face was Ronay's. Marcus was there, success in his eyes. Flushed with the kind of moments he was born for.

'I'd have given the world not to have you here,' he said.

She shook her head and held back her tears. 'I would never have forgiven you if you had,' she smiled. 'These days with you, with us as we were, all golden days, Marcus. You mustn't begrudge me them.'

He took her hands and buried his face into them. He could barely hear her as the truck roared to its eventual destination.

'When you left me that long time ago,' she said softly, 'I prayed to Saint Jude: Let me live again I asked, just once more, let me live.'

He saw her white face in the fleeting moonlight, her tears catching the half light but her voice triumphant. 'And you came back – you see how lucky I am, to be so blessed! To love you so much.'

With the last of his strength, he pulled himself up to her, her lips were on his, her warm live body pressed into his very soul.

Telfer sobbed again and Filch leaned back onto the rolling side of the speeding truck, trying to be brave enough for both of them.

The SS officer dragged Donna Maria down two floors into the bowels of the old building. The truck had taken the captives to one of the centuries-old salt mines that dominated that part of Germany. The Berchtesgaden mines were still in operation, but this building was semi-derelict and a monument of past diggings. The officer pulled her by the hair and threw her into what had once been a stable for mine ponies. She fell heavily. She heard the man leave and dragged herself back to the straw piled along the side of the wall. All was quiet.

At first light on the morning of May 26th the sound of jackboots came towards an outhouse of the old building. The door slammed open. Harvey Teckner was first inside. He watched Filch and Telfer dragged to their feet and out into the air. Ronay lay half-conscious, drained of all strength by his untreated wound. Telfer helped him up and pulled him after them without a word. They staggered across the open-mined face of the mountain and into the main building. Down deep into the basement they went and stopped by a high, broken door. It opened. As they entered, a generator purred into life and a bright light filled the dirty room. To the left and right were groups of grim-faced men, some in uniform and some civilian. Just above them, on a makeshift platform, a soldier stood with a film camera on a tripod. Ahead and in the middle of the room was another platform, with four chairs on it. Donna Maria was sitting there.

Tied hand and foot, she fixed Ronay with her dark, vital eyes, as he and the others were bound and then pushed towards her. He looked in pain. She too was in torment, the last injection had worn away long ago, her nerve ends were uncontrollable. But she knew it was not to be for long now – not too long.

They sat Filch and Telfer together on the far two chairs and Ronay next to Maria. He looked above the platform and saw four meat hooks swinging from the ceiling. A huge soldier came behind them and reached up to the hooks, tying glistening piano wire to them. Two more guards dragged the four to their feet and lifted them up so that they were standing on the chairs and the ends of the wire were tied harshly around their necks. Harvey Teckner walked to the edge of the platform and waited. Only the whirr of the cine camera interrupted the silence. The group edged closer, their faces ashen and expectant. Cameras clicked.

Harvey Teckner strode to the rear of the platform and suddenly kicked away Telfer's chair. A choking gasp came as the young man's legs trod the air. Another kick and Filch heaved into space, his head jerked upwards, his eyes bulged, his throat whistled, his large body swayed. Ronay watched the shape of Harvey Teckner come to Maria's chair.

'Forever,' Ronay said without looking at her.

'I know a quiet house,' she said before falling. Ronay closed his eyes and tried not to hear her choke. He felt the kick into his chair. The wire dragged at his neck, his windpipe closed, a feeling ran through him of enormous calm. He thought he saw Cheney. Then he realised it was the man from Alby and Son, the nameless man with the black sack and condolences.

Emily Villiers placed her best china gently on the tray and took the tea out onto the front lawn of the cottage. Hamble was bathed in sunshine and her guest blinked in the brightness of the rays.

'At the last count over three hundred thousand men,' she said. Her voice held laughter and tears.

Charlie Peake muttered inaudibly. He was thinking of the rumours coming out of Germany. If they were true, then Hitler had been hit and it *was* true that German forces were still not on the move. And the boys were still coming off those beaches.

'They are calling it a miracle, Charles,' she said. He closed his eyes, a sound like a snore came from the back of his throat.

'Dear Charles,' she whispered. 'It's all too much for you isn't it?'

She crept from the lawn, leaving him with his dreams. He thought of Ronay and the others and left her with her miracles.

EPILOGUE

As Adolf Hitler lay seriously ill, Rudolph Hess assumed the mantle of Führer. This was done under great secrecy. It lasted for ten days. In that time no decision was given for the German divisions at Dunkirk to attack the British Expeditionary Force on the beach and 338,580 men of the British army were rescued. Adolf Hitler recovered from his wound. On June 4th Hess was reprimanded for his part in the events and never recovered from the shock. Under great pressure, he escaped from Germany and parachuted into Scotland on the morning of January 12th, 1941.